Outspoken

Lora Richardson

Outspoken

Lora Richardson

Copyright 2015 Lora Richardson.

Cover Design by Beetiful Book Covers

www.beetifulbookcovers.com

To my mom, who taught me the love of books,

And to Ryan, who taught me love.

Chapter 1

Penny held her finger on the button and watched the window glide all the way down, letting in exhaust fumes and the scent of mown grass. She hoped the wind would blow away the panic rising in her. She had never been past the borders of Montana, and here she was, setting off across the country alone.

A few miles down the road, a flicker of excitement replaced the panic. She had an opportunity stretching before her, and she didn't intend to waste it. "I am on a journey," she said aloud, to no one but herself. No, this was bigger than a journey. "I am on a quest."

The No Quest, she thought, and laughed. It was a fitting title. She would seize this chance and say no as much as possible, until it felt natural. Up to this point, saying *yes* was her default. She had to admit, saying yes had its advantages. She was going to miss the ease of moving through life letting other people guide her and make her choices. But she had reached her limit, and it was time to practice speaking her mind.

She stuck her hand out and surfed the wind until her fingers tingled, asleep from the pressure on her elbow. Then she heard a most terrible noise. Flug-chunk. Flug-chunk. The car dipped with each flug and bounced back up with each chunk.

She pulled over and hopped out of the car. The right front tire was flat. She had changed a tire once before, but it was a group effort in her Driver's Ed class so it didn't count. She located the tire iron, and sighed at the smear of black grease it left on her fingers and palm. She lifted out the piddly little jack and went to work. The whole car swayed toward her each time another vehicle drove past, and she was glad the flat was on the passenger side. She had a wide grassy area in which to work.

Jacking up the car was easy, and she stood up to admire her work. Solid. Competent. Then she started in on the lug nuts. She pulled so hard trying to loosen the first one that she was certain her shoulder would pop out of joint. She tapped it gently with the iron, and then whacked it mightily. She tried wiggling it back and forth. She dug around in the tool box her dad packed for her when she was sixteen. It was the first time she'd needed it. Inside, she found some WD-40. She sprayed that on the lug nuts until they were dripping. She jerked and tugged and cursed and refused to cry.

She stood up and pulled out her phone. Fine. She would call a mechanic. She figured that knowing when to ask for help was a mark of maturity. She tapped on her phone, searching for the nearest gas station, when a pick-up truck pulled over and stopped behind her car. She glanced at it nervously. Penny knew her mom would advise her to get in the car and lock the doors. Worrying was her mom's hobby. Penny saw how much fear her mom had, and knew she was headed in the same direction. She didn't want to live that way.

Though her heart pounded, she stood still and waited to see what would happen. *Please let there be a woman in that truck. Please let there be a woman in that truck.* A man climbed out of the driver's side, but Penny squinted past the headlights and saw a woman in the passenger seat. Her shoulders relaxed and she smiled at him, motioning toward the tire. "I can't get the lug nuts loose. Do you think you could get them started, please? I can take it from there." It was important to her to be the one to change the tire, as if fixing this first problem would foretell how the rest of her summer would go.

"Sure thing doll, just step back and I'll take care of this for you."

Penny stepped away from the car, wrinkling her nose at the nickname. When he had the lug nuts off, she opened her mouth to thank him, but he kept going.

"I can do the rest," she said, her voice shaky.

"Oh, it's no problem. I don't mind helping out."

Numbness spread through her body, though her brain was firing left and right, thinking of things she should say. *Hey, thanks for your help but I really want to finish the job. It was nice of you to stop and loosen the tire for me, but sir, it's important to me to do the rest on my own. Dude, back away from my tire.* None of those thoughts made it past her lips.

She wordlessly watched him finish the whole job. He tightened the lugs on the spare tire and handed her the iron.

"Thank you, sir."

He smiled at her. "No problem. You're all set. Be safe now." He thumped the hood of her car with his palm, and went to his truck, merging back into traffic.

When Penny couldn't see his taillights anymore, she let the tears fall.

~

Penny felt better after a cheeseburger. She felt better still when her phone rang and she saw it was Vera.

"Hey, sis. Is mom doing okay?"

"Mothers of eight children don't have time to wallow when their firstborns leave home."

"Ha. You speak the truth."

"I, on the other hand, have plenty of time to wallow," Vera said.

"Are you mad at me, Vee?"

"Yes. Get your butt back home. Your empty bed is spooky."

"I need to get my butt back on the road."

9

"Okay. Bye, Pen. Don't do anything you would normally do."

Penny ended the call and grinned, sliding out of the greasy booth. She dashed through the parking lot, stepping over puddles and trying to keep the misty rain off her face. She stuck her tongue out at the spare tire.

She climbed behind the wheel, and breathed in the lemon air freshener. Penny's car was her haven. It was a bubble of space that she could fill up with whatever noise she wanted, whatever junk she wanted, and whatever people she wanted. At that moment, she wanted no people, no noise, and every piece of junk she could cram inside. She was a collector of junk, a connoisseur of stuff. Her car was packed to the gills. An atlas was spread out on the passenger seat. Penny petted the smooth page. No GPS for her. She liked the weight of the atlas in her hands, the dog-eared pages and highlighted routes, the realness of it.

Real. She tossed the word around in her mind. She was ready to be real, to feel real. She didn't know what that would be like, looking at the world from behind her eyes and knowing she was genuine. She hoped she'd recognize it when she felt it.

Chapter 2

Penny wove through the streets of Wells Cove, South Carolina, trying to locate her apartment building. She drove past one vacant building after another, eyeing the knee-high weeds popping up through the sidewalk cracks. There was a stray cat and a few parked cars, but there were no other signs of life. She had been expecting something brighter, something bustling. But this was not a touristy beach town. This was a dumpy small town between the tourist traps.

When she turned onto a main road, things looked a little better. There were a few stores and some people on the sidewalks. She saw a group of teenagers sitting on a bench in front of an ice cream shop. As her car approached, Penny dropped her gaze from their stares. She heard laughter as she sped past them. Even though she was one, teenagers still intimidated her.

The next street was shabby, desolate, and hers. She wasn't disappointed by the lack of shine. She picked this neighborhood for the proximity to both her grandpa and the beach, not the accommodations. If she walked a few blocks north, she would be at Grandpa's house. If she walked more than a few blocks east, her feet would touch the ocean.

She parked her car and searched for apartment 1A, where the superintendent lived. She found the correct door, and knocked. It swung open as her hand was still knocking. She jumped back and stifled a shout.

"Hi there! You must be Penny. Welcome to Wells Cove. I'm Gwen." Penny had envisioned her building super to be an overall-wearing, tool-belted man, which did not describe Gwen in the least. She was probably about Penny's age and had pale blonde hair, a cherubic round face, and wore a pile of necklaces. Some of them hung down to her belly button, and some were chokers.

"Hello," Penny said, and stood just inside the door.

"How was your drive? Wisconsin, right? Would you like some iced tea?"

"No thank you—"

"Oh, I love your hair! It's so thick and chocolaty. My hair's shiny enough, but it's thin as spaghetti."

After two days without much conversation, Penny's brain had a hard time processing Gwen's words. She touched her grungy, car-flattened, plain brown hair. "Um, thanks. The drive was fine, and I'm from Montana, not Wisconsin."

"That's right, I remember now. I always get those two states confused." Penny looked at her sideways, but Gwen just sat on her sofa and tucked her legs underneath herself, smiling.

"So Penny, sit down and let's trade stories," Gwen said, and patted the seat beside her.

Penny sat, though she did not want to. Recognizing that this was a low-risk opportunity to practice speaking up, she mustered her courage and said, "Well, actually I'd just like to get my keys and get settled into my apartment. I'm pretty tired."

Penny sat nervously and awaited Gwen's reaction, but she didn't seem slighted. She stood up and rummaged around in a drawer in her kitchen. She held up a key dangling from a hula dancer keychain, and then handed it to Penny. Penny took the key, and stiffened as Gwen wrapped her arms around her in a tight hug. Penny looked at the hula dancer's brown belly, and awkwardly patted Gwen on the back.

"Welcome, Penny, and if you need anything at all just give me a call." At last, she released Penny from the hug and the perfume cloud surrounding her.

Penny went back to her car to grab a few things. She balanced 3 boxes on top of each other, one more than she should have tried to carry, but she hated to make more trips than absolutely necessary. She peered around the side of them as she found her way to apartment 2D. As she reached the last step, the top box tumbled off the stack and landed with a loud thunk. She glanced around, embarrassed, to see if anyone noticed. Not seeing anyone, she set down the boxes and unlocked her door.

Inside, it smelled like Eau de Mildew with a hint of Clorox cologne. She flipped on the light and looked around. There was a kitchen on the right, and on the left was a small living room containing only a blue plaid sofa and a bookshelf. She followed the hallway, and found a bedroom on one side and a bathroom on the other. She made a mental note to buy a shower curtain.

She peeked into the bedroom. It was huge compared with her room back home. She had shared a small room with Vera and Corinne most of her life. Their three beds had enough space between them for a body to walk sideways, and their clothes filled the closet so tightly that the doors wouldn't shut.

She looked at the queen sized bed, and thought about a recent conversation with her sister. They had been lying in their beds, Corinne snoring softly in the third bed.

"So you're just going to go to this new town and change your personality?" Vera had said. She reached across the small space between their beds and tugged on a lock of Penny's hair.

"No, I'm not changing myself. That's the whole entire point. I'm going to start saying what I want to say without worrying about what people think, because I won't know any of them. It doesn't matter if I make a fool of myself, because after this summer I'll never see them again." Her heart pounded at the mere idea.

13

"So you're going to go there and let it all out. Just be rude and brash and say everything that pops in your head? That's a stupid plan." Vera sat up and moved over to join Penny on her bed. Penny made room for her, though she made a small noise of irritation at the intrusion. Vera's cold toes landed on Penny's leg, and she shrieked and pushed them away.

"Put some socks on, you brat. Anyway, I'm not planning on being *rude*. I'm planning on being *me*. I mean, maybe they *won't* like me. But it won't matter, because it's temporary. No attachments."

"So they're like practice friends?" asked Vera.

"I get that you think this is a dumb idea."

"It's not that. But I don't understand why you can't do that here. With me and the people who care about you. I think it makes more sense to feel safer being open with your loved ones."

"I've clearly proven that I can't be trusted to speak my mind around here," Penny said. Vera gave her a pointed look. "Okay, maybe I do with you, sure. But you're the only one. Think about Will, and everyone else in my life. So yeah, practice friends. That's the idea."

"I'm not sure it will work out like you're thinking, is all."

With that, Vera plucked out the silver leaf earrings Penny was wearing, and slipped them in her own ears. "You can't take my earrings with you."

Penny sat on the naked mattress in her new bedroom, and slipped her hands under her knees, surrounded by the silence she had so desperately craved her whole life. She was a solitary person constantly surrounded by people, and now she was alone. She swallowed thickly and watched a spider crawl up the wall and across the ceiling. Once it had traversed the entire length of the ceiling, she closed her eyes and tried not to wonder what she was supposed to do next.

Chapter 3

The next morning Penny was standing in her kitchen drinking water and thinking about food when someone knocked on her door. She didn't want to answer it, but she did anyway because it was the first knock on a door that was completely her own. Plus, it had to be the superintendent. She was the only one who knew where Penny lived.

Sure enough, Gwen walked in wearing a blue sundress, looking round and brown as a berry, with her hair in a complicated braid that Penny could never manage. She had on high heels, and Penny knew she could never manage those either.

"Good morning! I brought you some coffee and a ham and cheese croissant. There was bacon on it, but the smell was driving me crazy so I yanked it out and ate it. Sorry. Do you drink coffee? I figured you wouldn't have many supplies yet. Oh wait, maybe you don't even eat meat. If you don't want it, I'll eat it."

Penny smiled at Gwen's chattering, then noticed that Gwen was staring at her mouth. Penny's hands went to her lips, wondering what horrifying thing lurked there. "You lucky dog," Gwen said. "You have a gap!"

"Oh. Well, yeah." Penny had made peace with her gap-toothed smile years ago. Now she even kind of liked it.

"I'd kill to have a gap. In middle school I was obsessed with Madonna and I begged my dad to let me get braces to *make* a gap." She sighed.

Penny laughed and shook her head. "That's a little bit crazy. Anyway, I eat meat, so hand over that sandwich." She

15

took a big bite, closing her eyes in relief. She hadn't wanted to leave her apartment yesterday evening, not even to find food. She hadn't wanted to get lost in her new town in the dark. "This was really nice of you, thanks. I can pay you for it."

Gwen waved her hand in dismissal. "No problem. I'm going to the grocery store in a little bit. You want to come with me?"

Penny wanted to sit in her pajamas and alternately wallow in self pity and bask in self congratulation. But she needed food and had no idea where the grocery store was, so she figured she might as well.

"I'm still in my pajamas. Can you wait a minute?"

"Oh sure," Gwen said, and sat on the sofa and started playing on her phone.

Penny wished she had time to take a shower, but she didn't know anybody here and she reminded herself she wasn't trying to impress people anyway. She changed into jean shorts and a tank top, and brushed her hair into a high ponytail. That was about the extent of her hair skills.

"How on earth is your place so messy already? You've been here one night!" Gwen called from the other room.

Penny snickered. Her messy habits were a bane to Vera and Corinne. Now that there were no roommates to complain about her messes, Penny was going to enjoy tossing things about as she saw fit. "I only just moved in. You haven't seen messy yet," she called back to Gwen, who laughed.

Penny walked into the living room, and found Gwen stacking her books neatly onto a shelf. "You don't have to do that," she told her.

Gwen shrugged. "I like to organize things."

If she wanted to clean, Penny wasn't going to stop her. She grabbed her purse and counted the money in her wallet. "Okay, I'm ready. Let's go."

Gwen stood up and dug around in her own purse for a minute, and pulled out a lipstick. She twisted it up and Penny saw it was a soft pink. Gwen reached out and touched the lipstick to Penny's bottom lip. Penny jumped in surprise.

"Just going to freshen you up a little bit," Gwen chirped. Penny didn't swat Gwen's hand away. Without saying a word, she let Gwen pull out her ponytail and fluff her hair. Her shoulders sagged in defeat as she followed Gwen to the parking lot. Change was hard. She told herself it was okay to go slowly.

They rode to the store in Penny's car. She figured driving would help her remember the way there.

"What brings you to this little corner of South Carolina?" Gwen asked, tapping her fingers on the dash in time to the music that was softly playing.

"My grandfather was recently diagnosed with Alzheimer's," Penny said. "No one in the family has been able to come and check on him, to see if he's doing as well as he says he is. I'm just going to spend some time with him, help him out a little bit, and find out if he needs us to hire extra help."

"That's sweet of you," Gwen said.

Penny wouldn't describe herself as sweet. Everyone knew Mark, her fifteen year old brother, was the sweet sibling in the family. He was the kind of person who brought you a glass of lemonade just because he thought you might be thirsty. Penny was the responsible one. "Well, my parents didn't want to make the trip with all my siblings."

"You have a lot of siblings? That must be fun. I'm an only child."

Penny didn't know if *fun* was the right word, but she did appreciate her family. "There's me, I'm the oldest. Then it goes Vera, Mark, Corinne, Vincent, Art, Blake, and lastly Nedra. Vincent and Art are twins."

Gwen's mouth hung open. "God."

17

Penny nodded. "Yep. Anyway, what about you? Tell me about your life," Penny prompted, eager to shift the spotlight onto Gwen.

"So my dad and I had a fight yesterday," Gwen said, still cheerful. Apparently fighting with her parents didn't unsettle Gwen like it did Penny. "He thinks I need to get a second job, but I told him that being in charge of ten apartments is more work than he thinks. He thinks I have hours every day to sit around on the beach. Which, okay, I do that sometimes, but I'm always on call. I'm eighteen years old, I want time to *live*. He wants me in college."

"Don't you want to go to college?" Penny asked her, feeling that their situations might have a few similarities.

"I have no idea how I'd pay for it. Anyway, I'm a singer. Once I've saved up enough money, I'm moving to New York City. *Broadway is calling me, baby,* and all that. How about you? College?"

"Maybe someday," Penny answered, feeling like an ungrateful brat. Her parents would have happily paid for her tuition, even if she hadn't earned a scholarship. At this point, she figured they'd probably pay her just to go to college at all. She kept her eyes on the road, but could feel Gwen looking at her profile.

They were silent the rest of the short drive. As much of an open book as Gwen was, she seemed to know when Penny wanted to keep her pages closed. Penny watched her surroundings, and found herself smiling. Even dumpy places are exciting when they're new.

It turned out the local grocery store was only five minutes and two stop signs from the apartment building. Penny parked the car and they stepped out into the morning heat. They each grabbed a hand basket, and Penny felt giddy that she was only shopping for herself. At home, doing the grocery shopping was one of her chores. Her ten-member family went through a heaping cart of groceries every three days. She decided to buy one of those cardboard half gallons of milk, something she'd never done before.

They started out in the produce section, and as they chose fruit, Gwen talked. "My friend, Marissa, works here. If we run into her, I'll introduce you. Also, Justin should be here today," she said, dancing in small circles.

She looked at Penny expectantly, who obliged, "Justin?"

Gwen squealed, "Justin is the sweetest boy I've ever met. He goes to the College of Charleston, but he's home for the summer, thank God in Heaven. He's the drummer in a band called Someling. He works here stocking shelves."

Over Gwen's shoulder, Penny saw a tall guy pushing a flat cart full of boxes. He stopped a few feet behind Gwen, and winked at Penny. She laughed nervously, and asked Gwen, "What does Justin look like?"

"He has shaggy brown hair that always falls into his eyes. Someday I'll brush it back off his forehead and see what he's hiding under there. He's so tall, and a little lanky. I like boys like that. He is so hot I can't even believe he's real," she said, and fanned herself with her hands. Penny was entranced by Gwen's dramatic, lustful enthusiasm.

From behind Gwen, Justin laughed quietly. She heard him, and looked at Penny with huge eyes. "He's behind me, isn't he?" she said, her voice sounding tiny and high.

"Yes, he is." Penny cringed on Gwen's behalf. It was a relief for her not to be the center of an embarrassing situation for a change. "The way I see it, we have two choices here. We can walk away and pretend this never happened. Or we can say hello and pretend it never happened."

Penny had learned early on in life that embarrassment was to be her constant companion. There was the time in seventh grade when Tim Little told her he liked the pink sweater she was wearing. She had responded by telling him that her cat had peed on it the day before, and she'd washed it by hand three times and was sure all the smell was out.

After that incident, she expended a great deal of energy trying not to say anything stupid, which mostly meant she didn't say much at all.

That needed to change. She was ready to face the reality that she was likely to say something moronic. So she walked over to Justin, and stuck out her hand for him to shake. "Hi, I'm Penny. I'm new here and Gwen is showing me around. You're Justin?"

"I am. It's nice to meet you Penny. I believe you can see Gwen was exaggerating. She did get my name right, though." he said, grinning.

Out of the corner of her eye, Penny saw Gwen adjust her boobs before turning to face him. "Oh, I wasn't exaggerating." She gave Justin a sly look. "Maybe Penny and I will come see your show at Rocket this Saturday."

Penny was amazed, realizing that Gwen hadn't been embarrassed at all. How was that possible?

"Not this again, Gwen. You know you can't get into the club." He looked at Penny and said, "She tries to talk me into sneaking her in every week. I can't do it, because she doesn't go anywhere without Marissa, and Mike would kill me if I let Marissa in." Justin ruffled Gwen's hair. He actually reached out, and ruffled her hair. Penny winced, knowing that wasn't the reaction Gwen wanted.

Gwen smoothed her hair and said to him, "You say you can't, but actually you just won't. What has Mike done to scare you so badly?" She turned to Penny and told her, "Mike is Marissa's brother." Then she turned back to Justin and pointed a finger at him. "I have good reasons for wanting in that club and you know it. I want to sing a set with the band, and someday you'll say yes."

Justin smiled at Gwen and bent way down to kiss her cheek. "I have to get back to work now, but it was nice to meet you, Penny," he said easily, and went back to unloading cans from boxes. They were dismissed.

Gwen dragged Penny a few aisles over and blew out a heavy breath. "Isn't he amazing? Isn't he wonderful?" She held her kissed cheek delicately.

Penny looked at her in wonder. "He seems like a nice guy." She spied a box of macaroni and cheese, and tossed it into her shopping basket.

"He is. But he also still thinks of me as the twelve year old I was when we first met. The lead singer of Someling is this old guy who's moving to Oregon soon. I intend to take his place."

"Maybe you could start your own band."

Gwen's eyes brightened for a second. "Maybe," she said dreamily.

Penny felt a hollow in the pit of her stomach begin to expand. All the new names and faces swirled in her mind. And she didn't know where to find the chips and salsa. Everything was too new. What she wanted was to get back to her apartment.

"Gwen, I'm ready to go," Penny said, and turned toward the cash registers.

Gwen gave a puzzled look toward Penny's half-full basket, but said, "Sure. I need to grab some shampoo first. I'll meet you at the front doors."

Penny stepped in line at the nearest register. The cashier was a scowling older lady with tall gray hair. When it was Penny's turn, the woman scanned her items slower than was possible. Penny glanced at the bagger, who was holding her macaroni and staring out into the store. This place was weird.

The bagger's hair was black and messy; short on the sides but the front flopped down almost to his eyes. What she could see of his eyes looked so dark as to be black, too. He had a tattoo of a thorny, leafless tree on his right forearm. Penny, a sucker for good forearms, couldn't help but notice that his were very tan and corded with muscle. He was the kind of guy she'd never talk to, perhaps not even be brave enough to look at. In the spirit of her goal to quit being such a scaredy cat, she knew she should at least say hello. She didn't.

"Archer! Bag these things for the girl," the cashier snapped, startling him.

He looked down, and shoved all Penny's things into two paper bags as she paid the lady. He held the bags out to her, and moved his hands back quickly to be sure their fingers didn't touch when she took them. He turned away and focused on the bag he was getting ready for the next customer.

She hoisted her bags higher in her arms, and went to wait by the front doors for Gwen. There was a huge bulletin board on the wall, and she noticed a large *Help Wanted* section. Her parents weren't funding this trip, though they told her they would pay for anything her grandpa needed. Penny figured they hoped she'd run out of money and come home.

Penny scanned the ads. She wanted nothing to do with serving food, she wasn't old enough to work in a bar, and she didn't relish the idea of being a high school janitor. Then she noticed a simple hand written ad for this grocery store. It read, "Bellhill Grocery Store part-time delivery driver needed. Must have valid license."

She thought that over. She could be in her car with the windows down, listening to her own music. She could shop from lists and then deliver bags of groceries to strangers. She had lots of experience grocery shopping. She also imagined it was the kind of job that didn't have much close contact with coworkers. It sounded perfect.

Just then, Gwen appeared. "Sorry I took so long. I ran into Marissa and had to tell her every word Justin and I said to each other."

"It's okay. Now I need you to wait on me for a minute. I want to talk to the manager about this job," Penny told her, and set down her bags to point at the ad. Gwen smiled and waved Penny away. To the left of the bulletin board was a door with a name card on it: Hiram Bellhill. She took a deep breath and knocked.

"Come on in," said a jovial voice. Penny walked in and saw a tiny gray-haired man behind a messy desk. He was so small she could only see the top of his face over the stacks of papers, boxes, and other clutter. But his eyes were twinkling.

"Hello. My name is Penny Beck. I'm interested in the delivery driver position," she told him in her steady, clear, impress-the-teacher voice. She had never had a real job before. She had a lot of chores at home, helping take care of the house and her siblings. Her parents didn't want her to risk her grades by spending time at a job instead of studying. So Penny didn't know what to expect from Mr. Bellhill. He inclined his head toward an empty chair, and she sat.

Ten minutes later she walked out of his office with a job. A job, on her first try! She looked around for Gwen, and found her standing a few feet away from Archer the bagger, and glaring at him with her arms crossed. What could possibly be happening? Penny turned away, nurturing her intense aversion to any sort of drama.

A moment later, Gwen stomped over to her. "God, he is such a nitwit!" she said through gritted teeth, loud enough for him to hear. He didn't react, didn't even tilt his head toward them.

Penny smiled at Gwen's use of the word *nitwit*. "Let's get out of here, then," she said, and brushed past Gwen and out the door.

Chapter 4

Penny's apartment looked bleak. Scrubby and brown. Already sloppy and disorganized. It was a new morning, and she tried to summon some enthusiasm for organization. She half-heartedly put a few things on an empty wall shelf. She had pictured herself making this place a cozy, well-decorated home. Throw pillows, candles, and regular tidying. But her slovenly ways had followed her. She abandoned the mess and picked up her phone.

"Hello?" Vera sounded sleepy.

"Vera, it's me," Penny said. "Just checking in and hoping you'll tell Mom and Dad that I got here safely." She didn't want to talk to them yet.

"Pen! It's been *days* since you left." Vera's voice was no longer sleepy. "You could have called a little sooner, you know. Or at least answered my calls, you big jerkface."

Penny could hear her choke up a little. She repressed the simultaneous urges to laugh and cry. "How are you? How are things at home?"

"You know how it is here. People everywhere. Mom wringing her hands over everything and whispering her orders with an '*if you don't mind*' attached at the end. Dad in the den ignoring everything. Oh, listen to this! Corinne talked Mom into letting her go out with Johnny Reynolds, which is a disaster, but Mom was too tired to argue," Vera said.

"Johnny's your age!" Vera was seventeen, a year younger than Penny.

"Corinne just wears mom down. She's a diabolical thirteen-year-old. Whatever. So talk about you."

"I guess I'm fine. I met a girl named Gwen. She's like a tornado, sucking me into her life and blowing everything all over the place."

"Stop speaking in metaphors, weirdo."

"Fine. She's nice. She's a little too chummy."

"Hmm. An insta-friend. But only temporary, right, like those *washes out in three weeks* hair dyes?"

"Vera, don't pick on me."

"I'm right though. This girl is your first *practice friend.*"

"Maybe. But we've discussed this. I need the practice."

Vera was quiet a minute. Then she said, "I'm glad you have someone to know there, besides Grandpa. I didn't want you to be alone."

"I like being alone."

They talked a little more, and when Penny revealed she hadn't yet been to see Grandpa, Vera was appalled. Penny tried to explain that she just needed a chance to get her bearings. "I'm going there tonight, keep your shirt on."

After saying good-bye, Penny saw that she had an unread text. It was from Will, her ex-boyfriend. She deleted the text without reading it, and sighed. Their last encounter had been painful and traumatic, and she was relieved to be more than half a country away from him.

~

Later that day, she got ready to go visit Grandpa Cal. She hadn't seen him since she was ten years old. He used to visit every year, but then Grandma died, and he never made the trip on his own. Penny's family was too big and too busy to make the trip themselves. Looking at it with older eyes, she couldn't figure out why they never went, not once. They should have.

The Grandpa of Penny's memories wore plaid shirts and brown loafers. He gave hugs that were a little too tight and had a stash of candy bars he handed out randomly. He and Grandma Ruby had kissed a lot, and anywhere they pleased. Penny's mom had scolded them time and again for kissing (with tongue!) in front of the grandkids. Her parents, of course, kept their kissing secret, always stopping whenever a kid walked into the room. Penny planned to be *the kissing out in the open* type of grown-up.

She thought of all this as she walked down the steps of her apartment building, and breathed in the heavy evening air. Kissing wasn't yet relevant to her life, she thought, as she had only ever kissed one boy. Though she had crushed on him from afar for ages, their actual relationship hadn't lasted long. She had still been too skittish around him, still concerned about making a good impression, to kiss him with that sort of comfortable abandon.

She walked along the chipped sidewalks and through the shabby neighborhood. Some run-down neighborhoods feel dangerous, but this one felt okay. It was run-down in a lived-in, cozy sort of way. She liked it. This was a neighborhood she could settle into.

The walk to her grandpa's house took less than ten minutes. Penny leaned against his mailbox and studied the situation. His roof looked new. The yard was tremendously overgrown and weedy. Trash bags were piled up in front of the garage.

She pressed his doorbell, surprised that her stomach was jittery with nerves. She admitted to herself that she was afraid of what she'd find. What if he didn't recognize her? What if he no longer wore brown loafers? He opened the door, barefoot, but wearing a plaid shirt. He was bald now, with only a few patches of hair around his ears and neck. Her heart squeezed.

"Hi Grandpa," Penny said and stepped forward to embrace him. He hugged her back, not quite as tightly as she remembered, but then, she was bigger now. She caught a whiff of his shaving cream and tears pricked her eyes.

"Dear Penny, come inside," he said, stepping back and letting her go.

She followed him in the house and they sat in the living room. Some jazz music was playing, coming from down the hall. Penny hated jazz, but loved that he was listening to music. On the wall were several framed photographs of him and Grandma Ruby. In some of them, they were young. Penny stared at their wedding photo, and could find little of her grandpa in that young man. She thought the eyes would be the same, but even they looked different, with skin drooping in places and changing the shape. His smile hadn't changed, though.

"Ruby was a beauty, wasn't she?" he asked her, with that same lopsided, goofy smile as the photo.

"Yes, and you were handsome. Still are," Penny told him. They sat in silence for a few minutes, and it felt awkward for Penny, not knowing what to say to her own grandfather. Being a blurter, she was glad when Grandpa spoke and saved her from whatever thing was about to exit her mouth.

"Penny, I know why you're here. I know your mother thinks I'm incapable of even bathing myself. Well, she's wrong. I'm doing well yet, and I intend to for the foreseeable future," Cal said, in a voice that meant business.

Penny reminded herself that she was officially an adult now. She and Grandpa could speak as equals. Her throat suddenly felt thick, a sludgy soup of fear and the over-riding knowledge that she had no idea what to do for him.

"Grandpa, can I confess something to you?"

"By all means." He waited.

She sifted through some thoughts and memories, wondering what she could share that might make him understand.

Four weeks ago, Penny had stood by her bed folding up her graduation gown. She set her cap down on top of it, and turned toward her mom, who had followed her in, shutting the door behind them even though Blake was whining on the other side. Her mom smiled at her with warmth and pride. Penny was moved to hug her.

Then Penny dropped the first official *No* bomb, in what she hoped would be a series of attacks. "Mom." A lump formed in her throat, but she spoke around it. "I'm not going to Montana State this fall. I'm sorry."

Her mom's arms went limp, and Penny stepped back to look at her face. Her eyebrows were furrowed and her voice was shaky. "Of course you are."

"No, I'm not."

"Why?"

"It's hard to explain. It just isn't what I want anymore." In truth, it wasn't what she ever wanted. They both heard the doorbell ring, and Vincent shouted greetings at whoever it was. Soon there would be about fifty extra people in the house, eating cake, telling Penny congratulations, and giving her cards with money inside. Penny knew the timing of her news was terrible, and felt ashamed that she was using the guests as a buffer. She had hoped that if she told her parents right before the party, they would have a couple of hours to let it sink in before talking about it. It hadn't happened quite like that.

Picture it like this: Relatives and friends sitting awkwardly in metal folding chairs spread about the house, pretending they couldn't hear the muffled lecturing and crying coming from Penny's bedroom. Vera had known what Penny was planning to do, and she tried to play happy hostess. The great aunts and the cousins and the colleagues from the university hadn't been fooled. Finally, Penny simply walked straight out her bedroom and went downstairs to eat cake. Lots of cake. Nobody mentioned her puffy, red face, and no one asked about her college plans.

Fortified from that memory, she was ready to speak. "There are a lot of reasons why I'm here, Grandpa. The biggest reason is entirely selfish. I mean, don't get me wrong, of course I wanted to come here and see you. But I've disappointed my parents by not going to college, and they look at me as if I'm a misbehaving puppy that needs to be put in her crate until she learns her lesson. Mom kept saying she needed to come check on you, but couldn't manage to make it work out because who would drive Art to his piano lesson and who would keep Vincent from destroying the house and, well, she just couldn't make it work is all. It seemed like a good opportunity for me to maybe redeem myself the tiniest bit. And also be able to breathe for half a second. And escape their sad-eyed faces. And also have a visit with you."

Cal looked at Penny a long moment, his face sober. She began to wonder if he had lost more memory than she realized at first, and maybe she had confused him. But then, he laughed! It was loud, long, and filled Penny with relief and the tiniest pinch of fear. Was he laughing at her? She thought she must seem immature and awful to him.

"I think we got our wires crossed. I was afraid your mother had sent you here against your will, with the expectation that you would be my nurse-maid. Nothing made me feel old and useless more than that. I'm terribly pleased to hear that your reasons for coming are selfish."

"Well, I'm *not* here against my will." She chewed on the inside of her cheek, and thought about the night when she told her parents she was leaving town. It was two weeks after the graduation party nightmare. Everyone was still walking on eggshells. Penny had been sitting on the couch staring at nothing and trying to think without any thoughts coming at all. Her mom said to her dad, "Penny will do it, she won't mind." Penny had no idea what they were talking about, but knew she *would* do whatever it was, and if she did mind, she'd do it anyway.

She had sat on that couch and suddenly saw that her whole life was her own fault. She was a person who said *yes* when she meant *no*. She wasn't even brave enough to say *no thanks*.

She looked up at her grandpa. "I missed you. I wanted to be sure you were okay." She fell quiet. He waited, watching her patiently. She continued, "And, while I wanted to get away from home, the idea of going somewhere I didn't know a single person was just a little too terrifying. It's better knowing you're here with me."

Cal reached out and patted her arm. "Penny, perhaps we can be of some help to one another. I will be your familiar face in town, and you can tell your mother that I'm doing fine."

Penny hesitated, thinking of the garbage bags stacked waist high outside. She looked around at the clutter and dust in his house. Who was she to judge? She was a slob too. In another month her apartment would probably look just like this. Grandpa himself looked good. His clothes were clean, his hair was combed, and he didn't look sickly. "Deal," she told him. "But Grandpa, will you promise me that if you *do* need help with anything, you'll ask me? I won't go telling mom to put you in a nursing home, I'll just help."

"I will promise you that, if you will promise the same to me in return," he said.

They shook hands on it. She liked the feeling of being co-conspirators. Before she left, they played a game of checkers. She won. She figured he let her win, just like he always had. When she stood to go, he held out his hand as though he was asking for help standing. She took it and tugged, but he let go easily and she saw that he had deposited a miniature Mr. Goodbar into her palm.

~

It was now past ten o'clock, but Penny was walking toward the beach. She had gone to her apartment after leaving Grandpa's, and grabbed a blanket and a water bottle. After fifteen minutes of walking, she noticed sand on the sidewalks. A little farther, over a grassy hill, there it was. Her first glimpse of the ocean. She stood and looked out at it, waiting to feel something. It was kind of hard to tell the ocean from the sky, in the inky dusk.

A bonfire was burning farther down the beach, and the smell of smoke hung thick in the air. She could hear occasional barks of laughter and the low pounding bass of music, but it was far enough away that she felt like she was alone. She spread her blanket out, and lay down on her back. There was a skinny moon, and it was a little cloudy.

She tried to think about all the huge things going on in her life: her move, her new job, Grandpa. She was disgusted that her mind stayed only on Will. She couldn't believe he texted her. She partly wished she'd read it, just to see what outlandish thing he'd said. It might have given her something new to be angry about, which could have been fun. She was new to having this much anger, and a part of her enjoyed it.

Penny closed her eyes, and let herself remember him. She was a late bloomer at most things in her life, boys included. A new boy started at her school her senior year. Will. Penny liked his corduroy jacket, his curly hair, and the way he always had a book somewhere on his person. She was not brave enough to talk to him, but sneaked glances at him whenever she could. One day he smiled at her, and her insides transformed into electric jelly.

The only class they had together was AP English. One fall day, they had broken into groups to work on filling out college applications. Will was in her group. She focused on her laptop. Penny's list included only warm-weather schools. She wanted to be somewhere without a true winter. Suddenly, she felt a tap on her wrist.

"So, where are you going to school?" Will asked. He had never spoken to her before.

"I'm not sure yet," Penny said, her voice shaking. "How about you?"

"Good old Montana State. That's the plan. Maybe you'll end up there too."

"Maybe." She looked at her list of schools, and added Montana State to the bottom.

Months later, her acceptance letters started rolling in, Montana State among them. Will began paying more attention to her; waving at her in the halls, tapping her desk as he walked to his own seat, and chatting with her in the parking lot before school. He was stingy with his attention, saving smiles and conversation for, she guessed, special people. She was giddy that he considered her to be so. She moved the MSU letter to the top of the stack.

With just a few weeks left of high school, Will had walked up to her at her locker after the last class of the day. He handed her an orange lily, like the kind that grow in ditches on gravel roads, and asked if she'd go to dinner with him. She said yes. At dinner he told her she should go to MSU with him. When she got home, she placed her paperwork to Montana State University in the mailbox and put the flag up.

Looking back on it, it was clear how pathetic the whole thing was. At the time, it had seemed so romantic. She had been elated. Her parents were thrilled too, not only because MSU offered her a fantastic scholarship, but also because her father was a professor there.

Her last night with Will, however, was not romantic. It made her feel stabby. Or maybe she hadn't reached stabby level, but she was at least at *punch him in the throat* level. She was cultivating anger, but hadn't quite moved up to blood and guts imagery. She laughed to herself at that idea.

Images from that night flashed through Penny's mind, and she decided not to push them away. Maybe the more times she went over what happened, she'd finally understand it. It had been a few days before graduation. They had driven to a park near Will's house. There was a large grassy area and a stream a ways past the playground, where he surprised her with a picnic dinner. After they ate, they lay kissing on the blanket. She tried not to worry if she had fried chicken breath.

He had kissed her for the first time only a week before, after a date at the movies. Some terrible film with too many camera-shaking car chases. When he kissed her, she felt like she herself was being shaken. On that blanket, it still felt new and rather unreal. She had been surprised that he had waited five dates to kiss her, having assumed he was experienced. She remembered that gleeful feeling when he told her he was a virgin too. It felt like such a lucky thing.

They stopped kissing to catch their breath, and started talking about college. Penny jabbered on about the summer orientation program. There were four sessions, and she wanted to make sure they were going to the same one. Will wasn't making those kinds of decisions quickly enough to suit her.

As she talked, he looked down and took her hands. She closed her mouth and looked at his face, which had grown serious.

Without looking at Penny's face, he said that he wanted to continue to date her, but that when they got to campus, he wanted to date other girls too. Penny went numb. She forgot the rest of his speech, for that's what it felt like, a rehearsed oration. She only had snippets and visions of him addressing why it didn't make sense for them to stay exclusive, and how it was wise to consider all their options.

Penny remembered numbly nodding her head in agreement. She actually said to Will, "I don't mind, you're right it would be wise," and then wondered why on earth she'd said that. It was like she was a ventriloquist's dummy, and someone was speaking for her. He kissed her, and she kissed him back. He started touching her, edging around the boundaries of where they'd been before, but her body didn't respond because it couldn't. She was still numb.

Penny wished now that she had pulled away. She didn't know where her voice went, but it was gone. Here's what happened: She had sex with him. Except, it felt instead like he had sex with her. She was barely even there. Her body was there, doing those things with his body, but that seemed irrelevant. The only thing her brain was doing was repeating over and over, "If I do this, he'll like me. He'll take it back. He'll like me. He'll take it back." The whole thing took only about five painful minutes.

After it was over, Penny's voice returned, though she still didn't recognize herself in it. Will was buckling his belt when Penny told him that she couldn't be with someone who just told her he wanted to date other people. He got angry. "It's a little late to be saying that now, don't you think? I just gave my virginity to you!" he had shouted. Penny thought his anger was probably justified, because, after all, she had agreed to his terms. She had given her consent.

The thing was, she wasn't numb anymore. Now she had too many nerve endings. Will had tried to argue with her while she sat fuming, looking down at her bare knees on the blanket. He could not change her mind. She wasn't budging. She didn't ever want to see him again in her whole life. Finally, Will narrowed his eyes and clenched his jaw and climbed back into his truck. He drove off and left her there, sobbing next to the half-eaten peach pie.

That night in the park, shame had filled her as she realized how much control she had always given other people. Not just Will, but everyone. Suddenly, a thought came to her and she clung to it: she wasn't going to MSU in the fall. She didn't want to, hadn't ever wanted it really, and she just wasn't going to do it.

It wasn't simply that she'd had sex with a boy and regretted it and didn't want to see him around campus, though that was true. It was the pile-up of all the things she was going along with even though they weren't her idea: majoring in chemistry because her dad told her she should, not wearing red because her mom told her it wasn't her color, joining student council because her teachers told her it would help her get into a good college. Going to MSU would be a glaring reminder of her tendency to make choices to please people, that she was a person unable to speak her mind. That she gave away her virginity to a boy she didn't even love yet, just so he'd like her. She hated that part of herself.

Now Penny was sobbing on a blanket in the dark again, though this time she wouldn't need to call Vera to come and get her. This time she was alone because she'd started the night alone. She'd much rather be alone. That last night with Will had given her the fuel she needed to propel herself all the way across the country. That fuel was anger at her closed mouth, her ever-growing stack of yeses that should be nos, her numbness.

Penny sat up and wiped her eyes on the backs of her hands. Out of the corner of her eye, she discovered someone sitting in the sand about ten feet behind her. Embarrassed, she wondered if her crying had been loud. She felt depleted, so she stood up and shook the sand from her blanket, very much ready to go home and go to bed. The person, a man, stood too. Penny immediately went on guard. She tried to remember which pocket her phone was in, and froze with her hands holding two corners of the blanket. The man walked toward her, and grabbed the other two corners that were dragging in the sand. He brought them up to the corners Penny was holding, folding the blanket in half. He met her eyes, but for the second time, he made sure their fingers didn't touch. Archer. He took the blanket from Penny and folded it the rest of the way. He handed it to her and walked away toward the bonfire.

Chapter 5

Penny had another free day before she started her job. She lazed the morning away reading a book and taking a bath. After lunch, she decided to drive around and learn the streets, because she would need to be familiar with the area in order to deliver groceries. She wandered around in her car, trying to memorize street signs and neighborhoods.

The same group of teenagers was in front of the ice cream shop, just like the day she arrived. She tried to think of them as street art. She saw a clothing boutique next to the ice cream shop, and stopped in to browse. She needed more warm weather clothes.

As she was looking at the cotton dresses, someone shouted her name. It was Gwen, and standing with her was another blonde girl with an armful of clothing on hangers.

"Penny, this is Marissa, the friend I told you about yesterday. She works at Bellhill's too, so you'll be seeing a lot of each other," she chirped.

She waved to Marissa, and they smiled at each other. Penny was terrible at meeting new people. She couldn't get her cheeks to feel normal. She could tell by feel that her smile looked like the one in her third grade school picture.

"After this we're going to get some ice cream, then go for pedicures. You'll come, right?" asked Gwen.

Penny thought about her money situation. Between that and the fact that she needed to head over to mow Grandpa Cal's lawn this afternoon, the decision was made for her. "I'll come for ice cream, but I don't want to get a pedicure," she told the girls.

"You don't *want* one?" Gwen was incredulous.

"Why not?" Marissa asked.

Her first instinct was to tell them that she meant she didn't have time for one. But she took a deep breath and went for honesty. "I don't see the point in them. Feet are smelly and dirty and rub against shoes or the ground all day." She hoped that didn't offend them.

Marissa laughed. "I'm going to enjoy having you around, Penny."

Gwen grinned. "Told you. I knew you'd like her." She turned to Penny. "But my feet are not smelly or dirty, thank you very much."

Gwen went to try on some things, and Marissa and Penny looked through the rack of clearance stuff. Marissa added more things to her already large pile.

"Do you think this dress would look okay on me?" she asked, holding up a yellow maxi dress. Penny couldn't imagine anything looking bad on her, ever. Marissa was statuesque and tan, large-boned but thin. She was striking.

"It's a cute dress. I think you'd look lovely in it," Penny told her. "I'm too short to wear a dress like that off the rack. Most of my clothes have to be hemmed. I'd love to have your height."

"That's funny. I've always felt awkward being so tall. I wonder what it would feel like to be dainty," she replied, eyeing Penny's five foot two inch frame. "I feel like I take up too much space."

Penny had never thought of herself as dainty. Doilies and tea were dainty. "I think I'd rather be tall. I sometimes feel like I don't take up *enough* space. I'm easily overlooked, I guess." She shrugged. It was a confession, carefully made to match the weight of the one Marissa had given her.

Marissa studied Penny, and nodded her head slightly. "Okay, I'm going to try on this dress but first we're going to find you a mini skirt that will come to your knees."

"Maxi and mini, that's us," Penny said, and accepted Marissa's elbow. They linked arms and headed for a different rack.

After all three of them found some good things, they walked next door for ice cream. The shop was cute, if a little run down. The light blue trim around the windows and door was peeling, and the flower beds were full of weeds. Penny ducked her head and hoped to pass unnoticed through the usual crowd. "Step carefully around these urchins," Gwen mock-whispered into Penny's ear. The group of teenagers heard her, because of course she meant them to. One of the boys reached out and held Penny by the arm.

"Gwenny's right, ladies, guard yourselves around these bastards," a girl with pink hair chimed in, laughing. Penny snatched her arm away from the grabber. This crowd was the stuff of high school Penny's nightmares. They were at least 3 years younger than her, but they seemed to be more comfortable in their own skin.

"Nah, I'm not scared," Gwen said, and reached over to squeeze the cheeks of one of the boys. "I used to babysit little Darren, here, didn't I Pookie-Poo?"

Darren pushed her hands off him and grumbled at her, while the others laughed and called him Pookie-Poo in sing-song voices.

They stepped into the freezing, sugary air of the ice cream shop, which was much better kept than the outside. In fact, it was the polar opposite. Every surface gleamed, and everything looked shiny and new. A man holding a tray of waffle cones greeted them. "Hey Mike," Marissa said to him, and leaned over the counter to give him a kiss on the cheek. "Penny, this is my brother, Mike, the owner of this fine establishment." Seeing their exchange, Penny felt an unexpected and foreign feeling. She missed her four brothers.

Mike held his hand out to Penny, and she shook it. She noticed he and Marissa were almost the same height, and had matching green eyes and straw-colored hair. Mike reached out and patted Gwen on the top of her head. She seemed to have that effect on guys. She *was* cute, with her big blue eyes and round face. Penny figured *cute* wasn't what she was aiming for, though, as she glanced at her low-cut dress and high heels.

"Hey-o, Penny. This is your lucky day. My sister's friends eat here for free," Mike said, grinning at her, "I'm not sure I can afford it now that she has two of them, though."

"You're a brat. Give us each a Mad Mike and make it speedy. We have pedicures to get to," Gwen said. "Well, Marissa and I do. Penny prefers to have disgusting feet."

A laugh burst out of Penny. "I prefer for my feet not to be maimed by weird fungally-infused instruments."

Gwen rolled her eyes. They sat at a table to wait. "Did you work on Mike any more about taking us to Rocket this weekend?" Gwen asked Marissa.

"Of course he still said no. I promised him we won't drink, that we'd stay at their table, and even that we'd leave before eleven. He still won't go for it," she answered, frowning. "I lost ground when I reminded him that lots of eighteen year olds get in. He mentioned something about talking to the club security after I said that."

"Sometimes your brother sucks," Gwen said.

"Yeah, but I bring you free ice cream, so forget about Rocket and enjoy what's sitting right in front of your face," Mike said, and set a tray down on the table.

That was good advice, Penny thought. It turned out that a Mad Mike was a waffle bowl with chocolate, mint chip, and cookie dough ice cream smothered in hot fudge and strawberry syrup.

"So what's the big deal about going to Rocket?" Penny asked.

"Nothing, really. It's just a club," Marissa said. "We've been to clubs zillions of times. Rocket is where Someling plays the most. Nearly every weekend. And most of our other friends hang out there."

"And her brother is there every weekend, making sure we're not," Gwen added. "It's the lure of the forbidden."

"Well, he goes because that's where his friends are and Someling puts on a good show. He keeps us out because we are underage and for some reason he thinks he's in charge of my virtue."

Gwen snorted. "If I told him your virtue went down the drain two years ago, would he let us in?"

Penny was horrified by that comment, but Marissa just laughed and said, "Virtue isn't only about virginity. By the way," now she looked at Penny, "You'll have to come with us next time we go to Birch's."

"What's Birch's?"

"It's a bar we go to when our spirits need lifting. We get sad imagining our friends at Rocket without us, so we go to Birch's."

"I don't know. I've never been to a bar," Penny said.

Gwen narrowed her eyes. "Never been to a bar. A dance club?"

"Isn't that the same thing?"

"No."

"Well, I haven't been to a dance club either."

"House party?" Gwen's eyes widened.

"Not really."

"It seems your virtue is intact," Gwen said, gravely.

"What did you do for fun with your friends?" Marissa asked.

"Not much, by your standards. We just hung out at each other's houses. Ate pizza and watched movies." Penny had had the same best friend since kindergarten. Regina was studious like her, probably even more so. Regina moved

41

away junior year, and Penny had spent the last year mostly hanging out with Vera. She shrugged. "I'm a homebody."

Gwen bounced in her seat. "This will be fun! We can introduce you to lots of people."

Penny would rather clean a dozen litter boxes than do that. "I'm not sure I want to. Anyway, I'm not twenty-one."

"Birch's doesn't check ID," Marissa said.

"I think you guys have the wrong idea about me. I'm not sure how you managed that, considering how I look compared to you," Penny said.

"What do you mean?" Marissa asked.

She gestured around the table. "One of these things is not like the other. You're both manicured and bejeweled and shiny. Look at me."

"Uh-oh we have a self-esteem deficiency on aisle two," Gwen said. "That's ridiculous anyway. Marissa, have you seen the gap in her teeth? It's magnificent."

"I did notice that. I also noticed her fabulous boobs. Look at them!" She looked at Penny's boobs. "I'm probably eight inches taller than you, but you have several inches of boob on me."

Penny turned red, but laughed. She did appreciate her boobs. "I do *not* have a self-esteem problem. There's plenty about myself that I like. What I meant was, you're both wearing dresses, makeup, and jewelry. I'm wearing jeans and a tank top. Running shoes. I'm not a going-out type of person. I'm more in-staying that outgoing." She smiled at her joke.

"Your logic is flawed," Gwen said. "You can wear jeans to a bar. You probably *should* wear jeans to a bar. And you can't know if you're a going-out person until you *go out*."

Penny shook her head. "I thought peer pressure was for high-schoolers. Aren't we *weeks* past that stage of life?"

Marissa laughed. Gwen pouted.

"I'll think about it," Penny conceded, planning to be busy at her grandpa's next time they went.

~

Penny didn't bother asking her grandpa if she could mow his yard, she just went into the garage to find the mower. It was a push mower, and it hadn't been used in so long it was dusty. She pulled the starter cord, and against the odds, it roared to life.

The weather was good for mowing, dry and not too hot. The mower clunked its way through the grass, bumping over patches of tall weeds and foofing out dirt from mole hills. She'd need to rake, and was glad the yard was pretty small. Suddenly, the door flew open and Cal burst out onto his steps.

"What are you doing, young lady?" he shouted at Penny, with his hand raised to shade his eyes from the sun. He wasn't wearing a shirt.

"You caught me, Grandpa," she said, and turned off the mower. "I wanted to do something nice for you."

"What? Penny? What are you doing here?"

Well. She didn't know what to think. She had done some reading about the early stages of Alzheimer's, and knew that he was likely to have good days and bad days. She didn't realize the difference between the two could be so pronounced, however. The cold fingers of fear crept up her neck, and she swallowed hard.

"Grandpa, do you remember that I came by yesterday? We talked in your living room," she told him, and steered him back inside. "We agreed that you would be my familiar face and that I would tell mom you are doing fine." She was starting to regret telling him that.

"Of course I remember," he snapped at her, and sighed into the armchair. His eyes still had a bewildered quality

43

about them. "I'd just forgotten for a moment. I woke up from my nap because of the racket you were making, and I just needed to shake the cobwebs from my head." He patted Penny's knee, and she saw that his fingernails were long and gnarly. "I can't have you mowing my yard. I can do that just fine. I do it every week."

At a guess, his grass hadn't been mown in at least a month. "Fine, you mow, and I'll keep you company and run the weed-whacker."

Chapter 6

Penny was up before her alarm, arm slung across her eyes. If it was early enough that she would reasonably be expected to go back to sleep, she didn't want to know. She had been awake off and on all night, and her sleep had been full of nightmares. She chanced a peek at the clock, and sighed in relief to see that it was 6:20. She could finally get up.

She put on jeans and the baggy green polo shirt Mr. Bellhill gave her. It was the smallest size he had on hand, and it came to a stop mid-thigh. She knew it would be futile to make a shirt like that look good, but she tried. She pulled her hair into a high ponytail and put on her purple ballet flats. She added a little mascara and called it done.

The grocery store was eerily quiet so early on a weekday morning. Penny could hear the fluorescent lights buzzing as they warmed up. It wasn't one of those twenty-four hour stores. It opened at eight o'clock, seven days a week. Two of the cashiers were at their registers getting organized and ready to start. One of them was the grumpy older lady. She passed them by and went to Mr. Bellhill's office.

The door was open and the phone was ringing ceaselessly, ignored by Mr. Bellhill, who sat shuffling some papers. Penny stood in the doorway unsure if she should enter. He noticed her, and waved her in, smiling.

"Ah, there you are Penny," he said. He searched around his messy desk until he found the stack of papers he was looking for, and he thrust them at her. His voice was loud to be heard over the ringing phone, but rather than answer it, he just continued to talk over it. "Here are the delivery requests we have so far today. The three on top use the service frequently, the fourth is someone I don't know, but the addresses are all there. Let me know if you have questions, and come back to check for more once you've finished these. You'll be just fine." He winked at her, then turned and finally picked up his phone.

Penny backed out of his office and sat down on the bench under the bulletin board. She looked at the papers. Each one had a name and address at the top, followed by a shopping list. There was a space for her to write the total cost, and a note to bring the receipt to each customer. She was to make sure they paid with cash or a check before she left their home. Simple enough.

Penny wondered if she should shop for all the orders at once and then go on a delivery run, or shop and deliver one at a time. She considered the things on the lists. Three of the four had milk listed. She didn't want any food to spoil. She decided to do two at a time for no reason other than it sounded like the right choice.

She got up and took a cart. She put her purse in the middle of the basket as a divider for the two separate orders. Both of them had bananas on the list, so she went to produce first. After that, she had to do some searching because she didn't know the store well yet, but soon her cart was filling with eggs and cereal and bread. One list had pasta sauce on it. She found the correct aisle, and stared at the selection of sauces. The list just said "pasta sauce." She assumed that meant marinara and not pesto or alfredo. But which brand? Should she get homestyle, mushroom, spicy, or any of the other myriad types? Too many options. She grabbed the cheapest brand of plain sauce.

"Hi! You're the new girl. I'm Thea," a voice to Penny's left said.

She turned. Thea was a girl about her own age, with long braided hair and a big smile. "I'm Penny. It's nice to meet you."

"You too."

"It's my first day," Penny said.

"I think you'll like working here. If you have any questions, you can ask me. I'm in college now, home for the summer. But I worked here all through high school too so I know all the ins and outs of the grocery business."

Penny smiled at her. "That's nice of you, thanks." *Say something interesting!* Penny scolded herself. "I've done a lot of grocery shopping, so I should be fine." *Fail.*

"Okay." Thea chewed on her lip. "Oh, as soon as I heard we hired a new girl, I wanted to ask you something. Do you like sports?"

Penny furrowed her brow. *Be honest*, she coached herself. "Actually, no. I don't really get into sports."

Thea shifted from foot to foot. "It's just, my softball team needs one more player. You don't need to be an expert or anything. We'd love to have you on the team and to get to know you better."

Don't say yes! Why did her brain want her to say yes? Penny did not want to play softball. Heat crept up her neck. "Thanks for asking, Thea, but I don't want to play softball."

Thea stared at her. "Okay. Well, see you around, I guess." She walked off quickly, and didn't look back.

Oh no. That hadn't gone well. Penny groaned out loud at her lack of tact. Well, it would be fine. Maybe she could fix it later. It was a successful attempt at saying no, so she tried to shake it off and get back to work.

Her first list was finished. The other one had two more items Penny had yet to find: pickled eggs and canned tuna. She walked back and forth at the end of the aisles, peering down each one and searching the shelves. She didn't even know what pickled eggs might look like. Were they canned?

She got out her phone and started an image search for pickled eggs.

"I can help you find something, if you want," a deep voice said from behind her, startling her. "What are you looking for?"

She turned around. Archer stood with his arms crossed over his chest, leaning against the meat cooler at the end of the aisle. She didn't know how he did it, but he made the green polo look spectacular.

"Pickled eggs." She tried to force her cheeks not to flush. Those had to be the first words she ever said to him?

He pushed off from the cooler, and walked over to aisle six. Penny followed. As they walked, she gauged his height. Her eyes had a great view of his armpit. She sighed. All through high school her height had gotten her dubbed as *cute*. She feared she'd never be seen as a grown woman.

Archer stopped in the middle of the aisle, and she pushed her cart up beside him. He pointed to a big glass jar of pink eggs. They looked like specimens in formaldehyde. Whale eyeballs. It took two hands to grab a jar of them, and she put them in her cart.

"Thanks," she said, but he was already gone.

The tuna was in the same aisle, so she grabbed two cans and then went to the cash registers. She skipped the grumpy lady's line, and went for the only other open lane. The cashier was a woman about her mom's age. She was fast and loud, and had permed yellow hair. Her nametag said "Gloria" in block lettering. The unnecessary quotation marks were like a gnat buzzing around Penny's brain. She decided to assume Gloria was a nickname, and the buzzing quieted slightly. She collected the receipts from "Gloria," and went to deliver her first round of groceries.

Penny found the first house easily. This woman's groceries fit into four paper bags. She picked up two of them and knocked on the door. There was no answer, so she knocked harder. She was about to give up, when the door finally opened to a woman who had her eyes closed.

"Archer, is that you?" she asked.

"No ma'am, my name is Penny. I'm doing the grocery delivery now." So Archer had this job before she did. She wondered what his job was now.

"Oh, Archer didn't tell me he was moving on. Hmm. Okay Penny, first, you must not call me *ma'am*. Call me Irene. Second, you can see that I'm blind. Come on in here and I'll show you where to put things." Penny followed her through the dark house to the kitchen. She hadn't thought about that before; that blind people wouldn't care if the curtains were open during the day. Or maybe Irene just liked her privacy. Penny set the bags on the counter, and told Irene she had two more bags to get. When she brought them back, she dug around for the receipt.

"I need the cans on this shelf, in alphabetical order. Beans, corn, peas, then tomatoes," Irene said, as she opened a cabinet.

"Oh. You mean you want me to put your groceries away?" Penny asked, and then felt stupid. Of course she needed to put them away. All the cans felt the same, Irene would need them organized in order to tell them apart.

"Well, yes," Irene said, simply. She directed Penny where everything should go, and when it was done, Penny told her the total cost.

"I was hoping you'd stay and have a beer with me. Archer sometimes did, and the boy before him too. Would you like to stay?" she asked, and opened a drawer filled with cash.

Penny looked at the gobs of cash in the drawer, and counted out the correct amount. She swallowed as she realized how easy it would be for the wrong sort of person to take advantage of Irene. Being blind would require a lot of trust in humanity. Penny closed the drawer. "Well, I'm only eighteen. I can't drink beer."

"I won't tell." Irene rooted around in her fridge and pulled out two cans.

Penny dithered about what to say. She wasn't about to take an extra break, let alone drink on the job. And why was Irene offering beer to a minor, especially one who would be driving all over town for the next several hours? That seemed weird.

"I could have water or tea or something," she said, then remembered about the man's groceries that were sitting in the trunk of her car. "Actually, no, I can't stay today. I'm sorry. I have more groceries in my trunk to take to a different house."

"Those'll be George Baker's, I'm guessing. He lives three streets over. Next time, save my house for last so you can visit with me a bit," she instructed. She added, "If George says something awful to you, don't take it personally. He's just a mean old grump."

Penny raised her eyebrows and thanked her for the advice.

At Mr. Baker's house, she stood at her trunk and eyed the goods. He had two full paper sacks and the huge jar of pickled eggs. Never one to make two trips when one would do, Penny managed to cradle a bag in each arm and lift the jar with her hands. She rang the doorbell with her elbow.

Mr. Baker opened the door immediately and snatched the bags right out of Penny's arms.

"Someone as small as you shouldn't be carrying this much stuff." His voice was low, and he sounded like he was gargling rocks. Penny rolled her eyes. Was that supposed to be chivalry or an insult? He shuffled into his house, and left her standing there holding the egg jar. She didn't know if she should follow. Maybe he wouldn't want her to come in. She decided to wait.

"What are you doing out there?" he bellowed from inside the house.

"I'm coming," she shouted back, and made her way through his house. There was stuff everywhere. Empty pickled egg jars lined the wall in the dining room. A counter in the kitchen was completely covered with flashlights, stood on end. Messy as her own apartment was, Mr. Baker would win in a clutter contest. His clutter had a higher interest level than hers too, she thought as she eyed the tall stack of welcome mats blocking his kitchen door. Penny thought about Archer showing her where the pickled eggs were. How many of these jars had he delivered?

"If you're done staring, I'll write you a check."

"Yes sir. Let me get your receipt," Penny said, her cheeks hot. She had been staring, but there were just so many interesting things to see, no matter where her eyes landed. As he wrote the check, she noticed that the kitchen wall had 12 clocks on it, all hung in a circle looking very much like a wall-sized clock. She looked away and tried to find something neutral to look at, settling for the backs of her hands.

Mr. Baker tore out his check and handed it to Penny. "You'll hear people say I'm crazy or senile or mean. The truth is I'm old. I'm old and I'm tired of dealing with people's shit. You bring my groceries, you take my checks, and we won't have any trouble."

Penny nodded and backed away. In a way, she appreciated how direct he was. In a different way, he terrified her. She got in her car and went back to Bellhill's.

She met a few more people that day. She delivered chocolate and cheddar cheese to a young mother with an infant. A man with a broken leg was having his groceries delivered until his cast was off. When Penny wasn't on a delivery run, she bagged groceries. All things she expected.

51

Penny didn't see Archer or Thea around the store again that day. She did see Marissa and Justin a few times, but didn't have time for more than a few short conversations.

When she went home, she was exhausted, bone deep. A quick phone call with Grandpa revealed that he watched tv for half the day, and spent the other half sitting on his porch watching people walk by. He said the people were more interesting than the tv.

Chapter 7

Penny had just changed into comfortable clothes when someone knocked on her door. It had to be Gwen, she was still the only person who knew where Penny lived. She opened it, and Gwen and Marissa stood there, dressed to go out.

"You girls look hot. Have fun tonight, I'll be spending some quality time with my pillow," Penny said with a tired smile, then stepped back as Gwen pushed her way through the door.

"You can spare an hour. An hour! That's nothing. Throw on something good, and come out with us," Gwen pleaded.

"No thanks. I'm not going to a bar or dancing or wherever it is you're going. I want to stay here," Penny countered, proud of herself for that good *no*.

Marissa chimed in, "We're not doing that. We're going to the bonfire on the beach."

Penny raised her eyebrows, and pointed at Gwen's feet. "You're wearing heels! You can't wear heels to the beach. That's ridiculous."

"You can wear whatever you want, Penny. These aren't heels anyway, they're wedges," Gwen said. "Just come and hang out with us. Talk, don't dance, and leave whenever you like."

Penny sighed. "Fine. You are making it a habit, coming here and pulling me out of my cozy nest. You owe me. I think I'll make you come here this weekend for dinner and couch time." She went to her room to change into some shorts and flip flops.

As they walked the beach, Penny listened to them talking and marveled that she was part of a group of people on their way to somewhere. A bit of fear that had been lodged in her chest came loose. She felt lighter and a little bit free. She laughed out loud.

"What?" asked Marissa.

"I guess it just hit me. I'm almost two thousand miles from home. That's sort of crazy, you know?"

Marissa smiled at her, Gwen bumped hips with her, and she felt lighter still. They came upon the bonfire, which blazed higher than she thought possible. Music played, but softly, and there was a group of about fifteen people sitting around the fire. Penny recognized Mike and Justin, but no one else. The three of them sat on a log by the fire.

"Get your hairy hulk leg off me," Gwen said, as she scooted a little farther from Marissa.

Marissa laughed and lifted her leg and rubbed it on Gwen's. Gwen shrieked and pushed her away. "You're ridiculous, Gwenny. It's just hair. I bet you don't mind Justin's leg hair."

"No, I don't, that's true. I don't mind one thing about that boy's body," Gwen said. "At least you shave your pits. You haven't passed the point of no return yet."

Penny shaved her legs, and had never even considered why. In her house, it was something you were allowed to do when you turned thirteen years old. "Marissa, why don't you shave your legs? I mean, I don't find it appalling like Gwen seems to, I just never thought about it before."

"My mom never shaved her legs. She told me it was because she was clumsy and cut herself all the time, and my dad liked her body hair. She told me I could choose for myself." Marissa smiled.

Penny smiled back. "It sounds like your parents are really sweet."

"They were a perfect couple. My mom died when I was fourteen."

Penny was aghast. "Oh, I'm so sorry! I shouldn't have brought it up!"

Marissa laughed. "You didn't bring it up. Gwen brought up my hairy legs, and I brought up my mom. One reason I choose not to shave is because it reminds me of my mom. I like talking about her." Penny tried to relax.

"I loved your mother like crazy," Gwen said, "But her hairy legs were just as gross as yours." They both laughed softly. Penny watched them, feeling a little bit like an intruder on their memories.

A moment later, Gwen popped up and went to stand near Justin. Penny cringed when he merely glanced at her and gave her a vague smile, and went back to his conversation with some other guy.

"That girl is persistent," Marissa said.

"That's true. Although maybe her focus is too narrow." Penny nodded her head in the direction of a boy who was clearly trying to get Gwen's attention in much the same way she was trying to get Justin's.

Marissa laughed. "Yes, persistent but not observant. That kid's Jed. He was in our class in high school. I don't think she'd be interested in him even if she stopped gaping at Justin long enough to see Jed looking at her. He works at her dad's repair shop, fixing cars. She doesn't date mechanics because they remind her of her dad."

"Doesn't she like her dad?"

"Oh, she loves him to death. That's why she won't date a mechanic. It grosses her out to think about being romantic with someone like her dad."

They laughed.

"I met Thea, that girl at work," Penny said. "She seemed really nice but I don't think she likes me."

"Did she ask you to play on her softball team?"

"Yeah. I told her no, though."

Marissa laughed lightly. "Thea's great, but she is obsessed with her team. She was a star player in high school, and I think she's trying to hold on to the glory. You don't need to feel guilty for telling her no. She can't get anybody from work to play."

"I don't feel guilty for telling her no, it was the way I did it. I was just like, 'No, I don't want to play, nice to meet you, now good-bye.'"

Marissa snorted. "Well, you'll have other chances to talk to her. I wouldn't worry about it. I'm going to get a beer from the cooler. Do you want anything?" Marissa asked.

"No thanks. I might go sit by the water for a little bit." Penny stood up and walked over to the edge of the water. It washed up over her toes, a little bit frothy, and warmer than she expected. She still hadn't ventured into the ocean. She was nervous about sharks, and other things that lurked beneath the surface. When her family went to the lake back in Montana, she had to push thoughts of water snakes and dead bugs out of her mind before she could swim. There, she had a horde of people goading her to get in. Here, it was nice not to be pressured.

She sat back far enough that her shorts wouldn't get wet when the water rushed in, and let the steady rhythm lull her. She was so tired.

She glanced to her left, as someone sat down beside her. "Hi, Archer," she said softly. He always seemed to come out of nowhere.

"Hey, Penny."

"You know my name?"

"It's on your nametag at work."

"Oh. Right."

She glanced at him, wondering why he had joined her. The moon was bright in the sky, and she could see a splash of freckles on his nose. He sat with his head tilted forward, and his hair hung into his eyes.

Penny's mind was racing, trying to think of something to say to him that wouldn't be stupid. The only things she could think of were, *Nice weather tonight,* or *How about that bonfire?* Neutral, impersonal, safe. That described her in a nutshell.

She thought about what she really wanted to know, what she'd ask if she had any guts. *Why do you seem so sad sometimes? Did you hear me crying that night on the beach?*

She started to think it wouldn't matter if she never said anything at all, because the silence had been dragged out past the limits of her comfort. She was about to mention the weather out of desperation, when he said, "How'd those pickled eggs work out for you?"

She laughed softly, glad to trade the weather in for shop talk. "They were angrily received, I guess you could say. George is a little bit scary."

"Yeah, not surprising. He's testing your mettle."

Mettle. Archer used vocab words. She smiled. "So I should give as good as I get, is that it?"

"It worked for me," he said.

Minutes passed. Their arms were almost touching, and a strange fizzing was taking place in the space between. With no talking, all Penny could think about was how close his arm was to hers. When she couldn't take any more, she leaned forward and drew stars in the sand with her finger.

"Why does he keep all those jars, anyway?" she asked.

"I don't know. The real question is what's up with that jar of toenail clippings."

"What?" She laughed.

"I'm serious. Look for it next time you're there. It moves around, but I've seen it on top of the fridge more than anywhere else."

"Ugh. That is so disgusting. I guess he's a hoarder, though a very organized one."

Archer shrugged. They lapsed into silence again.

"Did you get a new job at the store? Now that I have yours, I thought you must have."

"Mr. Bellhill promoted me. Now I'm in charge of inventory."

"Congratulations," she told him, and peeked over at his face.

"Yeah, thanks. It's a dream come true," he said sarcastically.

Penny didn't respond for a moment, because she was surprised by the anger rising inside of her. Her first instinct was to tamp it down. She pinched her arm and reminded herself that she'd never see him again after the summer. She spoke softly. "Don't do that. Don't belittle it. Maybe it's not becoming chief of staff at a hospital or director of an airline, but it's still pretty great." She felt a burning embarrassment in her chest, but continued anyway. "It's something you earned. I'm lower on the rung than you are, so when you insult yourself, you're hurling an insult at me too, you know."

She knew she must have looked really weird, and she also knew her face was red. She was doomed. She had put an opinion out there, and didn't know what he was going to do with it. She held her breath and waited.

Archer crossed his arms over his chest and looked at her with wide eyes. After a minute, a small laugh escaped him. "Director of an airline?" Penny shrugged, but couldn't help but laugh a little too. Finally he said, "Okay. Yeah. I was glad when I got this job."

"Good." She looked at him. "Sorry about that. Feigned indifference is one of my pet peeves." She tucked her knees up to her chest, in an effort to protect herself from further embarrassment.

"I'll remember that," he said, and stood. For a moment Penny worried that she had driven him away, but then he held out his hand, as though to help her stand up too. She looked at his hand hanging there. She couldn't seem to make hers move.

"I'm going to sit here a little longer."

"Have a good night," he said in a quiet voice, and walked off down the beach, in the opposite direction from the bonfire.

A while later Penny noticed things were quieter over at the bonfire. She walked back and sat beside Gwen and Marissa on the log. They exchanged a secret look, and Gwen nodded. Marissa took a breath and said, "We saw you talking to Archer. I hate to intrude on your personal business, but I feel like I need to say something."

"About Archer?"

"Yeah."

"I don't think we should gossip about him," Penny said. She actually wouldn't have minded getting the scoop on him. She couldn't deny that he interested her.

Gwen said, "Penny, just listen. Archer has had a crazy life. I don't know all the details, but I know his mom is in prison in Tennessee. They say that—"

Penny cut her off. "Stop. Please. I don't even know the guy. If he wants to tell me about his life, he will. All of us have things in our lives we don't want people to discuss."

Marissa put her hand on Penny's arm. "What I want to tell you isn't gossip, I don't think. It's part of my own story." She paused and took another deep breath. "Archer and I went out a few times last fall."

"You dated him?" An uncomfortable feeling twisted Penny's stomach.

"Well, it's not like he was my boyfriend. I don't think he's ever had an actual girlfriend. I tried to get closer to him, but that proved impossible. He was prickly and distant. I stopped seeing him because being with him was exhausting. I realized I was trying to pry him open rather than grow a relationship. I wanted you to know."

"Don't forget to tell her about the drugs," Gwen added, nodding her head.

Penny's eyes were wide at this barrage of information. She looked at Marissa again. "Do you still have feelings for him?" If she did, Penny vowed to absolutely never again think another interested thought about him.

"I don't think I knew him well enough to feel anything very strongly. He wouldn't let me know him," she said.

Though it was a challenge to be so open, and she didn't want to think about why she cared, but Penny had to ask. "Did you have sex?"

"No, we only went out a few times. Any attraction we shared died somewhere between my badgering him to lighten up and talk to me, and quit drinking so much. I never saw him do any drugs, by the way. Well, maybe pot once, at a party, years before we ever dated. Anyway, I consider him a friend."

"Penny, what Marissa is trying to say is that Archer is messed up. Don't get involved with him," Gwen said. She hesitantly looked at Marissa and told her, "When you were with him, you weren't yourself. You took on all his moods. He brought you down." She looked back at Penny and said, "I like Archer fine, from a distance. I just don't want the same to happen to you."

Penny thought about this. She shook her head, none of it mattered. She was stressed from moving, Grandpa, her first break-up, her undecided college plans, living on her own in a new place.

"This is ridiculous. I've had one tiny conversation with him."

"Archer doesn't *talk* to people, Penny," Gwen said.

Penny looked at Marissa, who shrugged. "That's true."

"Well, I don't want to be in a relationship with anyone. And I don't know yet if I agree with your assessment of him, but you should know that I unequivocally do not date people who need saving. Not that he wants to date me, of course. Anyway, I'm probably not even staying here for very long," she said.

"What?" Gwen said. "What do you mean you're not staying here for very long?"

Penny shrugged. "I mean, I'll figure out what Grandpa needs, earn some money. But I'm still trying to figure out where I belong."

"What if that place is here?" Marissa asked.

She shrugged again. "I never thought about it."

"This isn't fair," Gwen pouted. "Marissa is leaving in the fall to save the manatees, and you're not staying either."

"Well, you need to make your way to New York City, right?" Penny said as she stared into the bonfire. "Maybe we'll all be leaving in the fall."

Chapter 8

Penny yawned as she walked into the grocery store. She rubbed her hands over her face to try and wake up a little bit before knocking on Mr. Bellhill's office door. There was no answer, so she did as Mr. Bellhill asked and went on in, feeling like an intruder even though she'd been doing it for more than a week already. On the desk was a green folder with her name on it, and inside were two shopping lists.

One was for the new mother Penny had delivered to on her first day. Today she wanted olives, diaper cream, and laundry detergent. That sounded serious, so Penny decided to do hers first and get it to her quickly.

Penny knocked softly on the woman's door, just in case the baby was sleeping. The door opened, and Mrs. Neilson stood holding her crying baby, and Penny saw that she had been crying too.

"Good morning, Mrs. Neilson," she said. "Would you like me to hold the baby while you take these things?" Penny set down the bag and held her arms out for the baby boy. Mrs. Neilson looked at Penny skeptically, so she added, "I'm the oldest of 8 children. Babies don't scare me a bit."

"In that case, you have more experience than me. Take him, and good lord, please call me Steph. I'm probably only five years older than you, though these days I feel about a hundred."

Penny took the baby while Steph picked up the bag and disappeared into the kitchen. There was a blanket on the couch, and Penny used it to wrap the baby in a tight swaddle.

Then she propped him on her shoulder and shushed softly in his ear. Still he wailed, punctuating his screams with hiccups.

Steph came back into the room, and flopped onto a chair. She laid her head back and closed her eyes. There was a familiar desperation in her level of fatigue. Penny's mom had postpartum depression after Blake was born, which had only just eased by the time Nedra arrived a year later. Neddie was a challenging baby, but by that time her mother was on good medication and doing well. Still, it was a tough time for the whole family.

"What's his name?"

"Gregory," Steph said. "He has colic, the doctor says. It could be worse though. He actually sleeps pretty well at night, only waking two or three times. The problem is that he cries nearly all day."

Steph looked at Gregory a moment, then closed her eyes to his screams. She stood up and took him from Penny's arms, then gave her some cash to pay for the groceries.

"I know this may be weird because you just met me recently, but if you want a break sometime, I'd be happy to watch him for a couple of hours," Penny told her. "I could even do it here while you nap. If you could sleep through this crying, that is."

Steph looked at Penny with watery, tired eyes. "You are my new best friend. I'll pay you whatever you want." Penny wrote her name and phone number on a slip of paper and gave it to Steph.

She headed back to the store to get started on the other list, which was really long. It looked like it was food for a party. She grabbed a cart, and noticed Thea talking with "Gloria." She smiled and waved. Thea lifted her hand but then turned back to "Gloria" without smiling. Penny's stomach twisted into a knot. *Not everybody has to like me,* she chanted in her head like a mantra until she was calmer.

Penny pushed her cart down the chips and nuts aisle, and saw Archer writing on a clipboard and studying the peanut section. She hadn't seen him around the store for a few days. The last time she saw him, she smiled and he smiled back. She had then given that exchange more examination than it warranted. She wasn't going to form attachments here, but that didn't mean she couldn't be friendly. She maneuvered her cart to where he stood.

"Hi," she said, smiling. "How's it going?"

He turned and looked at her with distant eyes. "Oh, it's just terrific. It's the best day in the fucking world." He turned and looked back at his clipboard. "Why are there so fucking many types of peanuts?"

Penny's face burned. So much for being friendly. She turned and walked quickly in the other direction, leaving her cart where it was. She'd come back for it later, when he was gone. The look in his eyes had been so cold. She went to the break room, hoping to sit for a minute and wait for her heart rate to return to normal. Maybe she was overreacting, but it had taken some guts for her to walk up and say hi to him, and his reaction was upsetting. And why hadn't she told him not to take his bad day out on her?

There was a man already in the break room, putting a filter into the coffee machine. Penny had seen him around the store a few times. He had greasy gray hair, and he put off a vibe that made her uncomfortable. Sure enough, he turned and leered at Penny. His teeth looked too wet, and his lips were limp and curled up on one side, in what she imagined was his version of a smile. Penny ignored him.

"Hi there, new girl," he said. "Don't I get a smile?"

Oh God, she thought, *not the smile request*. She was torn between not wanting to stoop to his level of disrespect, and annoyance at how often women are expected to be polite in the face of rudeness. It was a puzzle she hadn't solved yet. If she spoke her mind, she was almost certain he would call her a bitch, and the harassment would take on a different tone and certainly wouldn't end. If she played along as she always had when this happened before, and smiled or said something like, "Oh just having a bad day," she knew he would be encouraged and keep it up, while she silently seethed. There was no winning, and since she was at work she went with something in between.

Penny gave him an expressionless, glazed look and said in a monotone voice, "Say something funny then. Or juggle. That might make me smile."

Maybe that wasn't as neutral a response as she thought, because he narrowed his eyes and said, "Bitch." Well. Penny decided to leave the break room when Archer stalked around the corner and grabbed the man on the shoulder. He gripped him so tightly his knuckles turned white. The man winced. Penny's stomach lurched.

"Did you just say what I think you said, Lewis?" Archer spit out slowly. Penny felt sick.

Lewis squirmed and said, "She was being rude."

Archer bent down and looked Lewis in the eyes. "Get out of here." He let him go and shoved him toward the doorway. Lewis rubbed his shoulder and gave them both a hateful look. When he walked past Penny, she wrinkled her nose. He smelled like hot dogs.

Archer sat down on a chair across from Penny. One leg bounced up and down. He looked nervous to face her, and she thought he should be. This time she had no trouble working up the nerve to speak to him.

"Well that was lovely," she said, and glared at him. "First you snap at me for no reason about peanuts, then you come in here acting scary and bulldoze over a situation I had under control."

"I was scary?"

"Yeah. A little bit."

He didn't say anything. Penny waited. She wasn't going to say anything else until he spoke.

He rubbed his palms on his jeans. "I followed you in here to apologize about the peanut thing," he finally said. "I was standing on the other side of the wall, thinking of what I'd say to you." He paused there, as though expecting her to say something. She bit the inside of her cheek to keep herself quiet.

"So, uh, I heard Lewis call you a bitch. He has a bad habit of being a dick to the women who work here."

Penny pursed her lips, then said, "Maybe he doesn't have the market cornered on that."

He winced. "Okay. I deserved that."

Penny sat still, waiting to see what would happen next. She was used to rushing in and smoothing over things like this. She had to force herself not to say something like, *"No, no, it's okay, no harm done,"* and then bearing the weight of it.

He continued. "I *am* sorry for the way I talked to you out there. I'm having a bad day, but I know that's no excuse. It didn't have anything to do with you. I just didn't figure you'd...never mind. Anyway, I know it was a dick thing to do." He looked at Penny expectantly. "Okay?"

Penny released her arms from around her chest, and zeroed in on one thing he'd said. "I can't stand a *never mind*. I'll never be able to let it go. You didn't figure I'd *what?*"

He looked at her for a second, his eyes unsure. He shrugged. "Just didn't figure you really wanted to have a conversation with me. That's all. Anyway, I'm sorry."

"Okay. Thanks for the apology." She didn't know what to do with his explanation. She *did* want to have conversations with him. In fact, she craved it. She didn't dare tell him that. She wasn't that brave, yet anyway.

He rubbed his legs again. "And I thought calling Lewis out would be standing up for you. I didn't mean to be scary. But hopefully now at least he'll get off your back."

"What? You think you got Lewis off my back? I can live with him thinking I'm a bitch. Bitches are strong and they fight back. But because you had to be some sort of hero and rush in here and forcibly remove him…ugh!"

Archer looked confused.

"It's just, you made it look like I needed help, which makes me look helpless."

Archer leaned forward with his elbows on his knees, and his head resting on his steepled fingers. He looked like he was really concentrating.

Penny wasn't sure if anyone ever had gone to such effort to try to understand her. Her feelings thawed, and she shrugged. "I guess I should admit though, I kind of liked that you defended me." She was surprised that was true.

"You *kind of* liked it?"

"Maybe a little."

He thought some more, his brow knitted deeply. "I was scary though? Because I thought Lewis was scaring you, and that's why I did what I did. I *really* don't want to be scary."

Penny softened further at his earnest expression. "I don't like when people fight." She looked down at her feet. She didn't want to fear conflict anymore, but she knew she had a long way to go before that was accomplished.

Archer smiled. "I don't mind a good fight. Purposeful conflict. It can be rejuvenating, in fact."

"Rejuvenating? It is not." She thought he must be crazy.

He shrugged. "What about debates?"

"That's different from fighting. But to be honest, even debates set me on edge."

"Okay. What about constructive arguing?"

She glanced at him, not sure what to say that wouldn't make her seem weak.

Before she answered, he stood and rubbed his hands together. He grinned. "Better get back to counting those fucking peanuts."

~

"Now, you call me Miss Rita. Everybody does." The nurse patted Penny's knee as she sat down across from her. "I'm not allowed to talk to you about your granddaddy specifically, but I can answer any questions you have about dementia."

Penny smiled at her, a bit nervous. She was a large woman, with warm eyes and a commanding manner. "I guess I don't even know what to ask."

"Let's see. Start with your fears. That's always a good place to start. What are you afraid of? We can tackle that right off." She patted Penny's knee again.

"Okay. Well, I'm afraid he'll get hurt because, even though I visit or check in every day, most of the time he doesn't have anybody with him. He seems so capable sometimes, and so needy at others. I'm afraid I'll...trust him too much when he says he's fine. Because when he's not fine, he isn't aware of it."

Miss Rita nodded her head sagely. "Yes, yes. I hear that."

At her urging, Penny spilled her guts. She told Miss Rita how she had accepted the responsibility to decide what he needed. She told her how she hadn't accounted for his own opinion in the matter, and how he was not interested in any sort of live-in help. She confessed that sometimes he forgot she was even in town, sometimes he was angry for no reason, and sometimes he seemed to think it was years ago. It felt so good to unload.

Miss Rita kept nodding and patting Penny's knee. "You know what we need? We need one of those places like they have in Amsterdam," she said.

"Amsterdam?"

"Oh yes, Miss Penny, Amsterdam has it all figured out. They have constructed a whole little village. It's called Hogeweyk. There are stores, apartments, even bus routes. But see, it's all inside a secure wall, it's contained. The nurses and other caregivers work there, keeping an eye on the patients. They share households, and get help to do their own laundry and go to the market. They get to live normally, see?"

"So the whole village is full of Alzheimer's patients?"

"Sure thing, and other dementia patients. It's just like living in a town, only on a smaller scale. They can be free. They roam in the parks and streets."

"Wow, that is amazing!" Penny thought she had never heard of something so wonderful.

"Indeed, yes." Rita bobbed her head. "For your granddaddy though, he might not be ready for something like that, even if we had anything like it here. He's just not ready yet to accept help. Nothing wrong with that. He'll come around, you'll see. Or he won't, and you'll handle it."

Miss Rita showed Penny a list of medications, careful not to say which ones Grandpa Cal was taking, but explaining what they were all used for, and when a caregiver might need to administer which ones. Penny left feeling buoyed and more competent. Miss Rita was right. Her fears had been tempered by knowledge.

Chapter 9

A Saturday without work was not ideal. Penny was thankful for the time spent frittering away the hours as a hermit, but she also found that the excess of time burdened her with thoughts and worries.

She was irritated by how frequently Will crossed her mind. At least lately her heart rate didn't kick up at the mere idea of him. She figured it was finished cracking. Maybe the cracks were already sealing up a bit. What bothered her now was the mystery of why she'd gone through with it. The sex. What had happened to her brain and how could she keep it from happening again? Would she always react to upsetting things with numbness and shock and regrettable behavior?

After she put as much thought into that topic as she could, she moved on to dissecting her last phone call with her parents. She promised she would call them every Sunday before church. Her mom had cried because she missed her. She told Penny it didn't matter that she wasn't going to MSU, but she had to do something next year and she could sort it all out at home. When her dad got on the phone, he told her that he had fixed it so she had until the first day of classes to accept the scholarship. She appreciated that he felt he was giving her time to make a decision, but she didn't know how to explain to him that she'd already decided.

She was brought back to the present by her ringing phone. It was Steph, and she was crying.

"Penny, I'm a mess. Jeff's working today to earn a little overtime pay, and Gregory won't stop crying. I'm so angry at him and he's just a baby. I'm scared and I hate to ask, but is there any way you could take him for a couple of hours?"

"Absolutely," Penny told her. "I was just thinking that I need to get out of the house. I'll be there in ten minutes." She gathered up some things she thought might be useful, and slipped on her shoes. Her heart was pounding from hearing the desperation in Steph's voice.

Penny stood on Steph's porch waiting for her to answer the knock. She could hear Gregory wailing inside the house. She waited. She knocked again. Steph still didn't answer. Penny felt her pulse quicken and there was a rushing sound in her ears. She turned the knob, but it was locked. She raced around the back of the house.

As she approached the back yard, she found Steph leaning against a tree, sobbing into her hands. Penny went to her and knelt down to look at her. "I'm here," she said, trying not to sound panicky. "Do you want me to call anyone?" Steph shook her head.

Penny's mind raced. What to do? "Okay. You're going to be fine. Do you have a stroller?"

"Yes, it's in the garage," Steph said, and lifted her shirt and used it to wipe her eyes. The motion revealed a slice of stretch-marked belly, and Penny felt a wave of tenderness. "I'm so sorry you're seeing me like this. I'm acting like a child." She cried a little more. Penny grabbed her arm and helped her stand, and led her to the back door.

Penny got her settled on the couch, and went to check on Gregory. He was pretty mad, but okay. She picked him up and carried him with her to the kitchen. One handed, she made a snack plate. She put olives and cheese and chocolate on it, because those were things she had delivered and thought Steph must like. She poured a glass of iced tea, and brought the refreshments to the coffee table. She handed her the tv remote, a magazine, and a book that was on an end table. Steph took everything gratefully, though she was still in a daze.

"There are bottles of pumped breast milk in the fridge," Steph said, and choked back another sob. "He has a diaper bag that I keep packed, though we never go anywhere because he's always screaming. It's in his room. Oh God, his diaper. I haven't changed him in hours!"

Penny took Gregory to his room and cleaned him up. The diaper was indeed a disaster. She changed his clothes and wiped his face with a damp cloth. She gathered Gregory's things, and then handed him to Steph, who squeezed his little body and sniffed his head, then shut her eyes tight and took a deep breath.

"I'll be back in a few hours, and I'll keep my phone on," Penny said. "And just so you know, you're an excellent mother. Asking for help when you need it is proof of that." Steph didn't respond, only wiped her eyes with her hands. Penny took Gregory back. She carried him and all his paraphernalia to the garage, where she found his stroller folded up and leaning against the wall. She pondered how she was going to unfold it while holding him. She put down the diaper bag and wrestled the stroller open with one hand, and managed not to drop Gregory in the process.

She strapped the wailing baby into the stroller, and stashed his bag and her purse in the basket underneath his seat. She had an idea, and grabbed the quilt out of the trunk of her car and stuffed that in the basket too. She put her phone in her pocket and made sure it was on in case Steph needed her baby back. She rolled the stroller out into the sunshine, and looked around.

"First, we're going for a walk around the neighborhood," She told Gregory. "No, I have a better idea. Let's go visit Grandpa."

He cried the whole way there, which was not a short distance. It took twenty-five minutes to walk it. Penny wondered how Gregory managed to have any voice left. Grandpa Cal was sitting on a lawn chair in his grass when they arrived, loudly, and both red-faced; Penny from walking and Gregory from crying.

"Hello, Darling. Who is this young fellow with you?" Cal said. Gregory was sniffling and whining now rather than full on crying, so Penny was able to speak at a normal volume. After she completed the introductions, she asked her grandpa to hold Gregory while she went in the house to get them some drinks.

Things looked clean enough inside, and there was still plenty of food in the kitchen. She had taken to bringing him food every few days. She took two glasses out of a cabinet, and realized it would be a good opportunity to snoop around his house. She only felt a tiny bit guilty. In the bathroom she found some prescription pill bottles, and wrote down the names and doses of the drugs. She planned to look them up later, and match them against the list Miss Rita had given her.

Her spying complete, Penny filled two glasses with ice water and grabbed a package of cookies. When she went back outside, her heart warmed at the sight of her grandpa speaking sweetly to Gregory. Gregory wasn't exactly placid, but he wasn't screaming either. "Thanks, Grandpa. He seems to like you," she said.

"I've always had a magic touch with the diaper set," Cal said, taking the water Penny handed him. He adjusted Gregory on his lap so that he could look out at the cars driving past.

"So you enjoy sitting out in your yard like this?"

He gave her a level look. "To someone as young as you, I'm sure my life must seem entirely boring. But I find it peaceful. Not everyone needs to be in the center of the action."

"I wasn't making a judgment, Grandpa. I was noticing how we are similar. One of my favorite things to do is sit still and watch the world go by."

Cal nodded his head. They sat in silence a while, then he said, "So your mother told me you aren't going to study chemistry at the university. She was mighty upset you had changed your plans."

"Yes, Dad too. I changed the plan. They liked the plan," Penny said.

He smiled at her. "So they're angry. Are you?"

"I don't know that they're angry. I think they're disappointed. Concerned. They might think I'm being a flake."

"And you?"

"No, I'm not angry." How could she be mad at them when she had never given them any indication that she didn't love the big college plan as much as they did? "Not at them. They think the reason I'm not going is because of a boy. In truth, the only reason I was ever going to go was because of a boy, and now I've simply put that right."

"And you haven't told them that."

"No. They were so proud of me and all my plans. I don't want to disappoint them further. They don't need all the details."

He mulled that over. "Your mother might understand your situation a little better than you think."

"I doubt it."

"You should ask her."

Penny shook her head.

"Might I ask what your plans are?" he asked.

"How about I tell you when I figure it out?"

"There's time, Darling, there's time," he said, and patted Gregory on his fat cheek. For whatever reason, that started Gregory screaming again. "Now whose baby is this, again?"

74

Penny took him back from Grandpa Cal. "Steph Neilson's."

"Oh yes, I remember."

Penny changed Gregory's diaper. She tried to feed him a bottle. She swaddled and bounced and tried to soothe him. Nothing helped, and so they left Grandpa to his peace and quiet.

Penny walked quickly along the sidewalk, hoping the motion would help. "I sometimes cry next to large bodies of water, let's see if it'll do the opposite for you," she said to Gregory. They headed toward the beach.

She couldn't push the stroller onto the sand because the wheels just sank and refused to turn. She had probably three armloads worth of stuff to carry. She took it as a personal challenge, and tucked Gregory up by her neck and gripped him with her elbow while she lined the other arm with bag handles. She crammed the blanket against her chest somehow. She left the stroller where it was. She managed not to drop anything as she walked toward the water. It was crowded, which was no surprise as it was a Saturday in June. She found a bare spot in the sand and spread out the blanket.

She put Gregory down and went through the mental checklist. First she changed his diaper again, just in case. She was maybe an obsessive diaper changer, but better safe than sorry. Then she checked for anything that might be poking or scratching him. He didn't feel feverish. Then she offered him a bottle again. He ate one ounce of milk, no more. She held him to her shoulder and patted his back until he burped twice, and then swaddled him tightly. Still he cried.

Penny held him facing out to the ocean, and for half a moment he went silent and still. It didn't last, though, and so she surrendered and just held him without trying to do anything at all. He seemed to prefer it when she wasn't fussing over him and moving him around, so they sat still and eventually his cries turned to whimpers. She couldn't find a sunhat in the diaper bag, so she made sure her body shaded his, though her hunched position was uncomfortable. After about an hour, he fell asleep.

Penny's back began to ache from holding him on her lap without having anything to lean back on, but she didn't dare put him down. Her stomach growled. She inched an arm out toward her purse to grab a granola bar, but the movement jostled Gregory and he groaned in his sleep.

"I can help you reach that," Archer said, and Penny nearly jumped out of her skin. Alarmed, she looked at Gregory, but he stayed asleep.

"Why are you always sneaking up on me, especially on beaches?" she asked, trying to catch her breath.

"I'm just on the beach a lot. If you're here, I'll probably find you," he said with a shrug. "That looks like little Gregory Neilson. But he's not crying, so I can't be sure."

Penny patted the blanket, indicating he should sit. He did, stretching out his long legs in front of him. His feet were impossibly huge, and his shoes looked ancient. A piece of rubber was hanging off the sole, flapping around as he settled in. She wanted to reach over and peel it off, but thought that would be weird. "He's not crying now because he's been crying for hours and has no tears left," she said softly, so she wouldn't wake him. "Steph needed a break. Can you dig around in my purse and find a granola bar for me?"

He hesitantly picked up her purse and pawed his knuckly hands through her stuff. His tree tattoo dipped into the lavender bag, the branches like the bristles of a paintbrush. He pulled out the granola bar, unwrapped it, and handed it to her.

"Want me to hold him for a little while?" he asked.

"Nah, he'd just wake up if we tried to move him." A flock of gulls landed near the water. They eyed Penny's granola bar.

"Can you do one more thing for me?" she asked. "Can you find something for me to lean against? Maybe that giant diaper bag. My back is killing me sitting here like this, trying not to move."

Archer stood up, and then sat down again behind Penny, his back inches away from hers. "You can lean back on me."

For a moment Penny couldn't move at all. Slowly she leaned back, and felt the warmth and firmness of his back. She felt little shifts of bone and muscle as he adjusted and got comfortable. She couldn't even see his face, but still it felt extremely intimate to be sitting back-to-back like that.

After a few minutes, he cleared his throat and said unsteadily, "It was nice of you to babysit this little guy. So you know Steph pretty well, I guess?"

Penny was distracted by how good it felt, leaning together like that. How could he just chat as though their backs weren't crackling with energy? Her stomach flipped, and she forced herself to speak. "My sister, Nedra, had colic. My mom had postpartum depression with her and one of my brothers. Not that Steph is depressed, I wouldn't presume that. But colicky babies are an energy suck. Taking Gregory for a few hours isn't going to fix anything, but maybe it will help a little."

A silence fell, but not the kind that made her nervous. Penny looked at the waves, and listened to the gulls, who were no longer stalking her now that she had finished her snack. She soaked up the warmth from the sun and from Archer's broad back, and from Gregory on her lap. Sweat trickled down her neck, but she didn't brush it away even though it tickled. She closed her eyes. She wondered if Archer's eyes were closed too.

He turned a little and reached behind him, touching Penny's elbow lightly with his index finger. She stopped breathing. "I'm glad I ran into you today," he whispered. "I've been thinking. I hope I'm not really a dick."

"You'd know better than I would."

"I'm not sure that's true," he said, and she could feel in his posture that he was smiling.

"Hey, you should know two things," Penny told him, feeling brave. "First, I hate the word *dick*. Hate it. You've said it three times since I met you."

His back shook with laughter. "You've been counting?"

"Yes. Number two, just so you know, I generally don't hold grudges. It's one of the best things about me."

"Yeah?"

"Yep."

More silence. Minutes passed. She couldn't take it, and asked, "How old are you anyway?"

"Your crew hasn't already told you everything about me?"

"Some things. They tried to tell me more, but I asked them not to."

"Huh."

"Are you going to answer my question?"

"I'll be twenty soon. I graduated the year before Gwen and Marissa."

"And me. I'm their age too." She leaned back a bit, letting him hold more of her weight. She felt his muscles tense. She cleared her throat. "Are you on summer break from college?"

"No. I'm saving up some money. I have some ideas, but I'm not sure what I want to do. When I figure it out, maybe I'll have a little money to get started on whatever it is."

She nodded, knowing he felt the movement. It was impossible to be unaware of anything, sitting the way they were. "So, you come to the beach a lot." She couldn't seem to stop firing interview-style questions at him.

"Every day," he said.

"Is that part of your formula for a perfect day?"

He laughed softly. "Um, no. I've never had a perfect day in my life."

"Really? I mean, I've never had my fantasy money-is-no-object perfect day, but I've had plenty of days that have been perfect unto themselves."

"Today's not so bad," he said. She heard him swallow.

"Yeah." She looked out at the water. "Somebody's parasailing out there. That looks fun. Maybe I'll do that someday." Gregory stirred in her lap, but didn't wake.

"I've done it." He shook again, laughing silently. She really wanted to hear his out-loud laugh.

"Tell me."

"I tried it with my cousin Adam once. I was fourteen. No, maybe fifteen. Anyway, I hope you never meet Adam. He's a d..." He caught himself and changed the word. "He's a jerk. He was annoying the guy who was going to drive the boat. Being a know-it-all, telling him how to do his job. When Adam gave him the thumbs up, that I was ready, the driver hit the gas hard." He turned his head to ask her, "Is that what you call it for a boat? Hitting the gas?" She felt his breath across her hair. Goosebumps prickled her scalp.

Penny shrugged and tried to focus on the story instead of the way he affected her.

"So the boat took off and I started running, my legs going so fast I bet they were a blur, like cartoon legs. I got a little bit of lift and thought I was going to make it, but I face planted. Ate sand. I bounced up once and flopped down again, got an ear full of sand and water that time." He laughed again, this time out loud, and Penny loved the sound. His voice was so deep, his laugh rumbled like a bear. "I got dragged a while before the boat stopped. Had sand burns on my knees."

Penny laughed too. "When you started that story, I was sure Adam was going to get his comeuppance and he'd be the one to eat sand."

He shook his head. "Nah, even when he does get some sort of karmic punishment, he never believes he deserves it. He probably didn't even realize the boat driver was irritated by him and took it out on me. And if he did realize it, the driver's mistake was thinking Adam would care."

Penny tried to suppress a giggle. "Maybe the driver wasn't getting revenge on Adam, though. Maybe he was a professional about it, and you're just *that* terrible at parasailing." She couldn't believe she was teasing this big-footed, deep-voiced, freckled near-stranger.

He laughed hard, and the back of his head bumped lightly against hers. "Yeah, that's entirely possible."

"I like that you can laugh at yourself," Penny said, still giggling at the image of Archer flopping around and being dragged through the sand.

"I've had plenty of opportunities for practice," he said.

She nodded. "I can relate."

Gregory chose that moment to wake up, and he screamed loudly. Penny jumped up and swayed him back and forth, in what she knew was a vain attempt to calm him. "What time is it?" she asked Archer.

He pulled out his phone and looked at the screen. "It's just after five."

"I've had him nearly four hours! I better take him home now." She rushed around picking up their stuff. She was relieved it was time to leave. Being with Archer was intense. A little went a long way and her nerves needed a rest. He folded up her blanket, as he had done the night she cried. When he handed it to her, she thought he must be thinking about it. She hoped he wouldn't ask.

"Do you want a ride back to Steph's house? I have my car here," he said.

Penny shook her head. "No thanks. I don't have his car seat. I like to walk, anyway."

He helped her carry all the stuff back to the stroller, and waited while she got everything arranged and settled Gregory into his seat. Penny gripped the stroller handles and turned toward him. "That last hour would have done me in, if you hadn't turned yourself into a chair for me."

He tucked his hands into his pockets, and ducked his head, trying to hide the smile on his lips.

Penny pointed the stroller toward Steph's house and pushed the crying baby back home.

Chapter 10

Penny emerged from the safety of her blankets, surprised by how well she slept. She took a shower and dried her hair, watching it whirl around her head. Then she started cooking lunch. She had invited Gwen and Marissa over to eat and hang out. She was chopping vegetables for the salad when they arrived.

"Smells good, Penny. What can I do to help?" Marissa asked, walking directly into the kitchen and washing her hands. Penny set her to work slathering bread with butter and sprinkling on garlic salt.

Gwen, meanwhile, had flopped on the couch and thrown her arms over her eyes. She let out a little moan. "Gwen? Are you okay?" Penny teased her, "I'm worried because you haven't started cleaning yet. I even left that pile of laundry on the chair for you to fold."

"No. I'm light years away from okay. I will never be okay again," she whined. She dragged herself over to the laundry and started matching socks.

Penny looked over at Marissa, who rolled her eyes and said, "Gwen is being a big baby. Surely you've noticed her flair for the dramatic?"

"I'm not overreacting. I'm mortified. I think we should all leave town now, and not wait for the end of summer," she said with a huff.

"Tell me what happened," Penny said. She handed Gwen a glass of water and pulled her back onto the couch, away from the laundry.

Gwen stared at the water. "I wish this was vodka."

Penny cleared her throat.

"Ugh. Fine. Someling had a practice session yesterday afternoon at Rocket. A sound test or something, for their new set. Oh yeah, sorry we didn't invite you but Marissa said you were at your grandpa's. Anyway, Marissa talked Mike into taking us to watch. The bar was closed, so it was just us and I thought it would be the perfect time to show off my talent. I was wrong."

"You were not wrong," Marissa said. "They let you sing with them and you sounded great. Focus on that part." Penny appreciated the motherly aspect of Marissa's personality.

"What happened that was mortifying?" Penny pressed. She loved to hear embarrassing stories.

"Well, I was wearing this gauzy skirt. It was short and God, I looked hot. Everything was going fine, I was in the zone. The song I sang was one Justin had written recently, and I think he was impressed that I knew it. Anyway, at a vocal break, I came up with this little dance for the guitar riff," she said.

"And?" Penny prompted.

"Okay, so for part of the dance I turned my back to the audience to show off the many talents of my booty. I was feeling so awesome, and then Justin and the whole table started laughing. Cracking up. I turned around to look at them, and they were doubled over and cackling."

Penny was indignant. "They laughed at you? Those morons! That is the rudest."

"Well, they weren't laughing at my singing or my dancing. But thank you for that passionate defense of my dignity. They laughed because my gorgeous, gauzy skirt was tucked into my underwear. For real. Justin laughed more than any of them. It overshadowed my entire fabulous performance," she sighed and lay back on the couch again."That's not all," Marissa supplied. "The tucked skirt

83

itself wasn't such a big deal. Honestly Gwen, I could see you doing something like that on purpose."

"I would not!" Gwen said, rising up to glare at Marissa. "But maybe I wouldn't have been so embarrassed if I hadn't been wearing my period underwear. Penny, they were my big white ones. They were baggy, with a little hole on one side."

Penny knew it was juvenile, but she had to fight her rising laugh. One bark of laughter escaped, and that set off Marissa. The laughter took over, and they couldn't seem to stop. Gwen protested, but after a while, even she was laughing.

Penny sat up and wiped her eyes. "I admit, that sucks, Gwen. But it's really not *that* big of a deal. Did you talk to them at all after? Give them a chance to compliment you on your singing?"

"No. Marissa jumped up on that stage like a superhero, and pulled my skirt free. Then we escaped out the back door. I'm never talking to any of them again," she said. "I mean it. Not ever."

Penny fought her smile, and said, "It's kind of a classic skirt-wearing mishap. They've probably already forgotten it, and are trying to find you so they can invite you to sing with them again."

"Whatever. It doesn't matter anyway, because I'm not doing it. Not after that. Justin will never find me sexy now that he knows I wear a big white sack on my ass," she lamented.

At that, they broke into laughter again. Penny asked her, "Is that what you're after, though? If Justin finds you sexy, you've succeeded? If so, that's fine I suppose, but what about being human? Someday I hope for a relationship where I am accepted for all the various sides of myself."

"That was deep." Gwen rolled her eyes.

Marissa whacked Gwen on the arm. "Don't be stupid. Penny's right. He would have found out you're human sooner or later."

"I was hoping for later."

"Come on, let's eat," Penny said.

After the food and much badgering, Penny let them paint her toenails. She sat back and relaxed as they painted. When her phone beeped, she scootched over to pick it up and looked at the screen. Another text from Will. This time she realized her body wasn't revving up to panic. That was good. She tossed the phone back onto the couch, and it bounced onto the floor. She reached for it.

"Penny, stop moving! You're going to ruin your nails!" Gwen screeched.

Marissa reached out and picked up the phone. "Who's Will Sutton?" she asked, and passed it to Penny.

Penny took the phone and told her, "He's my ex-boyfriend. I'd rather forget he exists, if you don't mind."

"Did he do you wrong? Want me to hassle him for you?" Gwen asked, reaching for the phone.

"He was not entirely good to me. But don't hassle him, because I think *I* did me wrong in that relationship. More than he did, in fact," Penny said. "It was a classic case of Girl Becomes Whatever She Thinks Boy Wants Her To Be."

"I've been that girl before too," Marissa said. "I think most people do that when they're young and figuring it all out."

"Not me," Gwen said firmly. "No way. I am a doormat for no boy."

Marissa let out a deep belly laugh. "Gwen, you liar! You do it *all* the time. Maybe you're not afraid to say what you're thinking, but you still put on an act for boys. You are always trying to act sexy for Justin."

Gwen pouted for about a second, then she stood up and strutted around the room with her hips swaying. "That is no act, ladies. I'm just a sexy, sexy beast."

Once they stopped laughing, Penny said, "Okay, so we all know it's important to be your genuine self in a relationship. The guy will love you for who you are, big white underwear and all, blah, blah, blah. But what I want to know is, how do you get to that point? Just the idea of saying whatever's on my mind and feeling comfortable...yeah, I don't do that."

"You do it with us," Marissa pointed out.

"I guess so," Penny said, but deep inside she knew that she was putting on a little bit of an act, even with them. She was trying not to be a people-pleaser, but found herself holding back some opinions, and letting them talk her into stuff. She wanted them to like her. Maybe that was just the usual push and pull of relating with other humans.

Would she ever be completely soul-bare with another human? With a man? It probably involved arguments and making up, and the guy knowing all her weird habits. It didn't feel possible.

~

After the girls left, Penny went to her grandpa's house. She was pleased when he agreed to walk to the beach with her. It was boiling outside, and they were both out of breath when they arrived.

Cal picked a spot far back from the water. "I do not like the beach."

"Why on earth did you say you'd come with me then, Grandpa? For that matter, why did you move to a beach town in South Carolina?"

Cal blew out a frustrated breath. "The answer to both questions is the same. Your grandmother loved the beach.

That's why we moved here, and that's why I wanted to come today."

Penny sat back in her new purple beach chair and rubbed sunscreen on her face. "Okay. That's fair. You could at least take your shoes off though, and enjoy it a little bit."

"My shoes will stay on, thank you very much."

Chapter 11

Penny sat on her couch pulling at a loose thread on her stretch pants. She was up before the birds again, trying to ignore the anxiety pulsing through her veins. She was not used to living like this, feeling as though everything could collapse at any moment. She sort of missed the days when she had simply done what she was told and let the responsibility fall elsewhere. Her heart was pounding and she couldn't push away the what-if thoughts. What if her parents died in a freak accident before things felt normal with them again? What if Grandpa kept getting worse and worse and she didn't recognize he needed more help? What if she never figured out what to do with her life and ended up delivering groceries forever? The thoughts wouldn't stop intruding, so she got out of bed. It was mid-sunrise, and the sky was still pink. She thought that might be a nice view from the beach, so she threw on some clothes and rushed out the door to try and catch it before it was over.

As Penny crested the hill and walked out onto the sand, she saw a lone figure lying on the beach down by the water. She walked closer. He was flat on his back, arms and legs spread like he was making a snow angel. It was Archer. She recognized his floppy black hair and those junky tennis shoes. Because she was trying to calm herself down, she decided not to go talk with him. Archer made her feel many different things, but calm wasn't one of them. She turned and walked a few steps away from him.

"Penny? Hi Penny," he slurred, leaning himself up on his elbows. "Weren't you gonna say hello?"

Startled, Penny turned back to face him. "Good morning." She was wary.

He tried to sit up, but flopped back over against the sand.

"Oh. You're drunk," Penny said, taken by surprise. "Tell me, did you get an early start or is this leftover from last night?"

"I guess this is leftover? Come sit by me," he said.

Don't say yes, she ordered herself. "No thanks. I want some quiet time alone. I'll see you at work later."

"I don't work today. And I can be as quiet as this grain of sand falling." He pinched some sand and let it fall, a triumphant look on his face when it made no sound. "You won't know I'm here. Come sit," he pressed, managing to sit up this time.

"Archer, no." Penny spoke forcefully. He widened his eyes and looked at her. His face was puffy. She wasn't going to hang out with a drunk guy on the beach at dawn when she was feeling emotional. Her gut told her to stay away. "I'll see you around."

"Okay, okay. I get it. It's fine, you can leave. I'm used to it. People walk away from me all the time," he said, his voice thick and his words barely decipherable due to the slurring.

Penny's mouth fell open. "Oh no you don't," she said, infuriated. She clenched her teeth and tried to breathe. For far too long she'd let comments like that slide. She reminded herself that she wasn't here to make friends. She was here to learn to stand up for herself. She stepped close to him and poked her finger into his t-shirt. "You can't lay a guilt trip on me. Is it unreasonable that I want some time alone? Or that I don't think it would be wise to hang around you in your current state? I don't exist to make you feel better about your crappy decisions. I have done nothing wrong and I won't let you make me feel bad."

He barked out a short laugh. "I've said the wrong thing again, and you called me out on it, again. I like your guts, you know that?"

"I know I'm leaving. Bye Archer." As she walked away, she could hear him muttering to himself. In truth, she did feel bad that people walked away from him. But right then, she was glad to be one of them.

~

Penny was pleased to see that Irene had placed a small order. There were only a few other orders, and she decided to do them first so she could spend a little time visiting with her.

"Hi Penny, come on in and let's get this bacon frying," Irene greeted her. "Cooking with company is always more fun. Eating is more fun with company too, of course."

Penny set the bags down on the counter. She hadn't expected she'd be helping cook and eat a meal, but then again it was nearly noon. She could have her lunch break with Irene. The house smelled of vanilla, and light streamed through the open curtains in the living room.

Irene laid the bacon on a plate and put it in the microwave. Penny sliced a tomato while Irene tore lettuce into chunks. The whirring microwave, sizzling bacon, and the cozy silence lulled her, and she unclenched her shoulders for the first time all day.

"Let's sit here in the kitchen to eat. The dining room is my workshop," Irene said.

"What sort of work do you do?"

"I repair antique violins. The volume of work I do isn't high, but I'm good. I can get away with charging high prices."

"Do you play the violin, too?"

"Yes, I do. I began learning when I was just three years old. My mother taught me. She was a passionate musician herself. We connected through music. She told me that I didn't need to see her face, because hearing her play was seeing into her soul."

They ate in silence for a while. "I'm not musical, or artistic in any way," Penny told her. "I doubt anyone watching me balance a chemistry equation would somehow understand my soul."

Irene chuckled. "Your strengths lie in the sciences then?"

"I guess. The things I'm good at aren't the things I want to spend my time doing. It has made my dad happy, being a chemistry professor, so he must have found something special in it. But ever since I decided not to follow in his footsteps, I think he's mourning his visions of us sharing a ride to campus in the mornings, chatting about molecules while sipping coffee from to-go mugs."

Irene nodded.

"I feel sort of guilty about it." Penny took a bite of her sandwich, glad Irene couldn't see her reddened face.

"What do you have to be guilty for? That you aren't passionate about chemistry? In that case, ninety-nine percent of the population should be walking around feeling guilty."

"It's been drilled into my head how important it is for the world to have women scientists. And I could be one."

"Just because you *could* be does not mean you *should* be, I assure you. I *could* be a pole dancer if I wanted, but it's probably best that I am not one. I have rhythm, but I prefer to make the music, not dance to it."

Penny's eyes widened, and she laughed.

Irene continued. "Your interests and passions might change frequently through your life. There's no rule that you have to choose one career and do that forever."

"Do you think that will happen for you? Will you ever switch careers?"

"Well if I ever get the bug to be a topless dancer, everyone will be surprised but you." They both laughed. "But the thing is, I'm open to anything. To all of it."

Then Irene easily changed the subject. She was interested in Grandpa Cal's situation, and Penny's role in his life. She had been friends with Penny's grandmother. They had taken aerobic swim classes at the Y together for a time. She had met Cal a few times, but knew him mostly through Ruby's stories about him.

"I might understand him a little bit. I insist on living on my own in spite of my sister contending that I need to hire help. I don't need that kind of help, and I think I'd know it if I did. Granted, dementia might affect whether or not he knows it. Regardless, I believe you're doing a good thing, trying to keep him home as long as possible."

Penny was thankful for a new perspective from an adult who knew her grandpa too. "Thank you, Irene. Thanks for the food too. I better get back to work."

"Any time, honey. My grub is your grub."

Penny rose and counted out the correct amount of grocery money from the drawer she had been shown last time.

"Before you go, let me ask you something," Irene said. "Would you like to do any work on the side? I need a few projects done around here, and that's the kind of help I don't mind asking for. My friend Magnolia told me my walls need to be painted. She says they're faded and dingy and out of date. I'll get at least one other person to help you with that job, but most of the jobs are small. Would you be interested?"

When Penny drove across the country nearly a month ago, she hadn't expected to get so tangled in other people's lives. It seemed to be happening without her consent. Her eyes stung with unexpected tears when she thought of the people who had welcomed her and trusted her. "I can give you Wednesdays."

~

The next morning, Penny flipped down her visor and used the mirror to apply some lip gloss and check for breakfast caught in her teeth. She didn't want to leave her car and face work just yet, so she picked up some of the trash that had accumulated on the floor of the car. When there was only a minute left until her shift started, she climbed out of the car with a wad of trash in both hands and her purse swinging from her elbow. Before she shut her car door, she saw Marissa and Archer talking by the employee entrance door.

They were standing close together, and Marissa's hands were gesturing and waving wildly. Her voice was quiet, but Penny could tell by the way they were standing that they were arguing. Rather, she could tell Marissa was arguing. Archer wasn't responding in any way that she could see. His head was bowed, his hands in his pockets, folded in on himself. Marissa stopped talking and looked at him with her hands on her hips. He didn't say anything, but finally looked up at her. She gave him a frustrated glare and went in the door, slamming it behind her.

Archer sat down on the curb and put his head in his hands. She wasn't sure if she should approach him or not. She was still irritated with him because of the drunk-on-the-beach incident, but she wanted to practice facing these things. She went to the dumpster and dropped in her trash.

She walked over and sat down on the curb next to him. Neither of them spoke. After a minute, he bumped his knee softly against hers. An apology. She bumped his knee in return. A forgiveness. She sat there for a minute more, sharing the silence, then stood up and went inside the store to search for Marissa.

"Marissa?" Penny whispered, and touched her shoulder. Marissa was stacking apples in a bin, with an angry fervor. "Let me help. You're bruising these poor apples." They worked side by side, Marissa calming a little. "I saw you talking to Archer. Is everything okay?"

She paused in her work, and turned to look at Penny. "That boy makes me so mad. I saw him out on Sunday night. I was at the ice cream shop helping Mike, and Archer flung himself through the door. He was so drunk. He was falling all over the place, couldn't even get his ass in a chair. You should have seen it. Several people left because of him. Mike had to throw him out." Marissa shook her head in disgust.

"I saw him on the beach at dawn on Monday. He was still drunk," Penny told her.

"Ugh. His mom was a junkie, did you know that? Not just a junkie, she was a dealer. He just doesn't know what *normal* is," she said, and slammed a few apples onto her stack.

"I didn't know. So do you think…?" Penny let her question trail off, not wanting to put words to the thought.

"I know he's not using drugs. Having the family he did made it so he would never touch that stuff. But being drunk all over town? That has to stop. It's one thing to party sometimes, but I won't let him hurt Mike's business. Outside, I just told him to keep his drinking where it belongs."

"I spoke sharply to him when I saw him on the beach."

"Good," Marissa replied, and shrugged her shoulders. "I'm done trying to help him. Self-preservation and all that."

"That's good. You need to do what's best for you." Penny knew the same was true for herself. She would focus on her own concerns, and not insert herself into others'.

She sighed and went to get her lists and start work. She saw that her first customer was Mr. George Baker. She steeled herself to take his gruff attitude and not be intimidated. She didn't know how it was going to go, but at least this time she knew where to find the pickled eggs.

Penny knocked on his door, and lifted her chin to show him she wasn't scared. She planned to be on the offense. Not offensive, mind you, just on the offense. When George opened the door, Penny charged through it and said, "Good morning, Mr. Baker! Beautiful day, isn't it?" She walked straight to the kitchen and set his groceries on the counter. She yanked out the receipt and handed it to him. "Your total is twenty-six dollars and fourteen cents." Then she stood tall, waiting for him to respond. She looked at his face and ignored the intriguing clutter surrounding her. Out of the corner of her eye, she saw a pyramid of dice on an end table. She willed herself not to look for the jar of toenail clippings.

Mr. Baker narrowed his eyes and looked back at Penny. Steady as a rock, he retrieved his checkbook from a kitchen drawer, and filled one in. He tore it out and handed it to her. There was no tip, but that was fine with her. She wasn't sure she deserved one. She felt the whole transaction had gone as well as it could. She let her confidence go a little far, though, when she told him she liked his clocks.

"Mind your business," he said, and walked to his door and opened it. He waved her out, and she went, gladly.

~

Later the same day a call came in from Steph. Penny wondered how she and Gregory were getting on. She filled the order, and threw in a chocolate bar as a gift. As she loaded the bags into her car, she saw Archer across the parking lot. He was sweeping up the broken glass and debris around the dumpster. He lifted his hand to her, and she waved back.

At Steph's house, things were peaceful. She told Penny that Gregory was napping. "Would you like to hang out for a little bit?" she asked.

"Maybe that would be okay, for a few minutes," Penny told her. "I'll need to get back to the store soon."

"Sure. I guess I'm just starved for conversation. I feel like we've never had the most basic chat. So are you from around here?" she asked. Penny filled her in on her stats and lack of plans, then spent some time talking about her grandpa.

"I know Cal. He's been to my church a couple times. I'm glad he's doing okay. You say he liked Gregory?"

"Yeah, they got along great. It rejuvenated him or something, to be around a baby."

"Maybe I'll go see him. You let me know if I can help out sometime."

"Okay. Thanks."

"I did the road trip thing too, though I did it after college," said Steph. "I got my degree in journalism, and so I went traveling to see if I wanted to be a far flung news correspondent. After I spent about six months on the road, I decided I did not. So I came back home."

"Did you meet Jeff on the road?" Penny asked.

"No. Jeff and I went to high school together. He'd gone off to college too, and came back a few months before me. We found ourselves back in this place that we'd both sort of outgrown, but didn't want to leave quite yet. We don't plan to stay here forever though. I like it here fine, but I still hope to put down roots in a bigger city someday," she said. "Maybe someday I'll get back in the news business, too."

"At least you know the shape of what you want."

"I sure didn't know it when I was eighteen." If a bona fide adult like Steph wasn't sure what her future held, maybe it was okay for Penny too.

Penny's phone rang then, and she pulled it from her pocket and looked at the screen. "It's my grandpa. I'm going to go, but I'll see you soon." She answered the call as she closed Steph's door behind her.

"They told me I didn't have an appointment today!" Cal shouted.

Penny climbed into her hot car, and put the windows down. "Grandpa, what are you talking about?"

"I did have an appointment today! I think I know my own schedule!"

"Hang on a second, let me check my calendar."

"You don't need to check it, I know it was today," he grumbled.

From her purse, she dug out the day planner that she kept with all Grandpa's information. Today was blank. "Okay, Grandpa, but the doctor's office doesn't have you down for today."

"Then they made a mistake!"

"Grandpa, can you please stop yelling?"

"I am not yelling! You call that office back and tell them they got it wrong. They ruined my entire day!"

Penny hung her head. "I'll call them. Why don't you go sit out back and relax and I'll call them for you."

"I don't need to relax!"

Chapter 12

Apparently insomnia was going to be Penny's new roommate. Her now familiar roommate, anxiety, was there in the bed too. Anxiety doesn't have a memory, so any progress she'd made with Irene and Steph the past few days now seemed distant and untrue.

She glanced at her alarm clock, and saw it was once again too early to be up. She got up anyway. She took a shower and got dressed, then texted Vera. No response, of course, because it was ridiculously early in Montana.

She decided to go out for breakfast to kill some time. She drove through the main streets of town looking for someplace open. Mike's ice cream shop was lit up and she could see him moving around inside. She parked and went inside, thankful the usual crowd wasn't out front. To Penny's delight, there was a selection of pastries on a platter and some fruit in a bowl. She could also smell coffee.

"Good morning, Penny. What can I get you?"

"Hi Mike. I didn't realize you served breakfast here."

"Yeah. There's no donut shop or coffee shop in town, aside from the gas station, so I thought I'd take advantage of the market. I'm thinking of opening up a real coffee shop after I save up some more. Do you think it would do any business here?" he asked.

"I do. Diners are great and all, but a coffee shop with the right ambiance is special. If you put in couches and armchairs, I'd be a customer, for sure," she said, trying to picture herself still in Wells Cove in a year's time.

"In that case, your breakfast is on me."

"I thought it would be anyway. I'm one of Marissa's friends, remember?" she said, smiling. Then she thought better of what she'd said and added, "Not that I'm holding you to that, of course. I expect to pay for what I order."

He slid a steaming coffee mug over to her, a smile on his face. "You didn't order this. I just gave it to you."

She took a sip, surprised by the flavor. For a plain white mug, she wasn't expecting the creamy caramel coffee. She looked at him and nodded. "This is good."

"All right, now will you have a croissant? A donut?" he asked.

"Sure."

He laughed and put both on a plate for her. She ate while he quietly puttered around the shop. He wiped crumbless counters, rearranged already perfect stacks of cups, and counted bills in the cash register. He stopped for only a second, and looked up at Penny and said, "Do you like it here?"

"Didn't we just cover this? This is a great shop. It smells like sugar, and it's extremely clean." She pointed to the rag in his hand. "And the food is great." She held up her croissant for reference.

"No, I mean this town. Wells Cove, South Carolina. East Coast," he clarified.

Penny thought for a moment. Did she like it here? "I don't know. I haven't been here long enough to decide, I guess."

"Hmm," Mike said, and turned back to his puttering.

"Well, how about you then. Do you like it here? Did you grow up here?"

He walked into the back room without answering her. He came back carrying a box of napkins and began refilling napkin holders. Then he said, "That's the thing. I've lived here my whole life. I've never been out of the state. What you did, it was…big. I hope you don't think I'm being nosy, but Marissa told me a little about you. She thinks highly of you, by the way." He smoothed his thumbs across his eyebrows. "Anyway, I think about it sometimes, the way you left your home and traveled all the way across the country. I think I'd like to do something like that. Start fresh, you know?"

Now it was her turn to hmm. "Hmm." She took a long swallow of her coffee. "Hitting the restart button was definitely freeing. I wasn't freed from everything though. I think it's true that your troubles will follow you. Not to imply that you're troubled. Or that I am either. Sorry." She paused to try to think before speaking. "Yes, it was freeing. But only in the way that it is when you have a big test to study for and you decide to watch a movie and study later."

He nodded. "I got in trouble a lot in high school. Partied too hard, you know? I got my act together enough to go to the two year business school at the community college and then bought this shop and fixed it up a little. Still though, most of the older folks in town think of me as the troublemaker I used to be."

"Yeah? I cannot picture you as a troublemaker."

He laughed. "I seem so straight-laced to you?"

"Well, I'm definitely straight-laced, so I could be projecting."

He smiled. "Still, it would be interesting to see what it's like in a place where no one knows me. Maybe I'd get more business."

She chewed on her food thoughtfully. "You know what though?"

"What?"

"You'd be surprised at how quickly people begin to know you." She shifted in her seat uncomfortably while he glanced at her. She changed the subject. "Anyhow, with your reputation and your age, you draw a young crowd. That's not a bad thing."

He had to stop talking and help a customer who walked in. It was an elderly woman who ordered six apple fritters to go.

After she left, he said, "Well, so much for the young crowd." They laughed. "Seriously though, speaking of young crowds, I'm visiting a new all-ages club next Thursday. I want to see if it's a good place for Someling to play. Would you like to come?"

Penny didn't know what to say. Thursday. That seemed a weird night to go to a club. Or maybe she just didn't know anything about clubs. Did he mean for it to be a date? She didn't feel that kind of vibe coming from him. She tried to think it through, but the idea of being at a club was too weird. She didn't do night life. She was not used to being friends with a non-brother boy. She felt lame.

He noticed her hesitance. "Of course, I'm inviting Gwen and Marissa to come too."

At that, Penny smiled and nodded her assent. Not a date then. She threw away her doubts about her ability to function appropriately at a club and decided to embrace the opportunity to stretch the limits of her comfort zone. "That would be nice, Mike, thanks. Now I've got to get moving. Irene Solotken hired me to do some work around her house. Last week she had me replace a doorknob and clean the garage."

"That sounds like hard labor."

"Nah I like to keep busy. I'll talk to you later."

She walked out the door, already wondering if she should try to find a way to cancel the club plans.

~

The air still felt like early morning, crisp with a grayish light. Irene opened the door before Penny had even stepped out of her car.

"Penny?" she called.

"Yes, it's me," Penny responded.

"Good, I hoped you'd get here first," she said.

Penny walked into the house, and Irene held out a coffee mug. Penny took it, though she was already over-caffeinated from Mike's caramel coffee.

"So what's on the agenda for today?"

"Today you will be painting. Magnolia picked out new colors for the living room, kitchen, and the guest bedroom. Two coats each. You won't get all that done today, of course. I want to tell you that I hired someone else to help too, in the hopes that it'll make the work go faster. Archer Thomas."

"Archer?" Penny croaked. She took a big gulp of the scalding coffee.

"Yes. He's been a big help to me over the years. I assume you know him from the store. When I asked him to help you with this project, he jumped at the chance. But I want to make sure that will be comfortable for you. Do you like him fine?" she asked.

Penny wasn't quite sure how to answer that question. "He's...yeah. He knew he'd be working with me today?"

"Oh yes, he knew." Her face held a knowing smile. "He couldn't say 'yes' fast enough."

Penny raised her eyebrows and took a deep breath. "I can work with anyone." She wondered which version of Archer would show up. Hopefully not the hung-over one.

Since he wasn't there yet, Penny grabbed a roll of painter's tape and got busy in the living room. Irene told her how to place tape on the floor where the legs of each piece of furniture should go when it was moved back into place. It had to go exactly where it was before, so she wouldn't bump her shins on misplaced end tables. When that was done, she pushed the furniture to the middle of the room, with Irene hovering nearby. Occasionally she had a question for her about where to stash things, but after a while she was up on a stepladder taping off the ceiling. Irene went to her dining room to work on a violin.

The work was menial, and lulled her into a state of restful thought. It was still bizarre to Penny that she was on her own adventure without Vera. Though Vera hadn't said, Penny knew she had been hurt that she wasn't invited along for the summer. It wasn't that Penny didn't want her there, but she had wanted to find out what it would be like not being tethered to those people who had known her for her whole life. So far it was less different than she thought it might be. Maybe she wasn't trying hard enough to change her ways. She felt good about agreeing to go to the club, and reaffirmed her plan to be bolder.

She was pulled from her musings by a soft knock at the door. The knocker didn't wait for an answer; he just opened the door and came right in.

"Hello Irene! I'm here so the party can start," Archer called. He wore a big smile, and that messy black hair fell over his left eye.

"The party started an hour ago, lazy bones," Penny said, from up on the ladder. She silently congratulated herself for speaking to him first.

"Hey, I'm the least lazy person in this house," he said, and added in a shout towards the dining room, "And that includes you, Irene."

He walked toward the ladder and tilted his head up to look at Penny. She liked the height reversal. "I had to put in a few hours at the store before I could come. Tiny old Bellhill can't run that place alone." He smiled at her, and she loved the way it crinkled up his eyes.

Irene came into the room and put her arms out. Archer stepped into them, and hugged her tightly. "What's this about me being lazier than you? Ah, well, you might be right. I enjoy sitting around. Sue me. Now I do have to get some

103

work done, so you kids behave." She turned and went back to her violin.

Archer picked up a can of paint and a tray. "Is this the color for in here? It's yellow," he said, as though yellow was akin to evil.

"Yeah, Magnolia wants the living room yellow," Penny said, "In my opinion, yellow is the best color for any room, though maybe more of a soft butter instead of this." She gestured to the paint chip taped to the wall. It was bright goldenrod.

Archer shook the can a few times, and pried it open. He stirred it and poured it into the tray. He muttered, "Yellow. Well, Irene'll never see its horrid, hideous hue."

"Alliteration, Archer?"

"Precisely, Penny."

Penny hid her smile as she stepped down from the ladder. She found the plastic sheeting to spread on the floor and over the furniture. After that was done, Archer began to paint, and Penny looked around for another roller.

"There's a roller on the kitchen counter. Only one tray though. We'll have to share," Archer said, and gave her a sneaky grin. Penny went to get the roller.

She bit the inside of her cheek and waited her turn to dip her roller in the paint. After she did, she started painting at the opposite side of the wall from Archer. They could each paint toward the middle of the wall, and maybe by the time the paint met, she'd feel more comfortable.

For about ten minutes, neither of them spoke. Penny watched him out of the corner of her eye as they worked. He hummed softly. She found humming annoying, and tried to ignore it. He was wearing a gray t-shirt, and it kept riding up when he stretched his arm to paint up high, revealing his tan stomach. She did *not* find that annoying, and tried to ignore it too. The tree on his forearm was getting flecked with tiny dots of yellow, like little canaries sitting on the branches.

104

She decided to think about her family as a distraction, and just when she was getting lost in her thoughts again, Archer said, "Want to play a game?"

"Sure. What game?"

He paused in his painting and turned toward her, half his mouth curled up in a grin. Was he going to suggest *I spy* or something? "How about Two Truths and a Lie? You have to say two things that are true about yourself, and one thing that's a lie. Then I'll guess which thing was the lie..."

"I know how to play," Penny interrupted. She sighed. She had played that game hundreds of times over the course of her childhood. She was terrible at it, mostly because she hadn't done many exciting things that could be used to fool people. "Fine, let's play. Give me a minute to think." She felt nervous to say anything too personal. She thought of boring things like her shoe size and her favorite food. Then she remembered that night on the beach, at the bonfire. She also thought about the other day at the beach when they leaned back against each other. She thought she could be the tiniest bit brave with her truths.

"Come on, you're taking all morning," Archer said, as he dipped his roller again.

"Geez, give me a minute." A few more minutes passed. "Okay, I think I'm ready. Here goes." She paused to take a breath and Archer gave her a look that said *on with it already* and so she spoke, knowing her three things were duds.

"Number one: I hate spicy food. Number two: I am turning down a full-ride scholarship at Montana State University this fall. Number three: I have seven brothers and sisters."

"That's easy. I think you love spicy food," he said, without looking at her.

"You really think I have seven siblings?" She had thought for sure that one would trip him up.

"Yep. I'm sticking with the spicy food."

Penny breathed out heavily, and her hair flew around the front of her face. "Fine. You're right. Point for you. Your turn then."

"First we get to discuss your truths. Why are you turning down the scholarship?" he asked.

She felt dizzy. "We don't get to discuss my truths. That wasn't in the rules. Had that been listed among the rules, I would have chosen different truths."

He gave her a one-raised-brow look. "You didn't even let me finish explaining the rules. The point of this game, Penny, is to get to know each other."

"I thought the point was to pass the time while we paint, not delve into our psyches," she muttered. "I should have just listed my shoe size and my favorite color. But I didn't want to bore you."

"Not one thing about you bores me," he said casually, his arm making smooth strokes with the roller. "What size shoe do you wear?"

"Six."

"What? How is that possible? I wear a twelve. My feet are twice as big as yours."

"I'm not sure it works that way, but whatever."

"How tall are you?" he asked.

"Five feet two inches."

"Oh my God. I'm six feet two inches. We are perfectly mathematically balanced."

She laughed and shook her head.

"And let me guess. Your favorite color is yellow."

"Yeah. But it's tied with purple."

He grinned. "So, let's see. You kind of took the easy road with your truths."

She sighed. "One of them was a little bit of a big deal."

He shook his head. "It's okay. I can live with that. For now. Let me think of some middle-of-the-road facts about myself and maybe I'll inspire you to dig deeper." He grinned again and she knew he was teasing, but her cheeks burned. *For now?* She concentrated on painting and waited to hear his list.

"Number one: My mom is in prison. Number two: I lived with my cousin Adam for a while, until he kicked me out. Number three: My dad is dead."

Penny froze. It was pure luck that she didn't dribble a huge blob of paint onto the window frame. "Those are your middle-of-the-road truths?" she asked, trying not to sound as shocked as she felt.

"Only two of them. One of them is a lie. Which do you think it is?"

She thought about it. She'd already heard his mom was in prison. She didn't figure he'd lie about his dad being dead, so she said, "I think the lie is that Adam kicked you out."

"Wrong. My dad isn't dead. At least he wasn't the last time I heard from Grandma. He lives in Alabama with her," he said, no emotion in his voice.

"Oh." She didn't understand his matter-of-fact way of talking about that sort of thing. "So Adam kicked you out?" She wondered what had led to him living there in the first place, especially because she knew he didn't particularly care for Adam.

"The day I turned eighteen. But according to you, we're not discussing our truths," he said, a smile in his voice, "To make it not feel quite so personal."

Her cheeks burned again. At this rate, they'd be scorched off before lunch. She realized it was kind of dumb to share intimate facts with each other, but not expound upon them or discuss them at all. But it was what she wanted, that dipping in of one toe at a time. That was what she could handle. She didn't dare ponder why she was dipping any toes in at all.

"Your turn," Archer said. "So far I have two points and you have zero. You need to step up your game."

This time Penny was prepared with her three things. She wanted to make it more fun and less serious. "One: I sleep naked. Two: I've only had one boyfriend in my entire life. Three: I once ate a beetle on a dare."

He laughed. "The boyfriend thing. That right there is the lie."

"Wrong. Ha, a point for me! I knew you'd latch on to the idea that I sleep naked. But alas, I sleep in pajamas. Socks even," she said.

"Socks? No. No one can sleep in socks."

She shrugged.

"So you ate a beetle?"

"A little black one. My brother, Art, dared me to. I only swallowed it whole though, downed it with a glass of water."

~

After they cleaned the paint from their hands as best they could, they helped Irene make sandwiches. She put a pickle spear on each plate, something Penny's mother has always done. She felt a rush of affection for Irene, and reached out to squeeze her shoulder. She smiled, and Penny thought it was pretty neat that blind people smile even though they can't see other smiles.

"Irene, I'm curious about your family. Would you tell me about them?" Penny asked.

"Oh yes! I love to talk about my family," Irene said. The three sat down at her kitchen table, and she continued. "I have one sister named Sandra. She is only a year older than me, and we are close. I would like to make the trip out to visit her this fall. Our parents are deceased. They were in their forties when Sandra and I were born, and died almost 10 years ago, in their eighties."

Archer spoke then. "Irene, tell her about Jennifer."

Irene nodded her head and smiled. "Jennifer is my daughter. She is thirty-seven years old, and lives in Oregon. She was adopted by a lovely family when she was two days old. When she turned eighteen, her parents gave her my address, and now we exchange letters a few times each year."

Penny squirmed in her chair. Why did she never know the right things to say to people? To keep something stupid from tumbling out of her mouth, she chose to nod and smile.

Irene continued, her voice even and strong. "Jennifer was conceived by rape."

Penny blinked. "You were raped?" she whispered.

"Yes. That time I was seventeen years old. Apparently my rapist found it convenient to rape a blind woman, as I wasn't able to easily identify or describe my attacker."

"You said 'That time.' Do you mean," Penny breathed, "That you've been raped more than once?" *Why had Archer brought up this topic?*

"I've been raped twice. That time, and then again when I was thirty." She waved her hand dismissively at Penny. "I can tell you're over there freaking out. Relax."

Penny glanced at Archer, who shrugged his shoulders. She didn't know how to arrange her face. But Irene wouldn't see it anyway, so she focused on slowing her breathing.

"My parents encouraged me to make the adoption plan for Jennifer. I think they couldn't fathom how I would manage to take care of her, and they were already in their later years and didn't want to raise another baby," she said.

Penny looked at Archer again. He took a huge bite of his sandwich and didn't meet her eyes. She assumed he had heard this story before.

"People are often afraid to talk about the horrors of life, about rape, as if they can pretend it doesn't exist. That's rubbish. I don't live in fear. Living in fear would only diminish my life," she said. "I was angry for a long time, hurt for a long time." She chuckled incongruously. "My parents forced me into a lot of therapy. I fought it at the time, but I dare say now that I'm grateful. Do you want to hear the whole story?"

Penny didn't exactly *want* to hear the story. She knew her method of living in a vague swirl of fear about everything bad that could go wrong was pathetic. She decided hearing it would give Irene's experience the respect it deserved. "Yes."

"I was seventeen, as I said."

Penny listened.

"It was a Friday night, and I snuck out from my house to meet with friends at an old abandoned gas station. Sneaking out wasn't part of a rebellious phase. Rather, if it was, my rebellious phase lasted a good ten years. It was not unusual for me to sneak out on the weekends and meet with friends to drink, smoke pot, and sit and talk, being silly together. My parents knew about my behavior, and I was frequently grounded. It didn't matter, though. I would sneak out every weekend just the same.

"I sat on the cold tile floor of that gas station. The windows had been boarded over, and my friends told me it was pitch black. But of course everything is always pitch black to me. The darkness put us on common ground. We couldn't see each other, and we fumbled in the dark, passing a joint around. The place smelled of smoke and mildew.

"After several hours, the group dispersed. No one lived in my neighborhood, and no one offered to walk me home. They knew better. I would harshly scold anyone who tried to help me. I lived in a wholesome suburban neighborhood, which was why it took me by such surprise when a man grabbed me from behind.

"He sounded drunk, and smelled worse than a skunk in a dumpster. He had my arms pinned behind me. I screamed, kicked, head-butted. Anything I could think of. He taunted me for my blindness."

Penny shivered in her seat.

Irene continued her story. "He grabbed my breasts and told me I'd never know who he was. When he pinned me to the ground, I tried to gouge out his eyeballs. I thought that would be a fitting punishment. That infuriated him, and he lifted my head and banged it against the sidewalk. I blacked out, and consider it an odd sort of luck that I don't remember the actual rape.

"When I regained consciousness, I was a bloody, bruised mess. I hadn't been a virgin, but he had been rough and I knew the smell of sex. I stood and limped home. My parents took me to the hospital, and I willingly filled out a police report, my writing angry and sloppy and not staying confined to the little boxes on the forms. With no eye witness, there wasn't much to go on, and the case was never solved.

"I'm grateful to Jennifer's parents for all that they have done for her, not the least of which is encouraging the relationship I share with her. Rape is a horror, yes, but Jennifer does not represent that for me."

Archer had been sitting quietly through Irene's story, picking all the seeds out of his pickle spear.

"What a monster." Penny was outraged.

Archer scraped his chair back, and stood. He stomped into the living room.

Penny glanced at Irene. "Is he okay?"

"That'll be for him to tell you, Hon." She stood and picked up her plate. Now, let's finish our conversation. He can go be a grump on his own. Help me with these dishes." As they washed and dried, Irene answered all Penny's grisly questions. One thing she made sure Penny understood was that even though she was a bit of a wild child and had made some unwise decisions, Irene knew the rapes had not been her fault. She never blamed herself, only her rapists.

~

In the living room, Archer was aggressively rolling paint onto the wall by the floor. Crouched down like that, and with that scowl on his face, he looked like an angry troll. Penny stifled a laugh and painted in silence next to him. When their paint was about to meet, he took his roller to the last wall, leaving her to finish the remaining stripe.

She took the hint, and finished it on her own. Then rather than join him on that wall, she started a second coat on the first wall they painted, which was opposite the one where he was working. What was his deal? So he was brooding about something. That didn't mean he couldn't still be friendly. He had a bad habit of being rude when he was feeling dark things. Because it's hard not to let someone else's mood become her own, the more Penny thought about it, the more aggressive her own painting became. Now she was the angry troll painter.

There they were, both slapping paint on the wall, both angry. Penny slammed her roller into the paint tray. Yellow spatters dotted the drop cloth. She looked up to see Archer staring at her. He had finally noticed she was mad.

"Two truths and a lie. I know it's your turn, but I'm going anyway," she told him. "One: I am pissed off at the way you run hot and cold. Two: I also enjoy picking pickle seeds out of my pickle spears. Three: Irene would be better off to hire two seals to paint this room, the way we're slapping it on the walls." She glared at him.

The corner of his mouth lifted a fraction. He crossed his arms over his chest. "You don't like to dismantle your pickles?"

"No. I eat them like a normal person," she said. She looked at him, and saw that he was sucking in his lips to keep from smiling. She couldn't help it, she smiled. A laugh bubbled out, and she covered her mouth to try to keep its followers in. Then Archer barked out a laugh. All was lost after that. They laughed like loons.

112

"Why are we laughing?" she asked when she caught her breath.

"It's you. You just..." He sighed. "Somehow you change things around on me."

"What do you mean?"

He shrugged, and turned back to painting.

Chapter 13

It was late, and Penny couldn't wait to get into pajamas. As she walked up the stairs to her apartment, her phone rang. She dug around in her purse until she found it, and answered as she unlocked her door.

"Penny?" asked a male voice she recognized.

"Hi Mike." She dropped her purse on the counter and dropped herself on the couch. Her exhausted body was ready for bed, and she hadn't even had dinner yet. "What's up?"

"Sorry to bother you. I got your number from Marissa. There's an older guy here asking for you. When we ask him his name, he refuses to answer, but I think he's your grandpa. Cal Anderdoll? He is agitated and…wait, now he's trying to leave." Mike's muffled voice was speaking to someone, and Penny could hear other people talking loudly in the background.

Fear galloped through her and gave her the energy she needed. She didn't wait for Mike to explain what was happening. She hung up and scrambled to her car. It sounded like Grandpa had wandered. Penny tried to put all the information Miss Rita had given her into the forefront of her brain. She was determined to be calm.

When she pulled up to the ice cream shop, the usual crowd of kids was outside.

"Hey, what's your name?" One of the boys said in the kind of voice that would normally make her shrink. She didn't have any worry to spare though, so she held up her middle finger to them and stormed past.

"Whoa, whoa, sorry. We didn't mean anything by it," she heard as she swung open the door and was hit by the sugar fumes and agitated voices.

Penny went toward the small huddle of people at a table in the corner. She tapped Mike on the shoulder, and he moved out of the way. There was her grandpa, his fists clenched on the tabletop and his face in a scowl. One of the men had his hands on Cal's shoulders, as if to hold him in place. As soon as he saw her, he said, "Penny! There you are. These people won't let me leave. Is this a place to get a root beer float, or is it a prison?"

His voice didn't sound normal. "Hi Grandpa. I hear you were asking for me. What's going on?"

"Nothing! Nothing's going on. I came in here and asked for you, and here you are," he said. Penny had never seen his face hold that much anger.

"Well, why are you here?" She pressed.

"To see you, of course," he answered, now looking puzzled. "I need you to take me back home."

"But why didn't you just call me?" Penny rested her hand on Grandpa's cheek for a moment and looked around at the faces of the people in the shop. She didn't recognize the middle aged couple at the table with him, but the man still hadn't let go of Grandpa's shoulders. They made introductions, and she asked them if they'd sit with him for a minute. He didn't object.

"Mike, can I talk to you?"

Mike led her to a storage room in the back. "Penny, your grandpa didn't know where he was. He just kept saying your name over and over. When I tried to ask him questions, he yelled and slapped his hands on the table. Thankfully Della and Bill were able to calm him down a little, until you got here," he said.

Penny's eyes filled with tears, and her whole body trembled as she fought the sobs that wanted to take over.

115

She had never felt so overwhelmed and inexperienced in her life. Why had she thought she could handle this? If Grandpa was already at the stage of illness where he was wandering and not knowing how to cope out in the world, yet still refusing to accept help, his problems had outsized her ability to handle them. Defeated, she lowered her head.

Mike's large warm hands grabbed her shoulders firmly. "It's going to be okay, you know. You have friends here. We'll help you."

"Maybe it isn't going to be okay though. At some point it really isn't going to be okay. That's the whole point. Nobody will be able to help him."

Mike let go of Penny's shoulders and handed her a napkin from a huge box on a shelf, which made her laugh a little.

"What should I do?" she asked him, fully aware how juvenile that sounded. She hated how ineffective she felt.

"Take him home. Get him some supper. Talk to him about it when he can. It's going to be okay," he repeated, his voice reassuring in its certainty.

"Right." She wiped her eyes and blew her nose on the napkin. "Sorry I overreacted."

"I don't think you did," he said. "This is not an easy situation you're in."

She took a deep breath and walked back out to the front of the shop. Grandpa was alone at his table now, and Della and Bill were watching him from the opposite corner. He had his head in his hands.

"Penny, what's going on?" He looked adrift and vulnerable. But he wasn't a baby, and she didn't want to treat him like one. She didn't know how much of this evening he'd remember later, but she didn't want him to catch her coddling him.

"Grandpa, you just got lost, I guess. Let's go home and we'll talk about it later." Penny grabbed his arm and he looked up at her. While his eyes were familiar and blue, the man behind the eyes was vague and slightly foreign. Her heart lurched, but she pulled him up and he walked with her to the car.

When they got to his house, she made spaghetti and salad for dinner while he took a short nap on the couch. When he woke, they took the food outside to eat on the back deck. He was quiet, and he seemed more like himself.

"So, you wandered," Penny told him bluntly.

"I what?" he said, and sat down at the picnic table.

"Wandered. I did some reading about Alzheimer's, wandering is a—"

"I know," he interrupted, irritable. "I know what wandering is." He spun his fork around on his plate, but the pasta just flailed around it, not getting a grip.

"Has this happened before?" she asked.

He looked up at her for a moment. "I'm not ready to go to a nursing home."

"I know that. Who said anything about a nursing home?"

"Your mother. She thought it might be time for me to go to an assisted living facility. I hate the word facility," he said. Penny already knew that. Her mom wanted her to convince him of the merits of a facility.

"Well, what if you had someone come here instead? I could move in. There are lots of things we can do for when I'm at work. They sell special locks and nametag bracelets." A spark lit inside her, and she began to get excited about the idea. They could clean out his spare bedroom for her, and she'd worry less about him.

Suddenly, he stood up and slammed his palm on the table. Penny jumped. "You are not going to be my nurse-maid! I thought I made that clear to you when you came. You are my granddaughter." His voice softened, and he added, "You can be my friend. You may visit me. But dear girl, you are not going to spend your youth tending my old bones." He sat down with a thump.

She swallowed hard and nodded her head. "Okay," she said, meekly. Tears pricked her eyes and she was sick of crying and sick of being meek. She thought about arguing with him. She thought about all the valid points she could make. Then she shoved those thoughts away, deciding that keeping quiet was the wiser choice for the time being.

They spent another hour playing gin rummy, and after Grandpa was asleep she drove to her apartment. She sat on the dingy couch and rubbed her palm over the pilled fabric. Every plan she conceived to help him required his approval and consent. Clearly she wasn't going to be able to exert power over him. Anyway, the only power she had was to call mom behind his back.

Her parents were resisting using the power they had over her. They were trying to find ways to cooperate and communicate. They had even sent her a little cash in the mail last week. No, like her parents, she didn't want to use power and control to get what she wanted. She recognized that she was on the other side of the same coin. It was easy to see that neither side was a picnic.

Chapter 14

Penny curled the ends of her hair and dressed in tight jeans and a silver tank top. She threw on flip flops and only wore a bit of mascara, knowing Gwen would give her grief about both.

Her phone beeped. It was an alarm that she had set to go off every two hours so that she could call Grandpa and check on him.

"Hi Grandpa! How are you?"

"My dear, you ought to know. You've called five times today. I don't know how you got anything done. I know I haven't," he said, annoyed.

Penny sighed. "I know Grandpa. Thank you for humoring me. What were you trying to get done today?"

He sighed too, and ignored the question. Instead he said, "Your friend Steph and her baby just came by. That was unusual. I'm suspicious."

"Did she bring you dinner?"

"A lovely lasagna. Now go have a good time tonight. Be young. Let me be the old homebody."

She ended the call, and looked in the mirror. Reflected back was the face of a girl who had friends. Friends who were taking her out to a club. Club (*v*): To beat with a heavy stick. That sounded about right.

She grabbed her purse and went outside and down the steps. She sat on a parking block to wait. Gwen came bounding down the sidewalk and joined her. She was wearing a blue mini skirt and black high heels. Penny didn't know how a person could *bound* while wearing such clothes.

In spite of the fact that there would be no alcohol at this club, Gwen was excited to see it and had been thrilled to come along, but only once she'd been assured that Justin wouldn't be coming too. She still wasn't over the underwear incident.

"Sorry I took so long. I had to help loony Mrs. Limple with her trash compactor. At least once a week she calls and tells me it's broken, when she really just needs to change the bag." She paused in her rambling to look up at Penny. "Pen! You look fabulous. Your hair looks good tonight. Don't you own a pair of heels?" She took a tube of lipstick from her bag, and Penny slapped a hand over her mouth before Gwen could begin her ministrations.

"You leave my feet and lips alone. You have your own body, you know, do what you like with it."

A car pulled into the parking space directly in front of them, stopping a bit before their feet. Gwen shot Penny a pouty look, and then jumped up. She opened the back door before Penny even stood up, and climbed in. She poked her head out, beaming, and shouted, "You sit in front!" and then slammed the door.

Penny shook her head at Gwen's ridiculous enthusiasm and slid in the front seat beside Mike.

"Hi, Penny."

She tucked her hands under her thighs to stop them from shaking. She was not made for night life.

Marissa leaned forward from the back seat. "You look nice, Penny. This will be fun, huh?" she said. Then she must have noticed how nervous Penny was, because she added, "Are you okay?"

"Sure, I'm fine," Penny said, too quickly. Marissa patted her on the shoulder and sat back.

"You ever been to an all-ages club?" Mike asked her, his eyes on the road.

"No, I've never been to any club before. I hope it's not full of fourteen year olds grinding on each other and pretending to be grown-ups."

Mike laughed. "It's not any better when actual grown-ups act that way."

She smiled at him. "Either way, I'm sure I'll have a good time. Or, you know, an awkward and sweaty time."

"Aw Penny," Gwen said from the back, sticking her face between them, "You'll be fine. Nobody is a bigger fool than I am, and anyway, the fourteen year olds will be there to give you lessons."

Penny stuck her tongue out at Gwen, who darted back away from her.

"Let me set your mind at ease about this here club situation," Mike said. "Here's what I plan to do tonight. I'm going to order a root beer and sit at a table. I'll watch the band, and check out what kind of crowd the place draws. If I like what I see, I'll have a conversation with the manager. I'd like to have your opinion, and I suppose I'd like the opinion of those goobers in the back, too."

Penny was relieved. He hadn't said anything about dancing.

"Well, he can do all that boring crap, but we're going to spend the night dancing, Penny." Gwen poked her head back up front. "And you know, Mike is a really good dancer." She gave an exaggerated wink.

"Oh lord," Mike sighed. "She thinks she's being subtle."

"Gwen, stop your meddling. I'd be especially glad to sit and drink root beers with Mike while you and Marissa dance."

Marissa poked her head up beside Gwen's. "Just so you know, it's okay with me if you do decide to date my brother." She patted him on the shoulder.

"Well now I miss the subtlety." Mike laughed.

121

"Guys, just chill out. I think we're here." Gwen sat back and fluffed her hair.

Penny looked out her window as they pulled up to a large black warehouse type of building. It had a neon sign that read PUZZLE in blue letters. The parking lot was nearly full, which seemed like a good sign, especially for a Thursday night. Mike parked and they stepped out into the dusky night air. A group was standing in the alley behind the building, smoking. Their laughter and the smell of their smoke drifted over to Penny.

They entered the club, and it was more brightly lit than she had anticipated. She was expecting dark and smoky in the club too, but of course smoking wasn't allowed inside. Along one wall were upholstered benches with small tables in front of them. Her fears became real when she saw, on those benches, awkward tween girls sitting in the laps of awkward tween boys. They looked twelve. At twelve she was still playing with dolls. She'd never sat on the lap of a boy before, and honestly, did not see the appeal. Maybe it was because, as a lap-sized person, she didn't want to do anything extra to make herself seem childlike.

Mike chose a table on the opposite side of the room, with a good view of the stage. A band was playing a rock ballad. Penny sat down and watched the dance floor. A group of girls was dancing and ogling the lead singer. A couple of them were reaching their hands out for him, but he ignored them as he sang. Penny turned away in second-hand embarrassment.

A waitress came and took their drink orders. Mike did order root beer, so Penny did too. He leaned back comfortably in his chair. Gwen was not the *sitting on a chair* type, so she took a sip of her Diet Coke and pulled Marissa by the hand onto the dance floor. She didn't ask Penny to join them, which either meant she was getting to know her pretty well or she was still trying to match-make her with Mike and wanted to give them some alone time.

Penny turned toward him, and smiled. "This band isn't bad, huh?"

"They're decent. The vibe of this place is a little more wholesome than Someling usually goes for, though."

"Wholesome? Look over there in that corner." She pointed. "Let me count...I see four couples making out. Oh my God, that guy just grabbed her butt, right in front of everybody!"

Mike gave her a look. "Yes, Penny. Wholesome was the word I meant to choose."

She frowned. "Okay then. This is wholesome. That could be a good thing for Someling though. Maybe it's a way to expand their audience."

"I don't know if they're going for the boy band image. I wonder if there is an older crowd on weekends," he said. Then he sat up in his chair and leaned close to her so she could hear him without the need to shout over the music. "How's your grandpa?"

She started to tell him that Grandpa was having a good week, when she noticed a group of guys come in. Archer was one of them. She didn't recognize the others.

"What's he doing here?" Mike snarled. Penny wondered the same thing. This was not the type of place she pictured him. He was wearing dark jeans and a black t-shirt, and it looked like he hadn't shaved that day. Penny ducked her head and stared at her hands. Mike started to stand, for what purpose Penny didn't know, but she put her hand on his arm and held him in place.

"You're not best buds?"

"No. Marissa has never dated anyone I like. I think she does it on purpose."

Penny laughed, but he just scowled in Archer's general direction.

"Grandpa's doing okay. Steph has been helping me out, checking in on him sometimes while I'm at work. She brought him dinner tonight. I'm going to have a serious talk with him soon, and see if I can get him to agree to…well I'm not sure what. But we'll talk and see if we can come up with any ideas to keep him safe that don't involve assisted living facilities."

Out of the corner of her eye, she saw that Archer was watching them. She couldn't catch his eye; it was as though he was only focused on the back of Mike's head. His friends had gone to the pool tables in the next room, but he stood near the doorway. He looked like he was going to come over, but eventually he turned and joined his friends.

Mike relaxed, and refocused on their conversation. "That's good. But don't you think it seems like he needs help from professionals? You might have to force the issue."

"Maybe someone will have to force the issue, but it won't be me. I want to figure out all of his options before I call my mom and tell her what's going on. If I do that, maybe I can stay on Grandpa's good side. I guess I'm looking for a solution that includes his permission."

A man dressed all in black came over to their table and sat down. "Mike, good to see you here!" he boomed in a deep voice, and pumped Mike's arm up and down in a ridiculously rough handshake. Mike introduced Penny to Clyde, the manager, and they exchanged a few words. He invited Mike back to his office to talk.

"Is that okay with you? I'll only be a few minutes."

"Of course," Penny said and waved at the dance floor. "Gwen and Marissa are right there. I'll be fine."

After he left, she took a sip of her drink and checked her phone. She heard the scrape of chair legs on the floor, and looked up to see Archer swing the chair around backwards and sit on it, resting his arms on the back. For some reason, that maneuver had always appealed to Penny. His face was entirely too close to hers. It was such a strong face, with a wide jaw and straight nose. His eyebrows were black and thick, making it so he always looked deep in thought. His lips looked so soft and pink it was hard to believe they went with the rest of his face. She backed up a little.

"What kind of date leaves his girl alone at the table in a club?" he demanded.

"One who isn't being nearly as rude as you are at the moment," she retorted, suddenly angry.

"I don't like you sitting alone in a place like this."

She snorted. "A place like this? This place is crawling with thirteen year olds. How dangerous."

"I'm sitting here until he comes back. It's irresponsible to leave you here alone," he said, his voice firm.

"You're being ridiculous. Nobody here is even drinking alcohol."

"Three of the guys I came in with are wasted. I'm sure they're not the only ones."

"And you're not wasted?"

"Nope."

"If you think I need protection from your own friends, why are they your friends?"

"They're not my friends. Oh look, he found some sense and is coming back." Penny looked, and Mike was making his way through the crowd with Clyde and a gorgeous raven haired woman. They stopped by the stage to check out the setup, though, and Archer turned back to her. "Time for a quick round." He grinned. "One: I also sleep in pajamas. Two: Mike's a good guy. Three: I wish it was me here with you. Which one's the lie, Penny?" Before she could say a word, he stood up and walked away.

~

125

"What did he want?" Mike grumbled as he dropped into his chair moments after Archer's exit. He looked Penny over, as though checking for injury.

She sighed. "He was just saying hi. I'm fine." Mike nodded his head, but still didn't look happy.

"You know, he's not such a bad guy, Mike. Maybe he and Marissa didn't have the best go of it, but he's still a decent person."

He raised his eyebrows. "He's just trouble, plain and simple. He's weird too."

She pursed her lips at him. "Well aren't you Judgy McJudgerson. What's weird about him?"

"He's always alone, skulking around and staring at people. And what's he doing here, of all places?"

Penny laughed. "You're here, too! Maybe he thinks you're weird. Everyone deserves a chance. I like to think that if I met you when you were in high school, in your trouble-making phase, I wouldn't have pre-judged you. I can be friends with anyone."

"You can be friends with me, sure." He tapped her on the nose. She rolled her eyes but he just smiled.

"So who was the woman who joined you and Clyde?" To her surprise, he blushed.

"Mike! You like her. This is terrific!"

He dropped his head and groaned. "Like her? No. 'Like' is not the word. Anne has plagued me since the third grade when she wore a different colored bow in her hair every day. She'll never give me a chance. She owns this club, and that's the only reason she even looked in my direction."

"Don't sell yourself short. You never know what the future holds." She rubbed her hands together, as though forming a plan. "Just let me think—"

"No, no. Don't think or do anything. You better just go dance and leave me here to wallow."

126

"I don't dance, Mike," she said. "I wasn't joking. I have no rhythm, and I feel like a fool when I try."

"Look at them." He pointed to Gwen and Marissa. "No matter how you dance, nothing will look as foolish as my sister trying to do the robot." That was possibly true, but Penny had to admit they looked like they were having fun.

"I suppose I wouldn't look like a fool alone," she said.

She glanced in the direction of the pool tables. Mike noticed where she was looking, and as he was not the type to be coy about his feelings, gave her a look that showed his displeasure.

"I'm going to go to the restroom, I'll be right back," she told him. She stood up and grabbed her purse. As she walked, she could feel the pressure of a gaze on her back. She had to fight to keep from turning and looking again toward the pool tables.

She didn't skirt the dance floor, but instead pushed her way through, grabbing Gwen and Marissa in the process. In the bathroom, she wet a paper towel and wiped off her face. The place was hot, and she hadn't even been dancing.

"What's going on, Pen?" Marissa asked.

"Yeah, I was in the groove back there," Gwen added.

Penny laughed, picturing Gwen grooving with the preteens.

"Wait, is this about Mike? Are you guys hitting it off? I knew it! This is great." Gwen spoke a mile a minute.

Penny leaned back against the sink, and they stared at her expectantly. "Ladies, calm down. It's not that big a deal, and it isn't about Mike. You'll have to let that go, because he is interested in someone else. Anyway, Archer is here, and he sat down to talk to me for a minute, and when Mike came back it was obvious that he doesn't like the fact that Archer...exists."

"Hold up a second. Slow down. My brother is interested in someone? I never get any relationship dirt from him. How did you do that?"

Penny summarized what little she knew of Anne. Gwen stuck out her lower lip. "I'm still not giving up on you and Mike. We can make this happen."

"Whatever, Gwen. Let's get back to the point of this meeting. What did Archer say to you?" Marissa asked.

Penny thought about telling them the things Archer had said tonight. But a small voice inside her told her to keep it for herself. She looked at Marissa and Gwen waiting expectantly. She thought about what it was she really needed to discuss. "It's not what he said." She waved her hands dismissively. "It's what I'm feeling." She ran her hands through her hair. "When he talks to me, I just...I've never felt like this. I don't think I can handle it."

Gwen groaned. "You want him. This is terrible."

Marissa looked sternly at Gwen, then back to Penny. "Ignore her. It's clear to anyone who's paying attention that he feels the same way about you."

Penny furrowed her brow, thrilling at Marissa's words but trying to tamp it down. "Maybe. But I'm not staying here. And I'm not ready to date anyone. I don't have much to offer. Should I tell him this?"

"Are you sure you're not ready to date anyone?" Marissa asked.

"I guess. I mean, I don't know how to be ready for that."

"You *can't* be. You just have to jump in," Gwen said. "As much as I hate to admit it, Marissa's right. You two are like two sticks, just waiting for a little friction."

Penny couldn't help but laugh. "I don't feel like it's fair to start anything. I'm too scared to anyway, but if I did, it would probably be just another bad decision."

"Now you're talking," Gwen said.

"Maybe it wouldn't be though," Marissa said. "You can't go through life making no decisions for fear of making a bad one."

Penny knew this was true, and it was kind of the whole point of her being there. "You're right, but I hate taking risks, especially when they involve other people." She sighed. "Get this though. Archer told me he thinks Mike is a good guy."

"Everybody knows Mike is a good guy," Marissa said. "Even when he's annoying the crap out of me, I can't escape his goodness."

Penny wet another paper towel and wiped down her neck. The cold water was just the jolt she needed. She thought about what Archer had said back at the table, wishing he'd just come out and told her what he was thinking. Why the literal game-playing? She moved the paper towel to her cheeks, which had grown hot as she pictured him sleeping without any pajamas.

Chapter 15

Penny loaded three huge packs of diapers into her cart. She was glad to be going to Steph's house, and there was a lot on her list. She studied the shelf to find the right kind of wipes. She saw someone approaching out of the corner of her eye, and was instantly aware that it was Archer.

He didn't slow down as he passed, but whispered, "Tell Gregory hello for me," as he did. His breath stirred her hair, and her own breath caught in her throat.

She continued to fill the cart with Steph's things. In the freezer aisle, someone tapped on her shoulder. She turned, expecting it to be Archer again, but it was Mike.

"Hi, Penny. You left this in my car last night." He held out his hand, and on his palm was one of her tiny leaf earrings. She had worn them almost every day since she left. They were Vera's, who had changed her mind about Penny keeping them.

She reached up and touched her earlobes, as if to confirm that one was missing, though she could see it right there in his hand. She reached out and took it. "Thank you so much. I would have been frantic if I'd realized I lost it." She reached up and gave him a quick hug.

Over Mike's shoulder, she noticed Archer turn into the aisle with his clipboard. When he saw them standing together, he stood motionless. The look he gave Mike was colder than the frozen vegetables. He glanced at Penny with that blank look in his eyes, and walked back in the direction he had come.

Penny sighed. "I think he thinks we're dating."

"Don't bother to set him straight. It might keep him away from you."

"Mike, I don't play those kinds of games with people. Anyway, thanks again for bringing me this." She held up the earring.

Mike smiled and said, "I'm glad I brought it to you before you realized it was gone. Thanks for coming out with us last night."

"Yeah, of course. Oh wait, one more thing. I let it slip to the girls about Anne. I'm sorry." She looked at him, cringing.

He looked at the floor. "Damn. Oh well, it's not like they could change anything." He gave her one last smile and left. She put both leaf earrings in her pocket, because the one he gave to her was missing its back.

~

"Good morning, Penny!" Steph said as Penny lugged her bags to the kitchen.

"Hello, it's nice to see you so happy today. Where's the little dude?"

"Oh, he's taking his morning nap. He got up at seven this morning, and was happy for two whole hours before falling blissfully asleep for this nap. I think the world has maybe tilted on its axis or something. I almost felt energetic enough to come into the store in person."

"I'm glad you didn't. I like coming to see you. Hey, thanks for bringing dinner to my grandpa last night. Was he gracious about accepting it?"

"He was a perfect gentleman. He enjoys holding Gregory. I find that many older people like to spend time with babies." She was thoughtful for a moment. "Watching your grandfather's wrinkly, spotted hands stroke Gregory's smooth, pale arm, I thought, *One day, Gregory's arm will look like that*. It blew my mind."

"You'll be long dead by then, so no worries!" Penny teased her. They laughed and unpacked the groceries.

"Steph, did your grandparents ever need any sort of nursing home care?"

"My grandma did. My mom's mom. She lived with us for a few years, and then went into a nursing home and passed away a few months later," she said. "I don't mean that the nursing home had anything to do with her death, just that Mom couldn't meet all her needs anymore. At that point Gram was close to dying anyway."

"Was it good for you, when your grandma lived with you?"

"Oh, I loved it! She was never too busy to listen to me. Mom had to work, and then do all the things a household needs, but Gram was always available. Before she was too sick, she could do things like bake with me," she said. "As time went on and she was less able, she would sit and talk with me while I baked or did puzzles."

As Steph continued to talk, Penny's idea solidified. She thought maybe Grandpa could be content living with her huge, crazy family. Her youngest siblings hadn't even met him. She wanted them to get to know him before he was no longer himself. She could drive him home. That didn't mean she would stay there with him, but something about the idea felt right. With her gone, there'd be room for him in the house.

Gregory woke up screaming, so Penny left to get back to work. When she pulled in the employee parking lot, her eyes went right to Archer. He was leaning against the disgusting blue dumpster with his arms crossed over his chest. When he saw her car, he immediately pushed off the dumpster and strode toward her.

Penny unbuckled her seatbelt, and tried not to let her nerves get the best of her. When she opened her door, he had to step back a little, because he had been standing so close. She shut the door, and looked up at him. He loomed over her, just looking at her quietly.

"Um, hi?" she said.

"I want you to go somewhere with me tonight," he said. "Right after work."

"I have something I need to do after work."

"What?" he asked.

"Where would we go? And why?" she asked, ignoring his question.

"Say yes first."

"Nope."

The corner of his mouth twitched up, but he didn't allow the smile to take over his face. "I just want to talk to you."

Penny looked up at him and thought about it for a minute, shifting her weight from one foot to the other. "I really do have something I need to do. It wasn't an excuse. But maybe I could meet you after."

"Nine o'clock?" he said.

"Sure. Fine."

In spite of the annoyed tone in her voice, he allowed a smile to spread across his face. It was catching, and she found herself smiling back at him.

"Good. I'll pick you up," he said.

"No, I'll meet you."

He blew out an exasperated breath, and she snickered. It was fun to annoy him. "Okay. We'll meet there. Come to the beach where the bonfire was. I'll wait there." He started back toward the store.

"Wait!" she called. When he stepped back to her, she said, "I want to say something about last night."

"What about it?"

"Well, I didn't like it, the way you insulted Mike," she said.

"I told you he's a good guy, though."

"That's another thing. Can we agree to communicate in a more genuine manner, instead of through games?"

His eyes widened for a fraction of a second, then his face turned impassive. He nodded wordlessly, and she saw his adam's apple bob as he swallowed.

They walked to the building together, and when they got to the doorway, he opened the door and stepped back to let her enter first.

~

Penny leaned against Grandpa's porch rail, still in work clothes. He wasn't answering the door. She watched a cloud of gnats fly past. Her stomach began to feel like it had gnats in it too, but she forced herself to remain calm. There could be several reasons why he wasn't answering. Maybe he was asleep. She decided that this was the appropriate time to use the key he gave her.

She steeled herself as she entered, suddenly certain she would find him dead.

He was sitting on the couch, leafing through a book. He looked up at Penny and smiled broadly when she stepped inside.

"Hi," she said, but he turned back to his book. "How are you?"

"Oh, I'm fine. How are you?"

"Why didn't you answer the door?"

He looked up at her and beamed a pleasant smile, but didn't speak. He continued to flip through the book, and it seemed like he wasn't looking at the pages. She furrowed her brow, trying to puzzle this out.

Penny sat down next to him, their weight tilting them towards each other. She turned on the TV and found an old black and white movie. Grandpa put down his book and looked up. He leaned forward, and focused intently on the screen.

"Have you seen this movie before?" she asked.

"Yes, many times. It's called Sullivan's Travels. Ruby loved this one."

Penny sat back and tried to pay attention to the movie, but it was too boring. She breathed in Grandpa's scent, which was a mixture of Ivory soap, leather, and sweat. She put her hand on his knee and squeezed.

He startled, and looked at her, his face still as blank as it had been when she arrived. "When did you get to town, dear? I wasn't expecting you for another few weeks."

Penny sucked in her lower lip and bit hard, so that she wouldn't let the tears spill over.

"Oh, I came a little early," she whispered. She didn't know if telling him the truth would confuse him or anger him or help him remember.

"Well how lovely. I'm glad to have you visit." He smiled at her again, and turned back to the movie.

She needed some breathing room, so she left him on the couch and went to the kitchen to prepare dinner. She pulled out a frozen pizza and put it in the oven. She started chopping up some romaine, a little rougher than necessary. So that's how it was going to be? He was either going to deny he needed any help at all, or he was going to wander or forget she'd been in town for nearly two months. Her tears escaped as she grabbed a tomato, bruising it with her fingers.

Penny didn't understand why she was so angry. She had thought sadness would be the prevailing emotion. But she found herself mad at the way he wouldn't let her do anything for him. Mad that he forgot things. Mad that he was sick at all.

When the salad was prepared, she went to his back deck to set the picnic table. She sat out there for a while, listening to the neighbor's dog drag its chain over the matted grass. When she came back in, Grandpa was asleep. She picked up the book he had been looking at earlier. It was a thesaurus. She laughed to herself, then sat down and watched him sleep.

Twenty minutes later, he woke up and smiled at her. "Penny, dear. How was work today?" He came over and patted her on the hand. "I'm glad to see you."

She swallowed, and told him she had come to have dinner with him. She walked to the back deck, and he followed.

"I don't want to eat outside," he said, and crossed his arms over his chest, a gesture she hadn't seen from him before. His eyes darted from the back door to the front door.

"Why not?"

"I don't know." He squinted out the back door. "Never mind. This is fine." He shook his head.

Penny went inside to get the pizza, and when she brought it out he was already eating his salad.

"Ruby ate salad with every dinner," he said. She smiled. She loved to hear him talk about her grandma. He continued, "It doesn't seem fair that she was the one who ate so healthfully, and took care of herself, and yet she was the one to die first."

"I know Grandma loved to cook and bake. I remember when you both used to visit. She spent most of the time in the kitchen, and you spent most of the time playing board games with Vera and me. Mark would jump across the board in his Superman costume and we'd yell at him. But you told us to leave him alone. He was flying."

Grandpa put down his fork, and reached up to touch Penny's cheek. His fingertips were cold and smooth. "Those times were some of my favorites."

That reaffirmed for Penny that what she was about to suggest to him was a good idea. She waited until they had moved on from salad to pizza. "Grandpa, you haven't even met Blake and Nedra, and you haven't seen the twins since they were one year old. What would you think about going to see them?"

He took a sip of tea, and said, "I would like that very much. It was always Ruby who planned those visits. With her gone, I never had the wherewithal to plan anything." He paused to chew. "I'm afraid I wouldn't be the kind of grandpa to them that I was to you."

"You're the same person," Penny insisted.

He looked at her, his eyes firm. "I'm not."

She looked down at her hands and took a deep breath. "Well, mom will be really glad to see you."

"Oh yes, your mother. I imagine she will hover over me instructing my every move. Well, I could put up with that for a week or two."

Penny spit out the words quickly, to get it said and done. "Grandpa, there is an empty bed at home, now that I'm gone. I'm sure they could rearrange things so you could have the small room downstairs in the hallway to yourself. You know the one by the kitchen that we use as an office? Steph says her grandmother lived with them when she was little, and they all loved it. You could help out with the kids and the house. I know Dad would love help with the yard work. He never has time for that. And when you're having a bad day, they could return the favor and help you out. And about Mom, she's too busy to hover over you. You'd be a real help to her. Even just spending time with the kids would be so helpful…"

"You mean to say that you want me to move there?" he interrupted her nervous blathering. He didn't sound angry, just resigned.

"The other day, when I picked you up at the ice cream shop, that scared me. It really frightened me, Grandpa." She decided not to mention his memory lapse earlier tonight. "On your good days, which are many, you are obviously fine. But that day, I saw how serious this could be. Do *you* see it?"

He looked up at her, and his eyes were watery. "What ice cream shop?"

She didn't respond. She couldn't.

He continued. "But I do see it, dear, I see it. When I wake up and can't recall what happened earlier in the day. When I walk into the kitchen and can't remember why I'm there or how to make a sandwich. But just because I see it, doesn't mean I intend to let this thing beat me."

Penny knew he knew it wasn't a fair fight. Him against Alzheimer's. Alzheimer's would win eventually. "Mom has tons of photo albums, filled with pictures of you and Grandma. She also has a head full of memories she could talk to you about. Being around your grandkids could help. You've seen the pictures of Nedra, right? She's Grandma made over."

"I thought we had a deal, Penny."

"We did. We do. I haven't talked to mom yet at all, and haven't told her any of these things. This is something I'm thinking about. I just wanted to think about it with you."

He smiled at her then. "Perhaps to surrender is not the same as giving up. I will think about it." He reached out his hand, and she opened her palm. He dropped into it a tiny Milky Way.

Chapter 16

It was eight o'clock when she left Grandpa's house. She had been reluctant to leave, but he'd gone to bed and fell asleep in a blink. She locked his door behind her and hoped for the best. Back at her apartment, she showered and put on a green sundress. Maybe moondress would be a more fitting name, as the sun was setting.

She bent over and hung her head to blow her hair dry, and watched it swirl around her knees. The thought of seeing Archer again filled her with a blurry anticipation. Everyone was telling her that he wasn't a safe bet. Personally, she didn't feel like *she* was a safe bet either.

As she walked toward the beach, she wondered if it was wise to be walking alone at night in this part of town. She didn't feel unsafe, and as a big believer in following your gut instincts, she decided to just relax and enjoy the night. It had cooled down, and it was nice not to have rivulets of sweat streaming down various body parts. She enjoyed the crunch of sand against her shoes as she walked the sidewalks.

She looked down the beach, and there he was, sitting on a log a good distance back from the water's edge. His back was to her, and his head was tipped slightly up, watching the darkening sky.

"Hey," Penny said softly, as she came up behind him. She stood with her hands clasped, irritated with herself because her voice shook.

He turned and looked up at her. "Hi." His smile was timid. She relaxed, seeing that he had put away the swagger for the evening.

Penny sat next to him on the log, and joined him in his sky gazing. They didn't talk for a few minutes. She shifted around getting comfortable.

"I'm glad you came," he said, finally, and put his hand on her hand. He left it there for scarcely a second, lifting it off before she had the chance to brush it away. Fizzy warmth traveled through her. If he had left it there, would she have brushed it away? She didn't know.

"The water's peaceful tonight."

"Yeah." He picked at a knot on the log. "So, what would you think about having a sincere conversation?"

She laughed. "Well you just jumped right to the point."

"I thought that's what you wanted. Conversation, no games."

"It is, it's just, I don't think I'm very good at it."

"I'm probably not either. What does that even mean, to be good at talking?"

"In my case, it means I find some sort of sweet spot between sticking my foot in my mouth and not saying anything I really think. I'm not sure I've ever accomplished it." He laughed quietly. Her cheeks warmed, happy that she had made him laugh.

"Okay, here goes. I'm going to ask you a question. I hope it won't make you mad." He rubbed his palms on his pants. It made her more comfortable to see his nervous habit.

"Archer, I think I've been too hard on you. I don't want you to censor yourself, or worry that you'll stick *your* foot in your mouth. It's just that, I'm trying not to censor myself around you. So maybe I've been a little too free with my opinions, and too quick to jump on yours."

"No, I don't agree. Sure, you've jumped all over me and you question everything I say to you." He laughed as she ducked her head down in embarrassment. "But I like that you don't withhold yourself from me. That's what I want. You won't offend me."

"I might, someday. But so far you don't seem offendable."

"I'm not, mostly." He lifted his hand like he was going to touch her hand again, but dropped it without making contact.

"So what was the question you wanted to ask me?" she asked, bravely looking right at his face. God, his face. She wanted to run her finger along his jaw line.

He took a breath and let it out heavily. "Okay, this is probably rude and it's definitely nosy. But I'm going crazy not knowing, so I'm going to ask anyway. It's about Mike. Are you two...you know...just dating, or is it more serious?"

Penny looked down at her feet, a grin spreading slowly across her face. "I don't think it's rude to ask that. It's an honest question. I'm glad you asked rather than continuing to make assumptions." She looked back up at him. "I'm not dating anyone."

"Really?"

"Really."

He released a breath and let his head fall forward. His hair fell down and covered his eyes. From that position, he said, "Okay. I'm not dating anyone either, just in case you wondered."

She smirked. "People have warned me away from you. But they should probably be warning you away from me too."

"That's crazy," he said, and looked at her with those near-black eyes. They weren't blank tonight. They held something in them, and she wished she could take a picture so she could study it later. "Penny, my mother is a convict. My no-show dad is a complete lowlife, and also a convict. I used to drink too much, and you saw me the other day when I did it again. I live in a dump. I've got you beat."

141

"It's a contest now? Who's had a crazier life?" He raised his eyebrows, letting her know that he would win, if it was a contest.

"No, listen," she continued. "I'm not talking about that kind of thing though. It's not like I've done illegal things. This trip I took out here? It was me running away from having to face decisions I made. I told myself I was running towards a new life, and maybe it was a little bit of both. But I've figured out that I was mostly running away. You're acting like you're the devil and I'm a perfect person. You don't know enough about me to assume that."

"So why did you need to run away?"

"Um."

He smiled at her, his face open. "You don't have to tell me. I get it. But listen, nothing you've done could shock me."

She figured that was true. "I've never broken the law. I don't even think I've ever broken a rule."

He sat up straight. "Well you did manage to shock me."

She laughed. "Here's a question for you. When you want to prove your wickedness, you tell stories about your parents' lives, not yours. Why do their choices mean that I should stay away from *you*?"

"I'm a product of that. That's where I come from. I don't mean I'm scum or worthless or anything, but it's true that my life has been pretty messed up."

"Are your parents still in your life?"

"No. But they raised me." He huffed out a humorless laugh. "If you can call it that. I'm going to be different than them. I am. I'm going to do something good someday. But I can feel them pushing down on me."

She looked at him and didn't know what to say.

"What I'm trying to say is, I don't know how these things are supposed to go," he said.

"How what things are supposed to go?"

"This." He gestured between them. "Whatever this is. When you're not around, I spend my time trying to figure out how to *get* you around. Then once you're here, I don't even know how to act, so that you'll want to stay around." He looked up at the sky, avoiding her face. Penny could tell he was nervous about what he'd just said. Her stomach was flopping around like a fish on a dock, and she could hear the blood rushing through her ears. She reached out a shaky hand and laid it on his knee.

"We're not that different, you know," she whispered.

"Yeah?"

"Yeah."

They sat like that a while. He didn't move her hand, but he didn't try to hold it either. It was as though he knew that if he tried to touch her, she would bolt. Her hand just rested there on his leg, feeling strangely large. It was alternately thrilling and too bold.

Finally he swung the conversation back to something she said earlier. "So if my parents and my sorry excuse for a past don't determine whether I'm a good person to hang around, why do your problems, whatever they are, mean that people should warn me away from you?"

"Because I'm having an identity crisis." She pulled her hand away, and laughed to try to make her statement more light-hearted than it was, but he just looked at her with a serious face. She sobered and said, "I mean it. I don't feel strong in myself. I've been whoever people want me to be. Done what they wanted me to do. I allowed that, my whole life. I don't know how to be me."

He looked surprised. "I did not expect that. In fact, that's the last thing I expected you to say. That's not how I see you at all."

"How do you see me?"

"You seem so self-assured. You don't suffer fools. You're strong."

143

"Don't forget that you don't know me that well," she joked. He didn't laugh.

Penny was going to continue, but her phone buzzed in her pocket. "I'm sorry, I need to check this. It could be my grandfather."

It was Steph, and she was breathless as she hurried to impart information. "Penny, I'm sorry to call you so late, but your grandfather is walking around my neighborhood." She had glanced out her front window and noticed Cal walking past her house in the glow of streetlamps. She had gone to her porch and called out to him, but he didn't answer or look back at her. She couldn't leave, because Gregory was asleep and Jeff was out of town, but she thought Penny should know.

"Thank you, Steph, I'll...do something."

"My car is parked at the top of the hill. I'll drive you," Archer said, after she told him what was happening. She nodded numbly. They rushed up the sand, feet splaying out to get traction.

"It's the old rustbucket there," he pointed, as they got closer. Penny tore open the passenger door and threw herself inside, breathless. He sat down in the driver's seat, and buckled up far too slowly.

"Drive to Steph's neighborhood, he can't be far," Penny panted.

"Hey, try to calm down. He's just walking around town. It's going to be fine."

Penny knew he was trying to be reassuring, but it annoyed her. "You can't know that! Do you think we should call 911 before we start looking?" she asked, and he finally got the car moving.

"No, I do not think we should call 911."

"Just stop talking, so I can think," Penny said. She pressed her forehead to the glass, squinting into the darkness for any sign of her grandpa. Steph said he was wearing a light

144

blue shirt. She took a breath. "Archer, I'm sorry I snapped at you. I'm feeling guilty that I left him alone tonight. It wasn't a good day for him."

"Hey, it's okay. Snap at me all you need."

They wound through the streets, not missing one as they circled each block. After ten minutes, Penny was on the verge of tears. "I really think I should call the police now."

Archer didn't say anything.

"You still don't think I should," she pressed, and knew it sounded accusing.

He surprised her by smiling. "Why does my opinion matter? If you think you should, go ahead and call."

"You're right. I'm calling." She had been clutching her phone in case Steph or anyone else tried to call. She started to dial the number, but couldn't go through with it. "I'm afraid that if I call them, they'll take Grandpa and put him in the hospital or something. Could they do that?"

"I don't know the protocol for this type of thing."

"Me neither. He'd be so angry with me, if that happened. Maybe he's just out for a walk and didn't hear Steph calling his name." She wanted to believe that, but knew he wouldn't go for a walk this late.

"Let's check a few more streets, then go by his house and see if he's there," Archer suggested.

Penny chewed on her thumbnail, anxious and unsure. "Okay. But if we don't find him by then, I'm calling."

He wasn't on the streets or in the shops on the main drag, so they drove to his neighborhood.

"There's somebody ahead," Penny squeaked, and leaned forward as far as her seatbelt would allow. "Slow down."

Archer slowed the car, and after another block she could see that the walking figure was her grandpa. She sighed long and loud with relief. Archer pulled the car over and parked.

"Go ahead and drive closer to him. No need to make him walk back to us," Penny said.

"Hold up a minute. Do you think it might startle him if we pull up right next to him and call his name?"

"Why would that startle him more than us walking up behind him and saying his name?" She wanted to move quickly, driven by the need to go find out if Grandpa was hurt, lucid, lost, or scared.

"Let's just follow him, and see where he goes. That way we won't startle him and we can also make sure he's safe."

She thought about Hogeweyk village in Holland, where patients could roam free in safety. "Okay, let's do it."

Ten minutes later, she grinned up at Archer in the dark. He seemed even taller than usual, because she stood so close to him. They were behind a wide oak tree. "It's fun being a spy." Cal had walked another few blocks and then sat on the sidewalk. They were watching him sit. He seemed content there. He ran his hands over the grass in front of him, first his palms and then the backs.

"Yeah, but I'm ready for him to do something else. I want to practice jumping rooftops and slipping through narrow alleys."

"Oh look, he's getting up!" Penny said, whacking Archer on the arm in her excitement. It was surprising how fun this was turning out to be, in spite of the circumstances.

Archer peeked around the tree. Then he grabbed Penny's upper arms, and ducked down to whisper in her ear. "Let's go behind the houses, and get behind that gray shed three houses down. Do you see it?" He pointed. She nodded. They ran, she on tiptoes, to their next lookout spot.

They were almost there when a snarly voice whisper-shouted at them, "What arc you kids doing over there?"

Penny's eyes widened as she saw a man beside the front porch of the house with the shed.

"I'd know that growl anywhere," Archer whispered. "That's George Baker."

"What? Why is he lurking here?" Penny whispered back.

"I might ask you the same thing," Mr. Baker said, at full voice, and directly behind them. While they were whispering about him, he'd decided to sneak up from behind.

"We are not lurking!" Penny said, as she whirled to face him. "We're watching my Grandpa."

His eyes narrowed at her. "It's about time." He stalked across the yard to the sidewalk, and turned in the direction of his house.

"Wait!" she called to him, heedless now of the need to keep Grandpa from hearing.

She scurried after him, but Archer's warm hand stopped her when it grabbed her own. She turned to face him, and he looked down at her. In spite of the situation, her breathing sped up. She saw by the rise and fall of his chest, that Archer's had too. He was standing so close. "Let him go. Your Grandpa turned at Ripley Street, and I can't see him anymore."

Penny swallowed, mesmerized by how his palm felt against hers. "Can you follow him for just a minute? I'll meet you on Ripley."

She pulled her hand away and took off after Mr. Baker, and Archer turned in the opposite direction.

"Mr. Baker? What did you mean by that? By saying, 'It's about time,' I mean," Penny said, out of breath from stress as much as her effort to catch up to him. He didn't look like the kind of person who could speed walk like that.

"I have to get home now. It's late. I can't be doing this all the time," he spat out with a growl and a sharp glare.

"You mean you've done this before? He wanders and you follow him?"

"At least once a week, girl. Open your eyes. You're here now. You've been here all summer. Do something for him." With that, he turned and shuffled off down the sidewalk.

She called out after him, "But I didn't even know you knew him!" He just flapped his hand at her, and didn't look back.

Defeated, she headed toward Ripley Street to catch up with Archer and Grandpa. The knot that had been in her stomach for the last hour grew. They'd bring him home and he'd be fine. What about next time, though?

Chapter 17

The sun lit up the ceiling, and Penny lay and watched the swirling patterns. She replayed last night from start to finish. From her conversation with Archer on that log, to searching for and finding Grandpa, she was overwhelmed. She had stayed overnight with Grandpa, for lack of a better plan. She snuggled down into the musty quilt on the guest bed, and tried to organize her thoughts.

George Baker knew Grandpa and was keeping an eye on him. Why hadn't he ever mentioned it? Did Grandpa *never* remember his wandering? Would Grandpa know Mr. Baker if he saw him in a lucid state? Were they good friends?

Penny's belly filled with something that was half doom and half delight when she considered the other portion of her evening. Had she and Archer really discussed their mutual emotional-wreck status? Well. In the light of the morning, she felt a little wobbly and exposed, and more than a bit like she wanted to crawl in a hole and never have to face him again. But then she remembered how helpful and understanding he had been. And the way his hand had felt when it held her own. The way her whole body reacted up when he stood so close. She wanted that again.

But there was more to it than that. It was herself she didn't want to face. Penny still had not made peace with what she had allowed to happen with Will. Her parents were worried about her. She was still scared of how it felt to speak her mind, though she was proud of her progress. Biggest of all, she needed Grandpa to decide to go live with her family. Archer was a welcome addition, but she knew she shouldn't get in too deep without resolving some of the other issues in her life.

Or maybe they could figure some things out together? That was a new idea.

She pushed off the bed and went to the kitchen. Cal joined her a little later, and they sipped coffee and ate toast together. He kept sneaking glances at her, and he appeared nervous.

"Grandpa, do you know George Baker?"

He eyed her. "Yes, I know him. Darling, why are you here so early? I don't mean to sound rude, but I had thought our arrangement would afford me a little more privacy."

She stared down into her coffee mug. He didn't remember last night, and she wasn't sure of the best way to approach the situation. She settled on denial.

"Oh, you know. I just wanted to stop by and say good morning before I start my day."

He clucked his tongue. "I know what you're doing. You're checking up on me. As you can see, I'm fine. Now go, and do something worth doing."

She sighed, and kissed him on the cheek. "Bye Grandpa. But just so you know, spending time with you is always worth doing."

~

"I'm not sure about this," Penny said, letting the water slurp over her feet.

"Come on. What's the worst that could happen?" Mike called from the water. He was in deep enough that he was past the breakers and was bobbing with the waves.

"Sharks. Jelly fish. Crabs. Weird water snakes and things of that nature." Penny crossed her arms over her middle.

150

"Nah," Gwen said. She was lying on her belly, propped up on her elbows in the water, letting it just cover her back. Marissa sat beside her. "None of that will happen. Don't be such a worrier."

"How about you just come in this far? You can see the bottom," Marissa added.

Penny took a breath, closed her eyes, and waded in up to her knees. Then she sat and let the water tickle her waist. "Okay. I'm in. I just won't think about it."

"Now swim out to me!" Mike shouted.

"Give her half a minute to adjust, asshole!" Gwen shouted back to him. The girls laughed.

Mike made his way over to where they sat. "Sorry. I didn't realize it was that big of a deal," he said to Penny. He positioned himself like Gwen, leaning on his elbows and letting his legs stream out behind him.

Penny shrugged. "I like to be able to see any creatures that might approach anywhere near my vicinity."

Marissa smiled. "Being that you're from Montana, I thought you might be more earthy."

"Well, she does like to have bare, dirty feet," Gwen said.

Penny rolled her eyes. "I like dirt just fine. I mind *creatures*. Slippery, water creatures." She looked around at the surface of the water. "Oh no, guys. We've drifted out a little farther."

"No we haven't," Gwen said.

"Yes. Yes we have," Penny said, her shaky voice betraying her nerves.

"Look, the best way to do this is just go all in. Throw yourself into it. Push away all the fear and just do it," Mike said. He stood up.

Marissa smiled at him. "Yeah, for once I think my brother is right." She stood too and grabbed Penny's hand.

Gwen grabbed her other hand. "You can close your eyes if you want, and we'll guide you. I promise we won't let go."

At her words, something relaxed inside Penny. She wasn't good at going all in, or letting go of fear. She was getting better at doing it anyway. She let them pull her out into the water, past the breakers, until they were all bobbing and even her toes could no longer touch the bottom.

They bobbed there for a while, floating and riding the waves. "This is better than a wave pool," Penny said.

"The real thing is always better than an imitation," Mike said.

"Not always," said Gwen. "I prefer imitation crab meat to the real thing. I like my fake fingernails better than my flimsy real ones. My fake ID is better than the real one I don't have."

Mike groaned and splashed her, but she didn't even flinch. She wiped the drips off her face and said, "You only reacted like that because you know I'm right. Fake can be good."

"Whatever." He floated on his back and looked up at the sky.

The top of Penny's head was hot, so she leaned back in the water until it reached her forehead. She didn't dare go under.

"Mike, do you remember Shakes?" Marissa asked. "He was never fake."

"Of course I remember him. Nobody could forget Shakes."

"Who's Shakes?" Penny asked.

Gwen laughed. "He was this kid at our school. A year ahead of us. He was completely weird."

"Why was he called Shakes?"

"Because he went to all the school dances and his dancing was more like convulsing. He shook himself all around the gym," Gwen said.

"He dressed crazy all the time too," Mike said, "Like a yellow shirt and green pants and purple shoes. He wore a tie

152

every day, even if he had on a t-shirt. He always sang as he walked down the hallways."

Penny smiled. "That kind of eccentricity can go one of two ways. So was Shakes considered cool and revered for the way he bucked the trends, or was he considered a geek?"

"That's the thing," Marissa said. "People thought he was a dork. They made fun of him, even to his face. But *he* thought he was cool."

"Which made people tease him even more," Mike said. "Remember when some guys wrestled him out of his tie and hung it on the flagpole?"

Marissa sighed. "I always liked him. I didn't know him well, but you have to admire that kind of confidence."

"I didn't think of him as confident. I think he just wasn't very self-aware," Gwen said.

"I disagree. He knew the effect he had on people. How could he not, when they threw it in his face all the time?" Marissa said. "It just never mattered to him. He was real in a way most people aren't. It's not his fault he tried to let people know him and they refused."

"What ever happened to him?" Penny asked.

"I heard he went to acting school in New York. He'll probably become famous and have the last laugh," Mike said.

"But you don't understand what I'm trying to say. I don't think he ever felt like he needed to get revenge or have the last laugh or whatever. He was laughing along the whole time. He honestly, truly didn't care." Marissa smiled. "He was happy."

"It's risky letting people know that much about you," Penny said. "Letting them see the parts of you most people keep hidden." Her own goals to be more outspoken didn't even scrape the surface of that kind of self-exposure.

Gwen made a face. "No way. I do not want everybody going around doing all the things they do in private. It would be an off-key, disgusting world."

153

Penny floated in thought, sure of nothing, but content all the same.

~

Penny thumbed through the list of delivery orders. Archer didn't work today, which was a relief. She wanted some time to do more thinking and less feeling.

She saw that Mr. Baker had called in for a delivery today. She decided to do his first. He let her in with a grunt, and she set his bag of groceries on the counter.

"How's your grandfather?"

Penny blinked at him, surprised both by his tone and the fact that he initiated a real conversation. He had addressed her as though she were human, and as though he had manners. "Well, I'm not sure he'd like for me to talk about his business with you."

"You think I needed a can of tuna and some diced tomatoes? No. You're here because I wanted to find out how Cal is today. He's been telling me his business himself for years."

"Alright then, ask him yourself. But so you know, he had never even mentioned he knows you. And another thing, if you wanted to talk to me, you could just call. You don't have to place fake grocery orders."

He snorted and said, "It wasn't a fake order. I'll eat the tuna for my lunch." Penny rolled her eyes, but he ignored her and continued. "I can't talk to Cal about this. As you know, he doesn't like to speak of it."

The last part of his statement was said with kindness. She softened a little toward him. "So, you're friends with my grandfather?"

"Your surprised expression is vexatious. I used to see your grandfather at the Elks, and we played cards. He talks a lot, that guy."

"Grandpa doesn't talk a lot," she said, offended on his behalf.

"Yes he does. Anyway, anyone with eyes can see that his brain is going."

"People say the same thing about you, did you know that?" she retorted.

"I know it. But I also know it's not true. It is true for Cal. Now tell me, what is the plan for him?"

Penny sighed and waved a hand at his collection of jars. "Why do you have all these jars?"

"I don't answer nosy questions," he said.

"Well, neither do I," she said, and grabbed the cash out of his hand.

As she stalked to her car, she heard him mutter, "Keep the change."

Her face burned. The change was three cents, and he never tipped her. She dug around in her wallet and found the coins. She dropped them into his mailbox before peeling out of his driveway.

~

"You said you might do something good some day. Do you have something particular in mind, or did you just mean in general?" Penny asked. She knew it was nosy, but didn't know how you got to know someone without being at least a little nosy.

Archer looked at her.

"Oh no! You dripped a big blob on the cabinet," Penny said, and rushed to get a paper towel wet.

"Aw damn." Archer took the paper towel and scrubbed the cabinet. The paint wiped right off and he sighed in relief.

"You don't have to answer my question if you don't want to," Penny said, and took the paper towel back and

155

tossed it in the trash. She resumed her touch up work on the other side of the kitchen.

"Well, mostly I'm fighting the urge to make up something that would impress you."

Penny laughed. "Don't impress me on purpose. It only really works if it's accidental."

Archer smiled. "My dreams are small. I want to buy a house some day. I don't even care where. I don't have the usual hometown hatred that a lot of people get, so probably I'd buy a place here. Fix it up. Work a job that I don't hate."

"That's an admirable dream. In fact, it's the American dream," she said. He smiled at her. "Any idea what kind of job?"

"Don't laugh when I say it."

"I would never."

"Do you know Al Bloss?"

"I know Bloss Hardware," Penny said.

"Al owns it. I hang out there with him sometimes. He's like ninety, and none of his kids want the store. He might sell it to me cheap when he retires. If he ever does."

"Archer, that's brilliant!" Penny turned to him, looking ready to burst.

"Oh good lord, don't gush, it's just an idea. Don't say any more. I can't take it."

She tried to turn her grin into a regular smile. She failed. He shook his head and asked her, "What about you then? You never told me about why you turned down that scholarship."

Penny took a deep breath. "If I admit this to you, you have to promise to understand that I've grown as a person since then."

Archer drew a cross on his chest with his finger. "I swear."

She couldn't believe she was about to tell him this. "I only planned to go to Montana State because that's where my boyfriend was going. I didn't really want to go there."

Archer raised his brows, but didn't say anything.

"Trust me, I know what you're thinking. It was pathetic. I realized that, and decided I wasn't going to stay with him and I wasn't going to follow him to college. And I wasn't going to be a chemist like my dad wanted, and I wasn't going to stay home all summer and help take care of my siblings like my mom wanted."

"Wow." Archer grinned at her.

"Yep. Now I do what I want. Or, I try to anyway."

"And what is it you want to do?"

"For a job? I still don't know for sure what I want to do, but I'm thinking maybe something to help out people like Grandpa."

"See, now that's a noble aspiration," Archer said.

"Way more noble than hardware." She poked him on the shoulder to make sure he knew she was teasing.

He turned toward her. Their gazes caught. She swallowed, and she saw him do the same. They stared at each other. The way he was looking at her took her breath. The darkness of his eyes was lightened by fire. She could swear he wasn't breathing either, and that the air itself was buzzing. The kitchen felt suddenly crowded. She took a step backward and bumped into the counter.

He knew just what to do, knew exactly what she needed. He gave her one more smile and then turned and got back to painting.

Chapter 18

"It has only been a week since I went out with you guys," Penny whined. Gwen and Marissa were sitting on her bed, literally attempting to pull her out of it.

"It's been a week and two days," Gwen corrected. "And that barely counts as going out. Birch's on a Saturday night is the real deal." She tugged on Penny's leg.

Penny wriggled free and stuffed her leg back under the blanket. "I'm in bed! Seriously. Pajamas. Bed-head. I brushed my teeth!"

Marissa laughed. "It's not our fault you went to bed before nine o'clock on a Saturday night."

"Who does that?" Gwen put in, incredulous.

"I do! I like to sleep."

Marissa narrowed her eyes at Penny. "Do you have to work in the morning?"

"Well no—"

"Then come on." She pulled back the blankets and then went to the closet and pawed through Penny's clothes. "And anyway, I could use the company tonight."

Something in Marissa's voice made Penny sit up. "Okay. But only if you guys promise not to bother me tomorrow."

Gwen smiled and handed Penny her hairbrush. "You've got ten minutes."

~

"This place isn't so bad."

"Yeah, it's just your classic bar," Marissa said. "Look, the dance floor is empty."

Penny smiled at her. "Perfect."

They were standing by the pinewood bar, waiting for their drink orders. Gwen had found a table in the back and was waiting for them. Penny's heart pounded. She was sure they were about to be carded, thrown out, and then arrested.

Another minute later though, the bartender pushed three glasses toward them and then turned back to her work.

Penny picked up her gin and tonic and headed back toward Gwen. She had planned to skip the alcohol, but once she got there she decided she actually did want to try a drink. She'd always wondered what a gin and tonic tasted like.

Marissa handed Gwen her drink. They had copied Penny and ordered gin and tonics too.

"Marissa, look. It's that guy we saw last time. I wonder if he'll come over," Gwen said, and pointed at a cute guy sitting a few tables over.

Marissa shrugged. "I hope he doesn't. All I can think about is that I have a week left."

Penny felt a rock sink into her stomach. Summer was almost over. She sipped her drink. She liked it.

"Yeah, forget him. You're going to meet so many guys at college," Gwen said.

Marissa tilted her head back and finished her drink. She got up and went to the bar, and came back a few minutes later with another. "I usually get beer, but these are good."

"Want to play pool?" Penny asked, figuring it was what you did in a bar. "Oh they have a dart board! Let's do that."

Gwen laughed. "Darts would be dangerous. I'd take out someone's eye. And the wait for a pool table would be at least an hour."

"So we just sit here?"

"No," Marissa said. "We drink and we talk. After we've had enough to drink, we dance."

159

Penny wasn't planning to drink enough.

Two hours later, the bar was crowded. Wall-to-wall people dancing, talking close, drinking. Penny took the last sip of her drink. She had stretched it out as long as she could. She lost count of Marissa's drinks, but it seemed like an awful lot. She had switched shots. At one point Penny counted that she had three shots in a half hour. Maybe that was normal?

"Does Marissa usually drink this much?" she whispered to Gwen.

"No. But tonight is different." Gwen didn't whisper.

"Why?"

Marissa stood up and glared at them. "Tonight is different," she enunciated, "Because my mom died tonight." Then she giggled. "Not tonight, but tonight four years ago."

"Riss, sit down." Gwen patted her chair.

"No, I won't. Tonight I get to do whatever I want." She stomped off to the bar.

"Should we take her home?" Penny asked. She had never seen Marissa this way. She thought of her as the mature one.

"She won't let us yet. We have to wait until she reaches a certain level of drunk."

"She seems pretty drunk to me." She looked across the room. Marissa held a drink in one hand, and was dancing with someone, eyes closed.

"This happens every year."

"You could have warned me. Told me what tonight was all about."

"She didn't want me to," Gwen said. "She wanted to try to get through it without talking about it. But I think this year is hitting her hard because she's leaving soon."

They kept watch from the table. Penny noticed that Gwen had stopped drinking too. After another hour of partly talking and mostly watching Marissa drink glass after glass and dance with guy after guy, Gwen said, "Okay, it's time to take her home."

Penny gathered all their purses and stood to follow Gwen through the crowd. Gwen grabbed Marissa by the upper arm. "Okay, Marissa, time to go. Tell this gentleman good-bye."

"No, I don't want to go. This guy, this Robbie, he is so good to me."

Gwen pulled harder on her arm. "Hello Robbie. If you're good to her, you'll help me convince her to go."

Robbie shrugged. "Bye Marissa. It was nice to meet you." He turned around and started dancing with a different girl.

Marissa pouted. "Not fair, Gwenny. You sent away my boy. And he was taller than me and that is hard to find in a boy. I'll find another."

Penny stepped in. "Let's see if there are any boys outside."

"Good idea," Gwen added. "I bet all the best boys are out there getting some fresh air."

"Okay. Sure." Marissa wobbled, but was able to walk with them through to the door.

Outside, the quiet was like a slap on the face. Penny drank in the cool air. She kept hold of Marissa's arm and they steered her toward the car.

When they got to the curb, Marissa slipped out of their hands and sank down onto it.

"Come on, Marissa. The car is just a few feet away," Gwen cajoled.

"I'll just stay here." She leaned back, and Penny caught her before she slammed her head on the sidewalk. Marissa spread her arms out and stared up at the light on the side of the bar. Or maybe she was looking past it to the sky.

"Hey, let's just get you home. It'll be better there," Gwen said.

"No, it'll be worse. She's everywhere there. I can't escape her." Tears rolled down her cheeks and landed on the pavement. "Then I'll go off to college and I won't be able to find her anywhere. There's nowhere safe to go."

Gwen and Penny looked at each other helplessly. "I'm calling Mike," said Penny, digging her phone out of her purse.

"Mike, I hate to bother you—"

"Where are you? I'll be right there."

"Birch's."

He ended the call. Penny pulled the phone from her ear. "Does this happen every year too?"

"Every year so far." Gwen lay down on the sidewalk beside Marissa. Penny lay down on her other side. People walked past them, and one person even stepped over Penny's head.

"We're in everybody's way," Marissa said.

"Yeah, and that's absolutely fine," Penny said, and rubbed her arm. "Everybody gets a turn being the one in the way."

Gwen looked across Marissa's body to Penny. "Welcome to the inner circle."

Penny smiled. "I'm glad to be here." It was the truth.

Mike's car zoomed into the parking lot. He stopped right in front of them, and hopped out.

"Michael, what are you doing here?" Marissa slurred as her brother lifted her up by the armpits.

He looked at Gwen. "Beach?"

She nodded. "Beach. Penny and I will meet you there."

"No. Get in my car." He was firm.

"But Penny had one drink hours ago. She can drive," Gwen protested.

"Get in." He opened the back door and slid Marissa across the seat. Her eyes were closed.

Gwen climbed in the back and slipped herself under Marissa's legs. Penny got in the front. Mike pulled away from the bar.

"Is it always going to be like this, Mike?" Gwen asked.

"It's going to be like this for as long as it's like this."

"Well that was wise and helpful."

"Don't give me any shit, Gwen. You know what I meant. It is what it is. We just deal with it, we can't change it."

Penny sat on her hands and didn't say anything. She felt stupid now for assuming Marissa was in some sort of healed-grief stage. That probably didn't even exist.

Mike drove them to the beach, to the bonfire spot. "Do you know why we have our parties here?" he asked Penny.

"No, why?"

"It's where we used to picnic as kids. We had family reunions here. Birthday lunches. But usually just Sunday picnics with our parents. Mom died. Picnics ended. Parties started."

Gwen helped Marissa out of the car. When Marissa stood, she puked in the sand. Gwen ignored that, and supported her as they walked all the way to the water's edge. Mike walked over and kicked sand over the vomit.

"Is she going to be okay?"

"Yeah," Mike said. "Once she lets herself really cry."

They sat in a row by the water, not close enough to let it reach their toes. After a while, the first sob broke the silence. Then another. Finally, Marissa's body shook from sobbing. She didn't try to muffle the sound of her crying. The three of them put their arms around her until she was still. It took a long time.

After sitting quietly for a few minutes, Marissa stood and threw a handful of sand into the water. *Flomp.* The others joined her, pitching globs of damp sand into the ocean. *Flomp, flomp, flomp.*

When Marissa stopped, Penny put her arm around her shoulders. "I didn't mean it, you know. You can absolutely bother me tomorrow."

Chapter 19

"Here you go, Penny," Justin said as he placed a beer can in her hand.

Not even a half second later, the can was plucked out of her hand by Mike.

"Dude. She's eighteen," he admonished Justin.

Gwen walked up behind Mike and grabbed the can out of his hand and gave it back to Penny. "God, Mike. You're beyond annoying."

Justin was laughing, and Penny could see that Mike was about to explode, so she placed the can back in Mike's hand. "I don't even want this. Let's not argue over something pointless."

Gwen narrowed her eyes and crossed her arms over her chest. "Yes. Let's argue over something with a point instead. Justin, you need someone to sing with you next weekend."

"No. It's a stupid idea to let anyone under twenty-one in the band." Mike crossed his arms and mimicked her stance.

"It's not even your band, Mike! I was talking to Justin." She turned to look at Justin who was shaking his head with amusement. "One night, Justin. One set, even."

"Gwen, I haven't heard from you in a month. You disappeared. You sang for us, and it was awesome, and then I can't get a hold of you to talk about it."

Gwen's face turned red. Penny's own face burned from sympathy mortification. Gwen recovered nicely though. She shrugged, trying to play it cool. "I've been busy. You know how it is. Anyway, you play at Puzzle next week which is for all ages. Surely even Mike doesn't have a moral objection to me singing there."

Mike shrugged and motioned Penny away toward the logs surrounding the bonfire and said, "Let's give them some space to argue." Gwen and Justin took off down the beach, deep in conversation. Gwen's arms were flailing wildly as she spoke, and Justin's hands were tucked in his pockets.

Mike and Penny sat on a log next to Marissa, who was subdued. This bonfire was a particularly large one. It was the last of the summer. Marissa was leaving for Florida in a few days. Penny looked around at the people that were there, marveling that she knew most of their names. She hadn't expected it, but this town had absorbed her. The music was quiet, the whole tone of the night was mellow.

"I see Anne getting a drink out of the cooler," Marissa said, leaning around Penny to talk to Mike.

"Yeah, I saw her too," he said.

"Well, do something about it."

He only shook his head.

"Life is short," she said.

"Don't do that, Marissa." He glared at her.

Penny pushed on his back, trying to get him to stand. He tried to resist, but she was stronger than he expected. Marissa joined in, and they pushed with all their might while he laughed and tried to wrestle them away. He ended up on his knees in the sand. Marissa and Penny laughed, a little crazed, and Anne looked in their direction.

"Quick, get up! She sees you. Pretend you were looking for my contact lens," Penny said.

That made them laugh even harder, and when Mike patted around in the sand, they about lost it. "Yeah, she'll fall for that. Here's your sandy contact lens, good luck with that." He pretended to hand her something and stood up, brushing off his knees.

"There's no chickening out now. If you don't go over there she'll think you're ignoring her on purpose." Penny gave him a nudge.

He walked over to her, and when he glanced back at the girls, they gave him cheesy thumbs up signs for encouragement.

"Oh look, they're walking to a private log together," Marissa said. "Thank the Lord. Maybe Anne will keep him busy enough that he won't focus so hard on my life."

"You must admit you're lucky to have him."

"Yeah." She looked at the sand.

"Tonight must be the night for pairing off," Penny said, and pointed at Gwen and Justin, and then Mike and Anne. "If there's someone you're interested in talking to tonight, feel free. I can handle being on my own."

"Nah. All I can think about is getting to Florida and starting the next step."

"The manatees will be lucky to have you." Penny bumped her shoulder against Marissa's.

"What about you? Summer is ending. Where is the next stop on your journey?"

"I don't know. I thought I'd be ready to move on by now, but I'm not finished here yet."

Marissa tilted her head toward the water a short way down the beach. Penny followed her gaze and saw Archer sitting alone, looking at the water. She fidgeted, thinking of the way he's always on the periphery.

"Go ahead," Marissa said. "I'm going to grab a beer while Mike is distracted."

~

"So I got a message from Irene about her guest bedroom," Penny said, and sank down onto the sand beside Archer.

167

He looked over at her and smiled. "Yeah? I'm looking forward to it."

They had finished her kitchen last week, and had both been surprised at how nice the orange paint looked.

"I wonder what color she'll pick for the bedroom. Probably fuchsia."

He smiled at the water. "Any more spy missions for your grandfather?"

"Of course not. I couldn't do that without my partner." She dared a quick peek at the side of his face.

Their banter was interrupted by howls of laughter and splashing down the beach. Someone had dragged one of the logs into the water. They watched as three people, wearing only underwear, tried to climb on it. They were attempting to sit, yet the log kept rolling and they screeched and laughed as they fell off.

"Oh my God, Gwen is on that log," Penny said, laughing at their antics.

"Did you have any doubt that she'd be right in the middle of the action?"

"Well, no. But that's sober Gwen out there. Oh wow, is that Justin with her?"

Archer squinted at the crowd in the water. More people and more logs had joined the fray. "Yep, look, he's lifting her on the log. Oh, no, there she goes down again."

They laughed and watched the sea bathers, glowing from the moon and the bonfire.

"You want to join them?" Archer asked.

"Absolutely not," she said, pleased that he asked.

He looked at her with an open face. "We're kind of similar about some things, huh?"

"Seems so." It was odd how they had so many differences between them, fundamental differences in the way their lives had unfolded, yet they were more alike than she could have imagined.

"Are you thinking something and not saying it?" he asked.

She smiled up at him. "Most of the time." He laughed. The fact that he found her funny lit something up inside her. "I'm trying not to mention anything that might make you feel bad, like the wide variety of peanuts in this world."

He laughed again, but sobered quickly. She thought about the first painting day at Irene's, and how he had gotten upset so suddenly. She didn't know him well enough to know which things would be too hard to talk about. "Nah, don't worry about it," he said. "I'm not fragile."

She pointedly looked at his arms, and his broad chest. "I'd say not." She'd said it meaning to be funny and flirty, hoping he'd laugh again. But when her eyes traveled to his face, the force of their caught gaze made it so that neither of them could laugh. Her heartbeat danced a crazed rumba in her chest, which explained the feeling of footsteps treading around in her belly.

Archer was the first to look away. "Christ, Penny." He breathed out heavily.

Penny tried not to panic at his verbal acknowledgement of this swirling heat that blazed between them; that blazed inside her right that minute. She knew they were past the point of either of them denying it, but still she wasn't ready to face those feelings. They were too huge and wonderful and scary.

He reached out and touched her cheek with the tips of his fingers. She sucked in a breath, sure she was about to be burned to ash. He gave her a look filled with hunger, and murmured, "Not yet."

He pulled his hand away and straightened his legs in front of himself and rubbed his palms on his thighs. "So, uh, great party, huh?" He looked at her and tried to smile though it came out sort of pained.

169

She smiled back, looking equally pained, she was sure. "Yeah." She let out a relieved breath. Somehow he knew what she needed, like he could read her mind. She knew it was bigger than that though, he was paying attention. He could *see* her. After a few moments, she asked, "Can I ask you a question?"

"Please do."

"Why are you sitting out here on the edge of it? You're always on the edges."

He shrugged. "I don't mind being alone."

"I like to be alone too, but if I wanted to be alone I wouldn't come to a party and sit apart from everyone else. I'd just stay home."

He grinned at her. "You won't let me get away with being vague?"

"Nope."

"Okay then, I'll tell you. I came here tonight hoping to see you. You seemed to be having fun with your friends, so I was just waiting for a window of opportunity to talk to you alone."

"You don't have to wait until I'm alone. You can talk to me when I'm with other people too. You've known those people longer than I have."

He chewed on his lip. "Yeah, but it's weird how the people who are friends in kindergarten sort of stick together through high school, at least in small towns like this, you know? My best friend since I was six years old is Lee Avery. He's a year older than me, so he graduated two years ago. He went into the army right after graduation. We used to hang out all the time, and when he left, I just never found anybody to fill his spot."

Penny looked at him thoughtfully and nodded her head, wondering why he'd never mentioned Lee before. They had logged many painting hours together, with no shortage of talking, but he'd never talked about Lee. "What is Lee like?"

170

Archer chuckled as he thought about his friend. "You'd like him a lot because he doesn't take any crap from me either." Penny swatted him on the shoulder. "No really, I appreciate that about him. He's a great guy. If he ever comes home, I hope you'll meet him."

"I'd like that. But in the meantime, maybe you can come and sit by the fire with me and those other people up there? It's not like there's a limited number of friend spots to fill and you have to wait for one to become available. Look at Gwen and Marissa. I infiltrated that group."

"And they've been best friends since the womb," he said, smiling at her. "I like sitting here with you and having you all to myself. But if I must share, I guess I can go be social."

Penny smiled and stood up, brushing sand off her pants. As they walked toward the fire, she considered again that she didn't know how much she had to offer Archer. She couldn't see far enough into the future to make any decisions, let alone any promises. But maybe she could help him become a bigger part of this group of people that she had come to care for. She could help him find a spot.

When they neared the fire, Marissa jogged over and handed them each a lit sparkler. Since she was a little girl, the first thing Penny always did with a sparkler was draw a heart. She ordered herself *do not draw a heart. Do NOT draw a heart.* When the urge passed, she made a circle. She looked over at Archer, only to discover that he had drawn a heart.

Chapter 20

Grandpa had told Penny that mornings were his favorite time of day, and since she still wasn't sleeping well, she was up with the sun and jogging to his house while the sky was still pink. As she'd hoped, he was up and dressed when she knocked on the door at seven.

He waved her in and went to the table. He was eating breakfast, and he told her to pull up a chair and join him for a bagel.

"So, you're here early again," he said.

"Yes." She tried to make her eyes less sad, and her voice more sure. She took in a deep breath, but before she could utter a word, he spoke.

"You've talked me into it, my dear. Well, you and George Baker. I had an illuminating chat with him yesterday afternoon."

Penny set her bagel down and looked at him, and her eyes began to water. That turned into heavy sobs. Cal stood and walked around behind her chair. He put his arms around her shoulders, but didn't say anything. He waited for her to speak.

"That means you won't be here with me anymore," she choked out when she was able.

"I thought perhaps that since you had talked me into going to Montana, I could do the same for you."

"Oh."

"Yes. If it's the place for me, perhaps it's the place for you too," he said.

"Did you already talk to Mom and Dad?"

172

"I talked to your mother last night. She is annoyingly pleased." He pursed his lips.

"Isn't that the way it is with her? To please her is to be annoyed. Why is that?" Penny laughed a little, happy to have found someone with the same assessment of her mother as herself.

"She likes, a little too much, to be pleased."

"Grandpa, I can't move back. At this point, I don't think I would go back even if I thought it was the right thing for me to do. The pleasure she and Dad would take in it would bury me," she said.

"You'll grow out of that, I promise. Soon, very soon I think, you will make decisions to suit yourself, and you will do so even when other people take a bit too much of the credit. Thus, I have decided to go."

"Did you just call me immature? I think you did." She grinned and patted him on the arm and he laughed.

"No, no. Not immature. What you are, is unsure. Soon, you will be sure of yourself."

"I'm counting on it." She took a deep breath. "So how do we make this happen? You have a lot of stuff in this house, Grandpa. It's not like we can just put you on a plane."

"Will you drive me? There isn't much I wish to keep. Your parents will handle the house," he said.

Penny was jubilant. That could be really fun. She'd have hours upon hours with Grandpa, and it basically solved her biggest problem. She also relished the idea of seeing her family, just for a short visit. "Road trip!"

~

"Look who's late!" Archer said, a bit too enthusiastically in Penny's opinion, when she arrived at Irene's for their next paint day. He was carrying a ladder out of the hallway. He propped it on the wall in the living room.

"Yeah, yeah. Sorry," she said.

"It's for the best. I'm a better taper than you are, and I already finished that part." Penny stuck her tongue out at him, but he went on, "The glee that filled my soul when I arrived first and got my hands on that tape. Visions of straight lines and no touch-up work; the stuff of daydreams."

She crossed her arms over her chest. "It's only because you're ninety-four feet tall, and you don't have to wobble on the ladder as you work."

"I suppose your three inch height caused you to wobble while you were taping the baseboards as well?" he said, grinning.

"Fine, you win. I suck at taping," she said, smiling too. "So where's Irene today?"

"She's visiting Magnolia. She'll be back before lunch. The better question is, why were you late?"

"What? People can oversleep you know. It happens."

"Not to you. You're too high strung for sleeping in. What's up?"

She raised her brow, knowing that was true. The past two days had been overwhelming and busy. "I had to get some things my grandpa needed. Doctor records, boxes, and some other stuff. He's moving back to Montana to live with my parents."

Mike had given her several good boxes from his shop, and it had been nice to talk it through with him. He was good at making Penny feel like she could be an adult; like she too could be someone who knew what to do in situations.

"Oh yeah? That's good," Archer said.

"I think so, too. I'll be driving him back home this weekend," she said.

Archer froze. He leaned against the wall. He put his hands in his pockets. "You're leaving?"

"Grandpa's leaving. I'll be coming back."

The whoosh of air he breathed out was so huge it blew her hair around her face. She tucked it behind her ears and laughed. "Why Archer, you act as though you're relieved to hear that."

"Damn right, I'm relieved. It would be pretty hard to take you on a date if you lived in Montana," he said.

Her heart sped up. "Didn't we decide we're both undateable? You're burdened by your past and I'm trying to discover my own personality." She was only half teasing.

"We never finished that conversation. We were interrupted by your lost gramps."

She nodded. "It's just, I still don't know if I'm in the right place in my life to date anybody."

He clenched his jaw and disappeared into Irene's garage. He came back carrying a drop cloth. "I've done some thinking. What better way to figure yourself out than to have as many experiences as possible?"

Penny laughed. "And you're going to give me *experiences*, is that right?"

He shrugged and turned around to organize a box of painting supplies. When he was quiet for a while, she realized that he wasn't in the mood for teasing; he was serious. "And where would we go for our date?" she asked, quietly.

He didn't answer for a minute, and she started to think maybe her teasing had offended him—a first. Then he said, "There are lots of places I want to take you, but I thought first I would take you to meet a friend. Miss Zelda."

"Miss Zelda?"

"Yep. She's a palm reader. She's also my friend. Maybe she'd have some ideas for self-illuminating experiences we can do."

"Well, it's true that I've never been to a palm reader. So...do you go and get your palm read on a regular basis?"

"No." He laughed. "She used to be friends with my mom, when I was little. She lived three houses down, and

175

sometimes babysat for me. Made me breakfast when Mom was out of it. Anyway, she's a character. She *has* read my palm before, just not on a regular basis."

They continued organizing the painting supplies in silence as she thought about it. After a while she said, "Okay. When I get back, we'll go meet Miss Zelda. But can we just call it hanging out?"

He smiled at her. "Okay. Dating is just hanging out anyway." Before she could respond, he turned on the radio Irene had on a table in the hallway. It was Led Zeppelin. Not Penny's favorite. She knew it made her a musical blasphemer.

"Let's get painting," he said, and lifted the box of supplies and headed into the guest room. Penny followed, carrying rollers and a tray.

Archer filled the tray with light green paint, then held out a hand so she could give him a roller. "By the look on your face, you either hate this music or you hate this garish green."

She smirked. "It's a gorgeous green." He laughed and Penny glowed.

"Okay, yeah, my musical preferences are different. But I don't believe in music-shaming. Go ahead and listen. I'll torture you with my music some other time."

"I cannot believe you don't like Zeppelin. I mean, really. That's...wow." He disappeared in the hall and she heard the station switch. When he came back in, he said, "You're not allowed to listen to them if you don't appreciate them. It's just plain disrespectful." She grinned at him and continued to paint, now enjoying the sounds of some band she didn't recognize.

About an hour later, Irene rushed through the door carrying a large bag bulging with fabric. "It's hot out there today!" she said. "Magnolia gave me this bag of old curtains she had in her attic. I want you two to choose some for the living room and hang them while I'm gone."

176

"You're going out again?" Penny asked.

"Oh that's right, I hadn't told you two yet. My sister, Sandra, is sick. I think she'll be fine, but she has pneumonia and she's even older than me." She pointed her finger at Penny and shushed her. "I can't see you but I can tell you're about to tell me I'm not old. Tell that to my knees. Anyway, I have some errands to run and things to do before going to Knoxville."

"Your sister lives in Knoxville?"

"Yes. She's in the hospital. I need to visit her."

"Irene, how are you getting to Tennessee? Is Magnolia driving you?" Archer asked.

"No, she can't get off work on such short notice. I'll take a Greyhound. And before you say it, I can handle it just fine. I'm not worried and you shouldn't be either."

Archer looked at Penny, and she knew what he was thinking because she was thinking the same thing. "Irene, I'm driving my grandpa to Montana. We're leaving on Sunday morning. Would you like to ride with us? I'll be driving right past Knoxville. I don't know how long you'll want to stay, but on my way back here I can come get you. My trip will take about a week."

Irene sat down loudly on the bed, which was draped in a plastic sheet. "That's awfully generous. You're sure it won't be any trouble? You really are driving that way anyway and there's room in your car?"

"Yes."

"Well, never mind. I'm not sure I should wait until Sunday. I'll just take the bus."

Penny sat down next to her and took her hand. She thought that might help her know she was sincere. "I'm renting a big old SUV to pull the moving trailer for Grandpa's stuff. There will be plenty of room, he won't mind at all, and we are driving exactly where you need to go.

I understand if you need to go sooner, but really, I'd love to have you along."

"You'd let me pay you."

"I would?"

"Yes. The price of a bus ticket."

Penny shrugged. "Okay. You better go call your sister. I'm going back to Grandpa's house to tell him about all this.

Penny looked up and saw Archer standing there holding a drying paint roller, with a look of incredulity on his face. "You're sticking me with the painting. You only helped for an hour," he said.

Irene stood and said to Penny, "That's Archer, alright. Behind every silver lining is a dark cloud." They chuckled, while Archer mock-glared at them. "Archer, Penny can help you clean up the brushes and then I'd like your help packing, if you don't mind. And could you run me to the post office?"

Archer pressed his lips together in a thin line and glanced at Penny and then quickly away. "I don't like half-finished jobs. I hate leaving things incomplete."

Irene rubbed his arm. "Don't be so uptight." Penny laughed out loud. Archer grumped off to the kitchen, muttering something about getting a hammer to close the paint cans.

"He really is a dear," Irene said.

~

"You can move my bed into the den for him," Penny told her mom. They were on the phone discussing the plans for the Grandpa delivery mission. She was sitting in her car in the parking lot of the moving trailer place, and Grandpa was in the passenger seat of a newly rented SUV. Renting it hadn't been easy. She had been turned away after learning she needed to be twenty-five to rent a vehicle, and had to bring Grandpa along to sign the papers. He didn't drive anymore, so she was relieved that his license hadn't expired.

"But where would you sleep, then?" her mom asked.

"I don't mind taking the couch."

"You can't use the living room as your bedroom, honey. You'd last about a week without any privacy."

At that moment, a man walked up and handed Penny a clipboard full of paperwork she needed to fill out to rent a trailer, and at the same time Grandpa opened the passenger door. "Mom, I've got to go. We'll figure it out when I get there."

She took the clipboard from the man, and got Grandpa situated back in his seat. It wasn't until she started filling out her address and nearly put Montana in the box for her state, out of habit, that she realized her mom thought she would be moving back home. To stay.

Her heart dropped down in to her stomach. Oh no. When she called her mom to talk about Grandpa moving in with her family, she hadn't mentioned her own plans to return to Wells Cove. She hadn't thought to mention it, because not returning hadn't even crossed her mind. Of course now Penny realized it had crossed her mom's mind, though.

Her mom didn't know there were things tying her here, or that she had left for reasons other than to help Grandpa. Now that Grandpa's plans were settled, her parents probably thought hers were too. Well. She would fix it later. She pushed it from her mind and finished filling out the forms.

Chapter 21

"Penny, I don't need to bring all those record albums," Cal said, annoyed.

"Really? Why don't you want them?" Penny didn't know why he was grouchy. Maybe it was the stress of moving.

"My record player stopped working a couple weeks ago. My ears aren't the best anyway. Someone should take them who can enjoy them."

"Ooh, I'd love to have them, Mr. Anderdoll!" Gwen squealed, as she ran over to flip through the box of dusty albums.

It was mid-morning on Saturday, and Gwen had come to help pack the things Grandpa wanted to take. Mr. Bellhill had kindly let Penny have the next ten days off. She was glad for the deadline, because it gave her a good reason to leave Montana without lingering. She figured her family would try to talk her into staying, but they would respect her work commitment.

She was dusty from sorting through old boxes. Her grandparents had a lifetime of stuff packed away. Her grandpa didn't seem to want to bring much with him. Penny thought about the things she had left at home. Yearbooks, science fair ribbons, that kind of thing. She understood leaving some of the past behind. But the only personal mementoes he would let her pack were Grandma Ruby's jewelry box and a few photo albums.

"This is beginning to feel more complicated than it needs to be," Cal said. "Why don't I just tell you the things I want to bring? We can forget the rest of it."

"But what if you're sitting on the porch swing in Montana in three months, and realize you didn't bring something very special, like your old letters or service awards or something?" Gwen asked.

Penny looked at him, wondering what his memory would be like in that length of time. He looked back at her, and seemed to know what she was thinking. "In three months it will be too cold to sit on the porch in Montana. Besides, I carry my most special memories in my mind, and those are all I need to bring along," Cal said, and threw her a wink.

Penny went into the spare room and set out a large empty box. Gwen followed her in and Penny whispered to her, "If you find anything that seems like an important memento, will you put it in here?" She set the framed wedding photo of her grandparents in the bottom of the box.

Gwen pulled out an envelope from her back pocket and set it on the photo. "It's a letter from his mom. He told me to trash it. I mean, his mom! I wasn't about to throw it out. It was written in 1942," she said.

Penny grinned at her. "You are the best, you know that? Help me find that shoebox of letters from Grandma that he told me he didn't want. Maybe he doesn't want this stuff, but I do. Plus, he might change his mind."

"How late do you think we'll be here? I need to get ready for tonight," Gwen said. Justin and Gwen had decided her debut as the new lead singer of Someling would be that night at Puzzle.

"Gwen, you perform at nine o'clock. It's not even lunch."

"Yeah, I know." Gwen widened her eyes and gave Penny a serious look. "I hope I can fit it all in. My manicure is at two, and I need to get showered before that and do my hair after. Oh God. I'm going to pack one more box and then I have to get going."

Penny laughed and shook her head at her friend. And it was true, they were friends. Real friends, not practice friends.

Penny was glad she would get to see Gwen perform before she left. Justin was leaving on Sunday, to go back to Charleston, and Gwen was following him there. She was even going to stay at his apartment until she found her own place. Gwen had said, "It's going to take me a *long* time to find a place."

They poked around the room searching for other things of sentimental value, when the doorbell rang. Penny walked to the front room, where Cal snored in the recliner. He didn't wake when the doorbell rang a second time.

She opened the door, and Mike stood on the porch holding a stack of boxes. "I thought you might be running low."

She took the boxes from him, but said, "He's refusing to fill the boxes I already got from you. He won't take much beyond the bare necessities. But thanks for these. I'm going to pack a few things secretly just in case."

Penny set the boxes inside on the floor. She closed the door behind her and stepped onto the porch with Mike.

"Hey, are you okay?" she asked. He looked sort of sad.

"I just wanted to say good-bye."

"Aren't you coming to Puzzle tonight?"

"Yeah, but there won't be a chance to talk there."

"True."

"I feel like everything is changing," he said.

"I'm supposed to be at work in ten days. I'm coming back." She smiled up at him.

"Yeah. I have this feeling that you might stay there. It's your home. And Marissa isn't coming back."

Penny gave him a look. "I know this is a hard transition, but you're being a little dramatic. She's coming back at Thanksgiving."

A smile ghosted his lips. "I suppose. Will you come to our house for Thanksgiving? You'll have to bring a pie. All guests must bring a pie."

"I'll bring a pumpkin pie."

"If you come back."

Penny rolled her eyes at him.

"Maybe you can be a substitute sister for me while she's gone?"

"I may have a lot of brothers, but I can always use one more. I always wanted an older brother anyway, did you know?"

"Well good."

"And I really am coming back. I'm leaving my stuff here and everything," she said. "Is it just that Marissa is leaving, or is there something else?"

He crossed his arms and let out a moan. "I asked Anne on a date. She said no."

"Oh no! I'm sor—"

He cut her off. "Don't be sorry. It's the kick in the ass I needed to shake myself out of this run-of-the-mill life."

"What are you talking about? Your life isn't run-of-the-mill. What about your shop? And the coffee shop you wanted to open?"

He smiled then. "That's what I mean. I'm sick of waiting around for stuff to happen, worrying I'll fail. I'm finished making plans and not following through. I'm going to talk to some dude at the bank next week about getting a loan. I have to start doing things instead of just thinking about doing them, even if they fail."

Penny smiled back at him. "You might not know it, but you're someone I look up to when I don't know how a real grown-up would behave. You've got it figured out."

"Well I don't know about that. I may be older than you, but let me tell you, the only thing I've figured out is that nobody gets everything figured out. Just try stuff and see what sticks, you know?"

"Yeah." Penny didn't know if that thought was comforting or scary.

"I need to get back to the shop. I left a new kid in charge. Have a safe trip, and call me when you get back." They hugged tightly and then he walked down to his car. Penny sat on the porch steps for a minute, watching this little neighborhood she had come to love.

Cal opened up the door behind her. "Are you being wooed?" he asked, quite clearly amused. At least he wasn't grouchy anymore.

Penny laughed, "No, I'm not being wooed. He's my friend."

"He's not the wooer you want?"

"I guess that's one way to put it."

"Ruby thought I wasn't the man for her at first. She took some convincing." His eyes sparkled. Penny stood and hugged him tightly around the neck.

~

"She sounds really good!" Penny shouted in Marissa's ear. She couldn't believe she was back at Puzzle. It was an older crowd this time, both because it was a Saturday night and because Someling had a lot of fans.

"I know! She belongs on a stage. Do you know she made me check her teeth, look up her nose, and triple check her underwear before she went up there?"

"Yuck!"

"She's done grosser things for me," Marissa said, shrugging.

Just then, Gwen did a bizarre hip-swooping, arm-flapping dance from one side of the stage to the other, and both girls laughed. "Even on stage, she has no shame."

Penny was still laughing about Gwen's silly dance, when a low voice whispered in her ear, his lips almost touching it, "Can I sit by you?"

"Sure," she croaked out.

"Here, let me scoot over and you can pull a chair over from that table," Marissa added, moving her chair closer to her brother. Mike glared. Penny reached over and swatted him on the arm, and he shrugged.

"Hey, Archer," he offered.

Archer nodded at him. "Hey." He found a chair and fit it into the space between the girls, and sat down. He didn't seem to know what to do with his hands, and he eventually just laid them on his knees.

The music changed to a softer, quieter song. "I didn't know you were coming," Penny said to Archer.

"I wanted to see you one more time before you left. That, and I had to see our girl up there." He tilted his head toward Gwen but didn't take his eyes off Penny.

Chapter 22

Penny was close to tears. The rental SUV was sitting perpendicular to the moving trailer attached to it. How had that even happened? Driving to Grandpa Cal's hadn't been too bad. Parking in front of his house only involved driving straight onto the grassy strip by the sidewalk. But now she was in a parking lot full of cars. She sighed and pulled forward again until the trailer was straight behind her. Then she parked crossways, covering about seven parking spaces. Oh well, she was only planning to be a minute.

She ran through the side door and into the employee break room. Paychecks were kept in an unlocked cabinet by the microwave. Penny guessed that wasn't the way it should be done, but nobody seemed to care. She flipped through the stack of envelopes until she found the one with her name on it. She set the others back and turned around to see greasy, hot-dog-smelling Lewis. She bared her teeth in the biggest smile her mouth could make. She looked like a lunatic, and he sneered at her. She bet he'd never tell her to smile again.

When she came out of the break room, Steph was there pushing a cart with Gregory strapped to her chest in a baby carrier. "Look how happy he is! And you're out of the house!" Penny greeted her.

Steph smiled at her and gave her a hug. Gregory was smooshed sweetly between them. When Penny stepped back, she had to pry his fingers off her t-shirt. "I hear you're leaving us for a while," Steph said.

"This town should be named Snoops Cove. How do people know my business? I'll only be gone a week or so."

"I'll miss Cal. He sure turned up a lot of places all over town. I saw him out at least once a week. Well, that was before I became a shut-in with my screaming child, and also while his trips out and about were still intentional."

"Well, Gregory seems to be doing a lot better," Penny said. She felt melancholy about the tides of life. One shut-in was now a free bird, and one free bird would soon become a lot more shut-in.

"He is. Mornings are now his best time of day, so I take advantage of that fact, even though I'm exhausted. When we get out early, the whole day goes better."

Penny grinned at her and kissed Gregory's puffy cheek. "I have to get going. We're trying to get on the road before nine."

"Tell Cal I said good-bye, and tell Irene I told her not to do anything I wouldn't do."

Penny waved and walked back to the side door to leave. When she opened it, she heard someone crying. Not quiet sniffling, but the bark of sobs trying to be contained. She looked around and didn't see anyone. She about jumped out of her skin when glass smashed on the pavement to her left. Then the crying stopped abruptly. She stood frozen. Was someone in trouble over there? She pulled her phone from her pocket, her finger hovering over the nine.

Loud footsteps scraped across the gravel, and Archer came around the corner rubbing his face with both hands. He was muttering curses under his breath. He looked up and noticed Penny standing there. He stopped and looked at her, stock-still for a moment, and then walked right past her toward his car.

"Archer, wait," she said, hurrying after him.

He leaned against his car and didn't say anything. Penny didn't say anything. When she couldn't stand the silence anymore, she looked up at the sky and said, "It's a beautiful morning, isn't it?"

He let out one small *huh* of laugher, which was quickly followed by more. She didn't understand why he was laughing, but for whatever reason, she couldn't keep from laughing, either. They stood there next to his car, him laughing at who knows what, and her laughing at his laughter.

"You say weird, unexpected things, Penny," he said, and ran his hands over his shaggy hair.

"I do?"

"All the time." He studied her, and bit his thumbnail. "I thought you'd be on the road by now. Long gone and leaving all this morning beauty behind."

"I need to hurry. I had to get my check, and I'm supposed to go load up Irene, and then swing by to get Grandpa. I got his things loaded up yesterday. You wouldn't believe it. His whole life boiled down to seven boxes. Seven! Some of them are very small, too. I couldn't convince him to take much at all."

Archer watched her ramble with a small smile on his face. He took a few deep breaths and looked away. "Penny?"

"Yeah?"

"My mom is dying."

She gasped, then put her hand to her mouth in shame. He didn't need her to be dramatic. She had tried to distract him with talk of the weather and packing boxes and he stood there and listened and his mom was dying. She stepped forward and reached out for his hand. At the contact, she was struck with a thought.

"Wait a minute! Isn't your mom in Tennessee? I'm driving to Tennessee! I'm leaving in less than an hour. This will work out perfectly. Go home and throw some things in a bag. I'll come get you after we go to Grandpa's." She dug around in her pocket for the keys. "I have to drive this crazy contraption, so I better get going. I'll be at your place in a few! It's the apartment complex on Maple, right?"

188

"Wait, Penny!" he called, as she rushed off. She stopped and turned to him, impatient to get going.

"I'm not going with you."

"But you said your mom is dying," she said, confused.

"She is. That doesn't mean I want to see her," he said, and tucked his hands in his pockets.

Penny furrowed her brow, trying to understand. "But you're upset. This would give you a chance to say good-bye."

"Not everyone has good parents, Penny. Not everyone has parents who live actual lives that have meaning." His voice was turning thick with tears again. "Not everyone's parents love them."

Penny blinked, abashed. She hadn't considered that. The idea was completely foreign to her. "But do *you* love her?"

He laughed coldly, then went silent. He scrubbed his palms against his face.

When she spoke again, she tried to be sedate. "I'm going to go do the things I need to do. Then I'll come to your apartment. Be out front if you want to come. Anyway, you don't have to decide right now. It will be several hours of driving until we're anywhere near her. You could decide not to see her at any time, and that's fine." Then she left as quickly as she could, so he wouldn't have time to argue.

~

"Climb on in here, old man," Irene said as Cal joined her in the back seat. Penny put his lone suitcase in the trailer, and sighed at how much empty space there was. She could have put the back seat down in the SUV, stuffed everything in, and taken the impossible-to-park trailer directly back to the rental place. But they needed to get going, so she kept the behemoth attached.

189

"Why are both of you in the back seat? I feel like a chauffeur up here by myself," Penny said as she climbed in and started the engine.

"We're leaving that seat free for Archer, my dear," Grandpa said.

"What about respecting your elders and all that? You should get the prime spot."

"You don't need to remind me that I'm the oldest one in this vehicle. Irene and I will do perfectly fine back here."

Penny looked back and saw Irene pat him on the shoulder.

She had never been to Archer's apartment building, but knew where it was. It was in the worst part of town, but Penny didn't care. He had to live somewhere, and she was not a real estate snob.

Pulling up to the building though, she didn't feel very good about it. It was a terrible place. Her own building was not the best-kept place around, but at least it didn't feature a man putting a needle into his arm out in broad daylight. She took a deep breath and looked away from the man, deciding to pretend he was shooting insulin. The thought made her laugh, and she suppressed it with a guilty frown. She scanned the area for Archer. She hoped fervently that he would be there waiting. Saying good-bye to a dying parent seemed to Penny to be a necessity, no matter what that parent had been like. Parents were just…fundamental.

"Why are you both so quiet?" Irene asked. "Isn't he here?"

"Well, I don't know which apartment is his, and he barely had any time to get ready. Let's just wait here a little longer and see if he comes out," Penny said.

"This place is worse than a rat hole," Grandpa added.

"Archer could afford better than a rat hole," Irene said. "The trouble is, he doesn't think he deserves better."

"Oh! There he is. He's coming!" Penny was jubilant.

He loped toward them, a black duffel bag in one hand and a cardboard box in the other. He opened the back door and stopped in surprise when he faced Cal.

"Your seat is up front," Cal told him.

"No sir, you take the front."

"If I wanted to sit up front, I'd be there. You're sitting up front," Cal repeated. Archer shut the back door, and opened the front door.

"Archer, meet my grandpa, Cal. Grandpa, this is Archer." The men shook hands over the seat.

"This is a bad idea," Archer said to Penny, sliding the box onto the floor and setting the duffel on top of it.

"Good. It's about time Penny was part of some bad ideas," Grandpa said. Irene laughed.

"Grandpa! This is not a bad idea. Every person in this car needs to be here. Actually, I'm merely a facilitator, but I do believe my part is vital," Penny said. She looked over at Archer, who was trying to create some leg room around his stuff. "You can put your stuff in the trailer or the back if you want."

"Nah, I'll keep it up here." He sat down and shut his door hard. He somehow found room for his huge feet, and sat there looking crammed in. Penny raised her brows and gave him a pointed look. He got her meaning and buckled his seatbelt with a sigh.

"Safety first!" she chirped. She was pretty smug about this whole trip, and though she knew she was being obnoxious, she couldn't help it. She had convinced everyone in the car to come, and it hadn't been easy. Archer rolled his eyes at her, but she could sense a smile about to emerge.

Irene told her the name of the hospital her sister was in, and Penny input it into her GPS. She hadn't had time to plot all the stops for this trip on her atlas. "First stop, Knoxville. According to this, it'll take six hours and twenty-three minutes. So get comfortable." She managed to get onto the road without having to use reverse, so that was a good start.

For the first hour or so, the four of them made small talk. Somewhere in the second hour, Penny noticed they were becoming more comfortable with each other. Grandpa and Irene were chatting and laughing quietly in the back. She glanced over at Archer, and saw that he was looking at her.

"You have any music?" He smiled broadly. "It's your turn to torture my ears, and you have me captive. Take your best shot."

"As I recall, you changed the station when I didn't share your love of Led Zeppelin. So I don't plan to torture you. Take the wheel a second." He reached over and grabbed the steering wheel, keeping them from veering off the interstate while she found the right song on her iPod. She took back the wheel as "I Was Made for Sunny Days" by The Weepies played softly.

He looked out his window and didn't say anything, just listened. Penny felt herself shrinking down in her seat. Sharing her favorite music suddenly felt too intimate.

"It's folksy, huh?" she said, unable to wait for him to offer his opinion.

"Yeah. Don't change it," he said, and reached out to stop her hand from skipping to the next song. She smiled and sat back, enjoying the open road before her.

~

"They asleep?" Archer asked.

Penny was in the passenger seat now. They were back on the road after a lunch stop at an Indian restaurant where she indulged in the spiciest curry they had. Archer had claimed the role of driver. She glanced into the backseat, and both Irene and Cal were snoozing, each leaning on their respective windows.

"Yeah, they're out," she said. She glanced at the clock. There was only an hour or so until they would arrive at the hospital to drop off Irene.

She squirmed around in her seat, trying to find a comfortable position. There wasn't much room for her feet, because Archer still refused to move his things to the back. "This box is cramping my style. What's in here anyway?"

"All my secrets," he said, and waggled his eyebrows.

"So your old diaries and copies of your arrest records?" She grinned at him.

"All that and more. Trust me, you don't want to open that thing."

"I bet your diary is less scary than my diary," she said.

"Yeah? I thought you never broke a rule in your life."

"Exactly. Reading it would cause absolute cringe-inducing mortification. I wrote about school work. Gossip that I wasn't even a part of. My cat. It would bore you right into the grave. Or you'd read it and die of embarrassment on my behalf. Either way, you'd be dead."

He laughed, and they were silent for a while. She wanted to ask him about something that had been weighing on her mind. "Archer, do you remember the first time you saw me?"

"Of course I do. I bagged up your macaroni and your fruit. Your hair was draped over your shoulders and you were wearing a purple tank top. You were beautiful. You were nervous." After that little speech, he glanced at her cautiously.

She shut her eyes to keep them from popping out and showing her surprise. "I *was* nervous. That was my first day in town." She didn't know how to respond to him calling her beautiful, so she didn't. "You looked really sad that day."

"I did? What do you mean? I wasn't sad." He seemed flustered.

"I guess I assumed that, but you didn't look at my face. When I looked at yours, your eyes just looked sad. I'm sorry if I assumed wrong."

"I did."

"Did what?"

"I looked at your face. When you were putting your stuff on the conveyor belt, and when you were getting your money out to pay." He smiled. "I probably looked sad because I was thinking that a girl like you would never give me a chance." He laughed. "But I really wasn't sad." He was hammering home that point.

Penny remembered how she had felt intimidated by him that day. He had been feeling the same way about her? That was such a bizarre idea that it did not compute. He sure had looked sad, that day and others too. "Okay. Maybe sad's not the right word."

He grabbed his drink and gulped it so hard the sides of the straw sucked in and it squeaked.

"You know what, though? I wasn't even talking about that time when you bagged my groceries. I didn't think you saw me that day. I meant the night at the beach, when I was crying. Obviously, I was sad. I thought that was the first time you saw me."

"Oh."

She shifted in her seat, glad he had to keep his eyes on the road. "I wondered how long you'd been there, and what you thought of me that night. Why you didn't say anything."

His throat moved as he swallowed. "I'm sorry if you thought I was spying on you or something. I was already there when you arrived. I kind of didn't want you to see me."

"Why not?"

"I thought you'd leave. Maybe this is weird, but I did want to watch you. I thought I might work up the courage to talk to you. Then when you started crying, I felt stuck. I couldn't talk to you because I didn't even know you and I thought you'd want privacy. I couldn't leave because you'd notice and might be upset that I watched you cry."

"But then you helped me fold my blanket."

"Yeah. At that point I knew I had to reveal myself, so it wouldn't be a secret I'd have to carry. Also, I wanted to do something for you, and that was the only thing I could think of."

"Well I liked that you did. I just wondered if you thought I was weird that night."

"I didn't think that. Not that night, anyway. I've thought you were weird plenty of other times since, though." He grinned and looked over at her.

She poked him on the shoulder and sat back in her seat, content.

~

Archer held onto Irene's arm as Penny went to the trailer to find her suitcase. When she came around the SUV carrying it, she saw Irene shake him off.

"Archer, you let go of me. I don't need help."

"Sorry. You've never been here before. I was just trying to make sure you know where you're going," he said.

"Well, I only accept help if I ask for it first. Now, Penny, I need some help. Get my stick for me and point me toward the building." Penny grinned at Archer, who stuck his tongue out at her.

Cal was still sitting in the back of the car. Penny leaned her head into the open window. "Grandpa, you sure you don't want to come in?"

"No, no. I'll stay here. If I went in, they'd probably admit me." He chuckled to himself.

They found the information desk, and were told Sandra was in room 214.

"Good lord, children. You don't have to walk me directly to her door."

They ignored her, and walked her there.

Archer leaned her violin case against the wall and said, "You won't be able to carry all this stuff. How will you get it to your hotel or wherever you're staying?"

"Archer, I know you're just concerned, but you're getting on my very last nerve. Get back out to the car, and let me have a minute alone with Penny."

"Don't I get to meet your sister?" he asked, with a pout.

"Scat." She hugged him, and then shooed him away with a wave of her hands.

After he was gone, she leaned in close and whispered, "Penny, I love that boy as if he were my own son. If I told him that, I'd never hear from him again because he would be far too embarrassed. So we just pretend we get on each other's nerves."

"I think you may actually get on each other's nerves."

"Well, a little," she said, smiling. "I am worried for how he'll handle seeing his mother. If it doesn't go well, will you bring him back here to me, before continuing on, if he wants? I don't want him getting a bus home by himself. That wouldn't be good."

Penny frowned. She hadn't given much thought to how Archer would feel after seeing his mom. She had been too focused on the goal of getting him to agree to see her in the first place. "Sure, I'll tell him."

"Good." She patted Penny on the hand, and turned into her sister's room and shut the door. Apparently, Penny wouldn't get to meet Sandra either. She walked back to the parking lot with a new lump of apprehension sitting in her belly.

Chapter 23

When Penny arrived back to the trailer contraption from hell, which was once again parked across six parking spaces, it was empty. She panicked. Maybe Archer had gone with Grandpa to the bathroom or something. She hugged her arms around her chest.

Then she heard it.

"Cal! Cal, where are you?"

Archer's voice was desperate. Penny dashed through the parking lot, dodging cars and pedestrians, toward the source of the shouts. There was a small wooded area about fifty yards past the parking lot. She darted into it, and saw Archer's blue t-shirt.

"Hey," he said, out of breath.

"What happened?"

"I got back to the car, and it was empty. I figured he had just gone to the bathroom, so I got in to wait. Then I saw him walk into these trees. I've only been in here a minute, he can't be far."

"You got back to an empty car, and just sat down to *relax*?" She took off again, shouting as she went. "Grandpa!" Archer followed at her heels.

After just a few yards, he grabbed her arm and pulled her back. "What?" she snapped. "You're slowing me down."

"Look." He pointed to a tree on a small hill. Cal was sitting on the ground, leaning against the trunk. His face was flushed, and Penny knew he had to be hot in that sweatshirt.

She glanced at Archer sheepishly. "Thanks for finding him."

197

"No problem. Let's go get him."

They climbed the hill, and Penny sat down next to her grandpa. "I know you aren't thrilled about moving to Montana, but you didn't have to run away," she teased him. Her heart wasn't in it though, because she could already tell that he wasn't himself.

"Hello. Lovely weather for a hike," he said, with a distant smile.

"Yes, it's a great day for a hike. Let's hike this way. I have some water for you." She swallowed thickly, and grabbed his elbow to help him stand. She avoided his eyes, because she didn't like looking in them when he wasn't inside.

~

"You want me to drive?" Archer leaned against the trailer, his arms crossed.

"Nope. I need to drive. It'll give my mind something to do so I'll quit worrying." She also wanted to give him some time to think because his stop was next.

Grandpa looked at Archer and smiled, no trace of recognition on his face. He was placid, though out of breath. Penny got him in the back seat, and gave him some water. He drank it and then buckled his seatbelt.

"Okay, so I need to change the information in the GPS." She glanced at Archer, trying to force her nervous smile to look more confident. She hated to bring up anything to do with his mom.

"I'll do it. He grabbed it from the dash and typed in *Tennessee Prison for Women*. He shot her a look that clearly meant she wasn't to say anything about it, and sat back in his seat, closing his eyes.

She studied the GPS, trying to figure out how to get onto I-40. "Two and a half hours!" she exclaimed, unable to contain her surprise. Archer opened one eye, and if it was possible to glare with one eye, he did. "Sorry. I just didn't realize Tennessee was so...wide." He closed his eye again, but she could see a small smile on his lips.

"Hey, Archer?"

"Yeah?"

"I'm sorry about earlier. I wasn't really mad at you, and anyway, it's not your job to keep an eye on him. I was mad that I had been so careless."

"I know."

"Okay."

"Archer?"

"Yeah?"

"It's just, maybe I'm getting too good at arguing."

"That wasn't arguing. That was a five second freak-out."

"I guess. But I don't like that I snapped at you."

"It's really okay."

"So you're not mad?"

"No, I'm not mad."

"Okay. I'm not either."

After ten minutes of driving, they were on the interstate and Penny felt more comfortable. She looked in the rear view mirror to see that Grandpa was asleep. She hoped when he woke up that he'd be back to normal. Archer had his eyes closed too, but she knew he wasn't asleep. His brows were furrowed and his shoulders were tense. Several times she almost said something, but eventually decided it was better to let him choose to talk.

An hour later, he did.

"Do you wonder why my mom is in prison in Tennessee, instead of North Carolina?" he asked out of the blue, his eyes still closed.

Penny had been daydreaming about how she would survive if she only had four hundred dollars a month to live on, and she jumped at his words. She pushed aside the thoughts of Ramen noodles and a studio apartment, and considered his question.

"Well, I did wonder. But I figured it was a simple answer, like she moved there and that's where she got...in trouble." Penny sighed at herself.

"Nothing with my mother is simple."

"Okay. Do you want to tell me why she's here?" she asked, dying to know.

"I don't want to tell anybody shit like this. But if you want to know, I want to tell you." His tone was light, in spite of his words.

She pursed her lips in thought. Was he trying to make sure she could handle it?

"I hope you're not trying to think of the perfect, right thing to say," he said, his eyes still closed. "Get off your dang tiptoes, open your mouth, and let it fly."

She laughed. "Alright then, yes. I'm curious about your mother, and her past and your past. So if you're willing to tell me why she's in prison, I am all ears."

"Her boyfriend at the time was from Tennessee. He moved to South Carolina to be with her, but he kept his house back in Tennessee."

"I don't even know your mom's name," Penny said.

"Dana. Dana Thomas."

"She kept your dad's name. Does that mean she never remarried?"

"Right. Now can I tell the story?" He smirked.

"Because I know you'll want to know it too, the boyfriend's name was Peter. He moved in with us when I was sixteen. He made meth in the garage, and mom sold it. She drew the line at using it though. She took any pain pill she could find, but she did not use the meth."

Penny had to interrupt at this point in the story. "They were cooking meth in your garage! Fumes!"

He gave her a look. "The garage wasn't attached to the house. It was back thirty yards or so."

"That makes it okay then." Penny rolled her eyes, but he ignored her and continued.

"Mom was a mess, high half the day, out selling drugs half the night. Peter wasn't violent, but he was stupid. He used the meth he made. He had a mean mouth. There wasn't a shortage of shouting in my house. I started spending the majority of my free time at Adam's. But Adam's apartment was no picnic either, so occasionally I would sleep at home. Mom was usually gone most of the night, and Peter was asleep, so it wasn't that big of a deal."

Archer glanced at Penny, a nervous look on his face. "So one night when I was staying there, two policemen dragged Peter out, and a slew of officers surrounded the garage. Peter told them where mom was, and they found her that night. They arrested them both."

"How did the police know to go to your house though? Did someone tip them off?" Penny asked.

"I did," he said.

She shut her gaping mouth. She looked at him. He had opened his eyes during his story, but they were closed again.

"I bet your mom didn't like that much," she ventured.

"No she did not. Not at all. She said a lot of things that night at the police station. She told me she wished she had aborted me like Dad wanted her to do. Some other stuff, too." He trailed off and stared out the window.

Penny's heart pounded. She tried to absorb what he'd said, but the truth was that she couldn't ever picture her mom saying she wished she had aborted her. She had no frame of reference with which to try to understand.

"She was an addict," Penny said. "When she said those things, she wasn't in her right mind."

"Do *not* make excuses for her."

"You're right, I'm sorry. I can't believe I said that." She also couldn't believe her idiocy. Of course that wouldn't be comforting to him.

He didn't respond to her apology. She started to panic. She had really stuffed her foot quite deeply into her mouth. There might be no recovery from this.

"I can tell you're freaking out."

"I don't want to be," she said.

"It's okay. You didn't say anything I haven't said to myself a thousand times. I've just had enough experience with my mother to know what is bullshit and what is true."

Silence fell. After what Penny felt was an acceptable time for the awkwardness to pass, she asked, "But why is she in Tennessee and not South Carolina?"

"Okay, so Mom and Peter were personally delivering their homemade meth to Peter's brother, Rob, who had moved into Peter's house while he was gone. They drove up every month or so."

As Archer continued his story, Penny learned that Archer's mom made connections in Tennessee, and was doing a little dealing of her own when they were up making deliveries. One night an exchange didn't go as planned.

"A buyer pointed a gun at my mom. He was desperate and didn't have enough money and was going to shoot her and take her stash. Well, she pulled out her own gun and shot the guy. He ended up dying. They just came back home like it was no big deal. I heard them talking about it one night."

He looked a little bewildered, as though he was still in that moment. "Before that, I never told anyone about the drug stuff. Looking on it now, I don't know why or how I kept it a secret."

"You were a kid," Penny said. "She was your mom. I think I can understand that."

He nodded. "Maybe. But suddenly there was murder. I couldn't keep quiet about that. So I tattled. It was decided that she would serve time in Tennessee first."

Penny didn't like that he used the word "tattled." It meant he put part of the blame on himself. "Where was your dad during all this?"

"I don't want to talk about my dad."

The Tennessee Prison for Women loomed ahead. Penny glanced over at Archer, and wondered if maybe he had been right in the first place. Maybe they shouldn't have come.

~

"Want me to come in with you?"

"You need to stay out here and keep Cal from doing another disappearing act," Archer said, as he picked up the box from the floor of the car.

Penny looked in the backseat. Grandpa was still snoozing. "I know, but I could bring him in too, and have him sit in a waiting area. Surely they'd keep an eye on him."

"Nah, you'd have to wake him up."

"Well good grief, he wouldn't mind."

Archer smiled at her, the tiniest of lights in his eyes. "God, you're aggravating. Fine. I have a couple reasons why I would like it if you came in with me. I have bigger reasons why I do not want you to come. Not the least of which is that my mom would not be kind to you, deathbed or no. You're not meeting a murderer." He laughed, which Penny found quite incongruous. Then he added, "Even if she's unconscious, you would feel the venom rolling off her." With that, he tucked the mysterious box under his arm, shut his door, and walked around the front of the car.

Penny lowered her window and shouted after him, "I'll be out here if you need anything!"

He raised his hand in acknowledgment, but didn't look back as he said, "I'll meet you back out here in an hour." She could tell he was smiling, just by looking at the back of his head.

~

"I am prone to a good afternoon siesta, but I never sleep through until bedtime. It's getting dark!" Cal said, after finally waking from his post-wandering nap. After Archer disappeared into the prison, Penny had driven around for a while, not sure how to kill an hour with a sleeping grandparent in the backseat. Besides, there were no easy places to park with the trailer on the back. She ended up driving back to the prison and parking at the edge of the lot. She read a few chapters of a book and ate through a lot of their road trip snacks, including an entire row of Oreos.

"Finally! You slept almost four hours." A tsunami of relief washed over her, because he was back to himself.

"We're at the prison. I assume Archer is inside?" he asked, as he peered out his window into the dusky parking lot.

"Yeah. He's been in there two hours." Penny wondered if it was good or bad that he was taking double the amount of time he said he'd need. She passed back a jar of almonds to Cal, knowing he was probably starving.

"Thank you, dear." They sat quietly for a while. The parking lot had emptied out during the last half hour, and Penny assumed visiting hours were nearing an end. The only sound was Cal crunching his almonds. She wanted Archer to get out of there. She wanted to go to dinner and eat real food, and she was impatient to know what was happening with his mom.

"You shouldn't ask him about it, you know," Cal said, as if he had read her mind.

"Don't you think he'll want to talk about it?"

"That would be true if you were the one in that prison visiting your mother. You'd come back and tell us every detail and the telling would take longer than the actual visit had. But it's Archer in there."

"I get it, Grandpa."

He passed his closed hand over the seat and tapped her shoulder with it. She reached up automatically and opened her hand. She smelled the chocolate before the Snickers even hit her palm.

~

The door swung open with such sudden force that the vehicle swayed and Penny's head knocked against the window. She sat up and looked over as Archer sat down and slammed the door behind him.

"Where's your box?" she asked, without thinking.

"Penny," Cal said, a warning in his voice.

"They're going to cremate it with her," Archer answered.

Penny looked at him and saw that his eyes were swollen and red. She reached out to touch his hand, but pulled back when he shrunk away. "I'm sorry." It sounded lame and inadequate, but it was the best she could do.

"She's not dead yet," he said.

"Oh."

He didn't offer anything else. She glanced back at Cal. He nodded at her, so she started up the engine and headed out to find a place to eat.

~

"We can't eat there." Penny was insistent.

"Why not? It looks perfectly fine. Clean even," Archer said, and punctuated that thought with a growl from his belly.

"I refuse. Let's look down this road a little farther."

Grandpa Cal leaned forward and peered through the windshield at the diner she had vetoed. "She's right, Archer. We can't eat there. The name is misspelled."

"What's the big deal? I'm starving."

"It's a matter of principle. I never support a business that has a misspelling in the name," Penny said.

Archer grinned as they drove past Konnie's Kafé. "I thought you liked alliteration."

"Alliteration can be good," she said, and gave him a sly look.

"What if there's alliteration but no misspelling?" Archer asked, smiling. "Like Denny's Diner?"

"That would be fine." Cal and Penny nodded their heads in solemn agreement.

"Okay, well what about rhymes? Like The Shiner Diner or Bill's Grill?"

"Shiner Diner, no. Bill's Grill, yes," Penny said.

"That makes no sense," Archer said, laughing.

"That place looks good," said Grandpa, pointing to a Morning Café up the street.

~

They were all wide awake when they piled back into the car after eating. Dinner at the Morning Café had been mostly silent, but with full bellies and the road ahead, they were feeling giddy. As they approached the car, Penny remembered what she had promised Irene. "Archer, do you want to go back and stay with Irene while Grandpa and I continue on? I can pick you up on our way back through."

He looked at her like she was crazy. "No way. I'm coming with you."

She smiled. "Okay. It's just, she offered so I wanted you to know your options. It wouldn't be a problem if you wanted to."

He grabbed the keys from her hand. "I'm driving."

Penny took a turn in the back so Cal could have the best seat for a while. She knew they all had worries on their minds, but for the moment they were content.

Penny leaned back and listened to the music with her eyes closed. She could hear Archer and Grandpa talking up front, their voices a low murmur that infected her with peace. Her limbs felt heavy with exhaustion, and she allowed herself daydreams about what might happen when she arrived home. There were scenarios with happy tears where she was considered a heroine for bringing Grandpa home and for following her own path. There were also some with arguments that she carried out in her head. She could clearly imagine the things her parents would say, but had trouble coming up with clear, sensible responses.

"That kiss was a doozy," Cal said.

That shook Penny out of her thoughts, and she popped up and shoved her face between their seats. "What kiss, Grandpa?"

"Oh I'm just feeling young tonight, dear. We are reliving the past a little bit."

"Well, start over, because I want to hear this," she said.

"The first girl I kissed was called Della Matthews, and I was eleven years old."

"Eleven is awfully young for a first kiss," Penny said.

"No it isn't," both men said at the same time. They laughed, and she felt embarrassed that her first kiss had been at age eighteen.

"My God, you guys! Eleven. Tell me it was a peck on the cheek."

"It was a peck on the lips."

"Archer, tell us about your first kiss," Penny said. She didn't want to hear about it. She really didn't. She had no idea why she said that.

"It was fourth grade, at recess. I was ten, and she was a fifth grade goddess. Amanda. She put on some sticky, sweet goop before we kissed. Afterward, the kids around us clapped."

"Ugh." Penny flopped back against the seat. That was terrible. Maybe it was better that her first kiss had been at eighteen.

Archer looked at her in the rear view mirror and laughed. "There's more. After she kissed me, she kissed my friend Lee, then she kissed another guy named Rick. I don't remember all the details, but I think there was actually a line."

In spite of herself, Penny laughed. "That poor girl though. What was going on with her?"

"Yeah. Looking back on it, I think it's kind of sad," Archer said.

"I never stood in a line to kiss a girl, that's true, but I never had girls line up to kiss me either," Grandpa said. "Though there was another gal that chased after me at the same time I was chasing after Ruby."

"What did Grandma have to say about that?"

"She never knew. Your grandmother was no timid flower. She did what her mind told her to do. For example, she wanted to dance with a good dancer and I wasn't one, so she danced with my pal Johnny, not caring in the least if I was bothered. I had a heck of a time trying to convince her to go to dinner with me. If she'd known Nancy Rose was after me she never would have given in. She did not abide complicated entanglements." He smiled in a dreamy way that Penny remembered seeing on his face when her grandmother was alive.

After a minute, Archer said, "Okay, your turn Penny. Tell us about your first kiss."

"No way."

"Hey, we shared. You have to share."

"I do not. I may not be quite as headstrong as Grandma, but I'm working on it, and I know which secrets to keep. You can't goad me into spilling my guts."

They rode in silence for a while, all thinking of the kisses in the past, Penny was sure. She smiled in the darkness, happy knowing that her best kisses lay in the future.

Chapter 24

The bedspread was itchy on the backs of her knees. The room was terrible, all pink and blue and light green. There were framed pictures of seashells on the wall. Grandpa Cal had been in the bathroom for an age. Penny didn't want to turn on the tv, she wanted to collapse and go to sleep. But she needed to pee, so she sat upright and scratched at her knees and waited.

A bit past midnight she had noticed that Cal was dozing off. They found a cheap motel at the next exit. They also found an argument. She replayed the conversation they'd had at the front desk.

"We'll just get two rooms, it's not a big deal," Archer had insisted.

"It's also not a big deal to share a room. I'll sleep on the floor," she had argued back. She knew his funds were limited, and the motel was sixty dollars a night. There was no point in him wasting that amount of cash. Her funds were limited too, but her grandfather was paying for their room.

Archer swallowed and she watched his adam's apple bob. He gave her a look. "Penny. I'm going to get my own room. Okay?" It came out as a rough whisper.

"Okay."

So there she found herself, in dire need of a toilet and sharing a room with a seventy-four year old bathroom hog. She knew she was tired and grouchy, but she started to get more and more irritated. The day had been too long and emotional for this. She muttered under her breath and grabbed her key card. She left to go wake Archer up and use his bathroom.

Penny stepped barefoot onto the cool concrete pad outside the door. Archer had the room to the left, so she turned that way and pounded on his door. No answer. She growled in frustration, and knocked even louder this time. If he didn't answer, she was taking her pajama-clad self to the lobby bathroom.

"You looking for me?" Archer came around the corner carrying a bucket of ice.

"Ice? Why are you getting ice?" She knew she was being testy, but couldn't manage to stop. "I've never understood why people go get buckets of ice at motels. What purpose does that serve?"

"Um, ice water?"

"You're going to drink ten cups of water? That's how much ice you have there. You could fill up ten cups. Maybe even eleven."

He laughed and shook his head. It annoyed her that he seemed amused by her grumpy mood. "I don't know. It's just what you do. You go to a motel, you fill up your ice bucket."

"And in the morning you dump out the water from all that melted ice," she said, trying not to bounce from foot to foot like a toddler. "Anyway, can you hurry up and unlock your door? I need to use your bathroom."

"What's wrong with your bathroom?" he asked, as he put his card in the slot.

"Grandpa's in there. He's...taking a really long time. He's probably swallowing the gazillion pills he has to take every day. I have no idea. But I shouldn't have let him go first." She brushed past him and sped toward the bathroom.

When she came out, Archer was sitting on his bed sipping ice water from a small plastic cup. He held up another one to her. "Would you like a refreshing cup of ice water?"

Penny laughed and took the cup. She sat down on the second bed, facing him. Their knees were almost touching.

"So why aren't you asleep yet?" she asked.

He shrugged. "I should be exhausted. I'm not tired at all though. I could have kept driving all night."

"No thanks. I don't want to get there any sooner than I have to."

"Will it be that bad?"

She thought about it for a moment. Her parents had given her the space she asked for. They weren't calling every minute. On the phone they weren't being as annoying as they had been at home, weren't telling her she was making a mistake. Slowly, they seemed to be accepting that she wanted different things for herself than they wanted for her.

"No, it probably won't be that bad," she said, and looked down at her hands. Her fingertips were numb from the icy cup. She took a big swallow to empty it, and set it on the bedside table. "The thing is, I think they have the impression I'm moving back. That I'll be staying, as well as Grandpa."

"You didn't tell them you're staying in Wells Cove?" His eyes shifted around the room, nervously. She knew he wasn't quite convinced that she would be coming back with him.

"No, I didn't tell them. They didn't come right out and ask, but over a couple phone calls, Mom has said a few things that make me think they think I'll be staying home. I haven't set her straight."

Archer didn't say anything in response to her confession. He just looked at her and waited. He was good at conversational waiting. Penny was too quick to fill silences. She knew that about herself, yet she continued to make comments or say the first thing that popped into her head instead of letting a moment play out. This time was no different.

"It's not that I think they'll be mad or disappointed," she said. "I can survive that. I did before. But when you let other people tell you what to do, you are free from the consequences of your choices. Staying in Wells Cove is my choice. If it's the wrong one, it's all on me."

Archer nodded. "I get it. You want their approval of your choices, so you will feel more confident."

"Exactly."

He smiled gently at her. "But I do think you should know that you only need your own approval. And that if it turns out to be the wrong choice for you, it's okay. Just like everyone else, you're allowed to make a wrong turn here and there."

"I am trying to learn that."

Archer got up and refilled his cup. When he sat down again, she asked, "Do you want to talk about your visit with your mom? Grandpa said I shouldn't bring it up, but I think I should."

"It's okay that you did." He rubbed his palms on his thighs. "It was kind of awful. She looked puny and, well, disgusting, actually. Dirty. She wasn't mean, but she was vacant. It was her but it wasn't her."

"Did you show her the things in the box?"

"I tried. It was just pictures and stuff. She looked at a couple of them, but when I held up one of her, me, and my dad, she told me to put them away." He looked at the ground.

"It's still nice that you tried."

"I guess." He looked up at the ceiling. "I changed my mind. Let's not talk about it anymore."

The seriousness of the conversation made Penny nervous. He could probably tell. He reached out and put his hand on her left knee, and pressed down. The pressure stopped her leg from shaking, and she was grateful. She also

213

felt light-headed. She was too nervous to look at any part of him.

"Archer? Can I tell you something?"

"Of course."

"I think I might be bad at making decisions."

"Why do you think that?"

His thumb moved in small circles on the inside of her knee. Blood rushed through her ears. She couldn't breathe, let alone think. It felt so good. Too good. She stood up abruptly, and walked to the door. "Because it's true. I have to go make sure Grandpa is okay. I should get some sleep. So should you."

Archer stood up too, but didn't come toward her. "Are you okay?"

"Sure. I'm fine. Okay, good night!" To keep the infernal, inescapable tears from coming, she smiled widely and backed toward the door. She hated that she was such a stress case. Behind her back, she searched for the door handle, still grinning crazily at him and trying to just get out of there.

"You do this sometimes, huh?" Archer said, calm as ever. Penny's embarrassing display of nerves and anxiety didn't seem to faze him. At least there was that.

She paused in her attempt to escape. "What do you mean?"

"You leave when you feel scared or uncertain," he said.

"No, I don't do that! I mean, I used to. But that's why I came here. Well, not here. We're in Missouri." She took a deep breath. "I came to South Carolina to start over. To finally start doing what I want to do and saying what I want to say."

"I know that, you told me before. But why are you running out in the middle of our conversation?" He took a step toward her.

"I'm not. I'm just tired. I needed your bathroom, and now I need to sleep."

"Say what you want to say." He took another step.

"It's stupid."

"It's not stupid if it's true."

Her eyes watered and she blinked furiously to make the tears disappear. It didn't work, and she felt one slip out and run down her cheek. Once that tear was free, so were the words. They came out cloaked in sobs.

"I do things and then I regret them. I don't think before I act." Will's face flashed in her mind. "I'm too scared to make any decisions because sometimes making the wrong one could hurt someone other than myself."

She stood there, waiting for numbness to begin its familiar creep up her body. It didn't come. He was about four feet in front of her, with his hands in his pockets. He didn't say anything. She fought the silence.

She lost that fight, again. Her chest rose and fell heavily, and her breathing was loud in the room. "There's something else. I like it when you sit close to me like you were. I want to kiss you. I almost feel like I'll die if I don't. But I won't, because I don't know how to be sure if I should." She turned around and opened the door, shutting it hard behind her.

~

Penny flung her overnight bag into the back of the trailer, shut it firmly, and walked to the driver's seat with her head held high. She hoped that if she acted confident, Archer would forget about last night. He was already in the back. She thought maybe he didn't want to sit by her after her clumsy word-vomit.

She had felt, for a long while, that she and Archer were zooming towards each other. Now she worried the feelings she had were more one-sided than she assumed. Either way, he hadn't come after her last night. He hadn't spoken a word to her, aside from *hello*, this morning. She reminded herself that he was dealing with bigger issues and tried to get her ego in check.

Cal shuffled around to the side of the car and opened the back door. He got into the seat beside Archer.

"What is this about? Why am I the only one up front? Get up here, Grandpa."

"I ride better in the back," he said.

"That's not true. The best seat is up front. It can tilt back and has all this leg room."

"It's too bright up there. Back here there are tinted windows," Cal argued, his voice mild.

Penny turned back and looked at both of them, deciding to be brave. "Archer, do you prefer the back, too?"

"No. I was trying to be polite to my elder and let him have the front."

Cal sighed and rolled his eyes. The corner of Penny's mouth curved up. She liked when Grandpa was sassy. She turned back to the front and set up her iPod.

The passenger door opened and the car shifted as a weight deposited itself in the seat. She didn't look over at him, and he didn't look at her either. She started the car and maneuvered around the other cars in the motel parking lot.

She breathed in the crisp morning air, and was thinking about the prospect of getting some greasy breakfast food, when she heard and felt a thunk-scrape. Being neither a stoic nor calm sort of person, she screamed in startled fear. Tears of frustration sprang to her eyes. She turned off the car and went out to inspect the damage.

There was a small dent low on the side of the trailer, and a large area of paint was scraped. It was streaked yellow, from the base of the light pole she had grazed. Relief paused her tears for an instant, and she was grateful she had hit a light post instead of another car.

"Well, I've done it now," she said aloud, to herself. Then she lost it, just a little bit. "This damn trailer needs to die!" She smacked the side of it with her palm, which stung. She wasn't proud of entering full-on tantrum mode, but it also felt kind of good.

Archer laughed softly. She wheeled around in surprise. She hadn't heard him walk up behind her. "Go ahead and laugh, whatever." Any remaining frustration seeped away. She was too exhausted to even feel embarrassed.

"Hey," he said softly. He reached up and touched her cheek with the pad of his thumb. His fingers went behind her ear, tucking her hair. His pinky grazed her neck. The gesture was so tender, that she was surprised when he said, "Give it another whack, maybe it will help."

She laughed. "No, the fight has gone out of me. I'm resigned to this unwieldy beast."

"Penny?"

"Yeah?"

"What you said last night? You're not the only one." He moved his hand from her face and let it trail slowly down her arm.

She looked up at him even though she was afraid to. Her pulse was racing. "I said a lot of things last night."

"I think you know the thing I mean."

Her body filled with a blurry anticipation.

When his hand reached her hand, the one she had used to punish the trailer, he turned it so her palm faced up. He brought it to his lips and kissed it, then let both their hands drop.

He took a step closer. Their bodies were not touching anywhere, but the cotton of his t-shirt brushed against the cotton of hers. He leaned down and hesitated for only a second. He kissed her. Fire raced around her belly and through her veins.

217

It was soft and quick. They were surrounded by the fumes of asphalt and running engines.

If someone were to have seen that kiss, there in a motel parking lot just after sunrise and next to a dented UHaul trailer, Penny bet they'd assume it was a three hundredth kiss, not a first kiss. They'd probably think it was a simple thing of very little consequence. They'd be wrong.

Archer tried to step back but she brought her arms around his back to stop him. His breath came fast, which made her own come quicker, and she hadn't known that was possible. She felt his fingertips touch her lightly on her lower back. This time she pressed her lips on his, and the fire blazed, melting her clear through to her skin.

"I thought that was the thing you meant," she whispered. Thoughts swirled around her head, and the only one she could grab onto was that whispering after kisses is practically mandatory. As if using your full voice would scare the new feelings away.

~

"All the food places are in the other direction," Penny said, as Archer pulled out of the lot. She could not, would not get back behind the wheel after what just transpired. Both the kisses and the light pole crash left her too unsettled.

"We have an errand to run first," Archer said.

"What's he talking about?" she asked her grandpa, turning in her seat. His eyes were twinkling. She reckoned he saw what had happened by the dent.

"I might have an inkling," he said and reached out to pat her hand. "Take these, and give one to your friend." He placed two Hershey's Kisses in her hand. Yep, he saw.

Archer fiddled with the GPS on his phone while at stoplights, and with minimal cursing under his breath he managed to navigate the city streets to the one place that could cure all Penny's ails.

He pulled into the moving truck rental lot, and she said, "Take that, trailer!"

A man came out to help unlatch the trailer. When that was done, they put down the third seat in the SUV and transferred over the boxes and bags. There was a little paperwork to do. It didn't take long, and Penny's relief overshadowed her annoyance that she hadn't done that sooner. They went through a drive-thru for breakfast, something they hadn't been able to do with the trailer attached.

Back on the interstate, Penny felt free and light. The trailer was gone and Archer had kissed her. She looked at him sideways, without noticeably turning her head, hoping he wouldn't catch her looking.

The air thickened with their awareness of each other.

His lips quirked up. He was fighting a grin.

"You're smiling," she said.

"You would be too if you were thinking about that kiss." He stopped fighting and let his lips do what they wanted.

"I can think about a kiss without smiling." She tried to play it cool.

"Go ahead then. Try it. Think about that kiss, the kiss to end all kisses, and don't smile." He looked at her, still grinning widely.

It was no use. The smile escaped, plastering itself to her face and making her look ridiculous, she was sure. There is no room to be cool when you've shared that sort of kiss.

"See what I mean?" he said, his voice holding surety and simple happiness.

They sat there grinning, looking out at the wooded hills in front of them. He reached over and took her hand. This time, his touch was confident. He knew she wouldn't pull away, and he was right.

She flipped their hands over so she could look at his tattoo. She ran her finger over the branches. "So is it just a tree, or does it have a special meaning?"

"I got it thinking it would remind me to grow."

"Has it?"

"Turns out it's just a tree."

Chapter 25

"I do not need to take another nap. Stop fussing over me!" Cal shouted. He held his hands in front of his face. He'd been grouchy at her before, but the grandpa looking at Penny red-faced and austere wasn't like any version of her grandpa that she knew. She was useless to him.

She'd experienced his memory lapses and strange behaviors plenty of times, and still wasn't always able to find her center and stay calm. She rummaged through his bag of medications with rough and frustrated hands. She kept grabbing the same wrong bottle over and over. Where was the damn Trazadone?

"Here, let me look," Archer said, reaching for the bag. She was glad to let him have a try. They were standing at the back of the SUV, with the hatch open. Archer dumped the bag's contents on top of a box, and methodically read each label.

Penny realized she hadn't told him which meds to look for. "Look for the Trazadone. His doctor told me he could take that if he was agitated."

"I know which drugs are sedatives, Penny. Don't forget that I'm somewhat of a drug expert. It runs in the family."

"Oh. Right." She went and sat by Cal, in the back seat.

He looked at her, his eyes bewildered and distant. She put her head on his shoulder. He patted her hair and said, "It's going to be okay."

"I'm sorry Grandpa. I should be comforting you, not the other way around."

"I don't need comforting!" he shouted right in her ear, causing Penny to jump. Then softer, he said, "I'm perfectly fine."

Archer appeared at the door, and handed her a pill and a water bottle.

"Grandpa, take this." She held the items out to him, bracing herself for resistance.

Cal didn't fight it though, he just took the pill. He sighed. She hugged him around the waist, and tried not to be hurt when he pushed her away. She moved to get out because it was her turn to drive.

"Sit back here with me a while?" he asked, surprising her.

She glanced at Archer to make sure he was okay extending his turn as driver. He nodded, so she settled in for the afternoon. When they stopped for dinner later, Cal stepped out of the car and Penny looked at him. "You should button your shirt before we go in, Grandpa." He didn't respond, but looked at her blankly. She buttoned it for him.

~

"Oh my God, can we *please* stop to pee?" Archer begged.

"No. My house is in the neighborhood just over that hill." Penny gripped the wheel, her nerves climbing along with the car.

"I don't exactly want to meet your family while tap dancing my way to their toilet."

She grinned and looked over at him. They hadn't kissed since that first time. The space around them was different though, as if the air was aware of their feelings. Even in a conversation about pee, she was aware of how close his arm was to hers, and how something was brewing in that space.

"That's a fair point. But seriously, there is no place to stop, unless you want to pee beside a tree in someone's yard," she told him.

"That tree looks good. Maple. Nice wide trunk." He laid his head back on the head rest and groaned.

"Penny, it would be polite to take the poor young man to a restroom," Cal supplied from the back. "Would you like to meet *his* family in such a condition? Let's take him to the nearest gas station. What's another five minutes?"

"You're just trying to postpone the inevitable. Look, it's that yellow house up there." She pointed to the house that she would always think of as home. It was a butter-yellow two story with a deep porch and a large yard. Several huge oaks and a redwood dotted the lawn. It was a comfortable house, welcoming and sunny.

"You put on a new roof since I was here last," Cal said.

"I imagine many things are different, Grandpa," Penny said. "It's been ten years since you were here. Half the people in the house are new, let alone the roof." She pulled into the driveway and parked behind her mom's van. Nobody made a move to get out.

"You're bitter that I didn't visit more," Cal said, and it wasn't a question.

"Well, I missed you. I shouldn't hold it against you, though."

"Now you're pitying me."

"Good grief, I can't seem to say the right thing here," she muttered.

Archer reached out and grabbed her hand. "You're not supposed to say the right things, remember? You're supposed to say the true things."

In the back, Cal sighed. "Your young man is right. It seems a bit of my wisdom is leaking out of me and into him. Alright, Penny. Let's get this finished."

It seemed to her they were about to start something, not finish it. Facing the beginning of something scary can end the torment of anticipation, though, and she was ready to finish that feeling.

Archer sprung out of the car first and strode onto the porch.

"Now hold on a minute," Penny said, scrambling after him. "Are you planning to introduce yourself to my mother?"

"Sure, why not? I bet she'd show me to a toilet, unlike her evil progeny."

At that moment, the door swung open and Vera flung herself into Penny's body. Penny's arms reacted on instinct and clung to her.

"I can't believe you're back! I think your boobs got bigger." Vera stepped back and squeezed one of Penny's boobs.

Penny laughed and pulled Vera's hand off her boob. "They did not! Get your hands off. And I missed you too."

Vera grabbed her up in another hug and whispered in her ear, "Is this one of your practice friends?" She let go and waggled her eyebrows suggestively. Penny shook her head to try to shut her up, but Vera had moved on to Cal. She walked around Penny and hugged her grandpa wordlessly. He didn't say anything either, but he patted her hair and Penny saw him slip a candy bar into her palm.

"Let's get you taken care of, yeah?" Penny said to Archer, and they walked into the house leaving Vera and Cal on the porch.

~

It was oddly still inside. The leather sofa felt cool and the house was tidy but not stiflingly so. Penny sat in the unexpected quiet, listening to the rhythmic groan of the

224

porch swing where Vera and Grandpa were talking. He was easing his way in.

She looked up and saw her mom coming down the hallway, pushing her hair out of her face. She looked tired, but perked up when she saw her daughter. Penny stood, and all the things she'd planned to say got stuck in her throat. They embraced, and Penny realized she didn't want to talk right then. She just wanted to be hugged by her mom.

"It's so good to have you back. The house hasn't felt right without you. Do you want help carrying in the boxes and bags? I bet that car is packed full," her mom said.

"Uh, there isn't that much, really. Let's get it later." Penny knew her dad was at work. She wanted him to be home when she told them she wouldn't be staying.

"Okay." Frances squeezed Penny's ribs and she jumped because it tickled. "You're too thin, Love. Come and let me feed you." She led the way to the kitchen. Penny thought it was strange how it felt like home, but also not. She was just a little bit of a stranger here.

She sat at the kitchen bar. Her mom busied herself making a plate of crackers and cheese. "Where is everyone?" Penny asked.

"The usual places. Your dad's at work. So is Mark. He got an after school job at the grocery. Isn't that funny, you're both working at grocery stores? Vera's around here somewhere. The twins are being pests at Uncle Saul's. Blake and Nedra are napping. At the same time, miracle of miracles."

"And Corinne?"

"Oh, Corinne. You know her. She's…somewhere."

"With a boy?"

"Probably with a boy." She waved the cheese knife dismissively.

Penny shook her head in sympathy. Corinne was advanced in the dating department. It was fascinating how all

225

sorts of different people could come from the same house, the same parents. Eight children grew up here, and among their ranks you'd find book worms, yellers, artists, clumsy people, athletes, and so on.

"So where is my papa? I see you here alone, and I'm afraid he refused to come," her mom said, and handed Penny the plate of crackers and cheese.

Archer wandered around the corner then, his hands in his pockets.

Frances raised her eyebrows at Penny. "Not completely alone, then."

Penny fought to keep the smile from her face. "Archer, this is my mom, Frances. Mom, this is Archer. He made the trip with Grandpa and me. Grandpa's on the porch with Vera. He's not going to want to talk about how he's doing, just so you know."

Frances shrugged. "That's fine. There's time. Well, have we covered the whereabouts of everyone yet?" She smiled at Penny and held out her hand to Archer. "It's nice to meet you, Archer. What is your last name?"

"Archer Waylon Thomas, Mrs. Beck. I'm pleased to meet you." He smiled at her, but Penny could see his hand shaking as it hung in the air.

"Hmm. Was your mother a fan of Waylon Jennings?" she asked, shaking his hand.

"I don't know. I never asked." He turned away from her and sat down on the stool beside Penny.

"Next time you see her, you should ask. I bet I'm right."

"Mom," Penny said, eager to change the subject, "Let me tell you a few things before Grandpa comes in and stops me."

Frances leaned on the counter. "Yes, tell me how the trip was."

"He's okay. He wandered out of a parking lot once, but it wasn't that big of a deal. He's really fine most of the time."

226

"You maybe don't need to gloss over things. She'll find out for herself soon enough," Archer said.

Penny narrowed her eyes at him, still wanting to protect Grandpa's dignity, but he only shrugged and continued. "He is mostly fine. He just doesn't see it when he isn't, and it's not always easy to predict. You never know when he might wander. And make sure you keep his sedatives handy."

Penny looked down.

"Thank you two for giving me the meat of the situation," Frances said. "I'll get down to the bones on my own." She wiped her hands on a towel. "I'm going to try to coax him into the house. Make yourself at home, Archer."

"Waylon, huh?" Penny said, after her mom left.

He shrugged. "Not like I can help it. What's your middle name then?"

Penny let a smile escape, excited about all the small things they still had to learn about each other. "It's Alice."

Vera came in then, the screen door flapping behind her. She joined them in the kitchen.

"Okay, Penny. Tell me who this is." She came around behind Penny and started finger combing her hair.

"Did you mention me to no one?" Archer asked, and though Penny knew he was only teasing her, she detected a kernel of worry in his voice.

"Oh don't worry about that, strange man in my kitchen," Vera told him. "Penny never tells anyone anything. She likes to keep all the good stuff to herself." She parted Penny's hair, beginning a French braid. "Stingy girl."

"I'm not stingy. I've just never had a personal life before."

"Hmm," Vera murmured and kept braiding.

"Vee, this is Archer, my...friend. Archer, this is Vera, my pesky younger sister and provoker." Penny gestured between them.

Archer leaned in toward Penny, and put his arm on the back of her chair. She felt the warmth from his arm through her shirt. "I'm your friend?" he whispered, his breath tickling her ear. His breath felt cool. He must have eaten a mint. She couldn't look at him.

"Well, yeah. Of course you are," she said, trying not to panic, letting Vera's fingers calm her.

"So of all the words you could choose, you think 'friend' is the most fitting?" he pressed. He was smirking, which annoyed Penny no end.

She stared at him. "There is no need to go into detail right this moment. Geez."

He shrugged, not at all minding her discomfort.

"Introduce yourself, Archer, the way you think Penny should have," Vera prodded. Penny slumped her shoulders, feeling like any progress she had made being bold and true while away had disappeared the moment she stepped foot inside this house.

Archer stood up and grinned down at Penny. Then he offered his hand to Vera, who had finished with Penny's hair, and said, "I'm Archer, the guy who sits with your sister on beaches, paints rooms with her, and kisses her in parking lots."

Penny sucked in a breath. "Archer! That's private!"

He looked at her with those black eyes, and the magical fizzing started again.

Vera laughed. "You're so silly, Penny. There was no need to tell me anything, it's written all over both your faces." She turned toward Archer and continued, "Welcome, and I approve of the way you torment my sister."

Penny whacked her on the butt as she scurried out of the room.

"I'm glad you interfered in my business and convinced me to come with you. It's been eye-opening," Archer said.

"I didn't interfere." Penny raked her fingers through her hair, pulling out the braid.

"No? The only reason I'm even on this trip is because of your interfering," he said softly, and moved his head an inch closer to hers.

She tilted her head back to look at him. She could see the bottom of his chin. There was a patch of whiskers there that was longer than the rest. He had missed a spot shaving. She surprised herself by lifting up a fraction of an inch and pressing her lips against those whiskers. Their roughness was satisfying against her lips.

He sucked in a breath and leaned down and put a hand on each of her armrests. "I like meeting your family. Seeing where you grew up. I wish I had this kind of place to show you." His eyes turned distant for a moment, then he grinned, pulled back and exhaled. He straightened up and wiped his expression clean. "Later. Your mom is coming back in," he said, and sat back in his seat.

~

In spite of the fact that darkness had descended, the scratchy shingles were hot beneath Penny's legs. She wished she had changed into long pants. She kept the window cracked open a couple inches, so she could feel the cool air from inside on the small of her back. She leaned against the siding and closed her eyes. She could smell the green sharpness of the garden below. Her dad must have mown the lawn recently.

She smiled without opening her eyes, thinking about the dinner from which she'd just escaped. It was everything she was used to from her childhood, and like nothing Archer had ever seen before. He had sat there with wide eyes and tried to answer every question thrown at him. With eleven people at the dining table, it was impossible to follow along with all the different conversations. She laughed, thinking of the valiant effort he made. His head had swiveled so fast from person to person, she bet he had a headache now. Corinne had not made it easy on him at all.

"Have you ever ridden a motorcycle?" she had asked.

"Yes," Archer answered.

"So what, you think that makes you a bad boy?"

"Corinne! Stop it," their mom had interrupted.

Archer responded anyway. "No, I think it makes me a person who has ridden a motorcycle. What do you think makes someone bad?"

Corinne narrowed her eyes at him, making her face as mean as possible. "Littering," she said sarcastically.

"Corinne, just...stop talking," Mom had said. On the roof, Penny laughed again. Corinne was a scary thirteen-year-old.

She took a deep breath in, and looked around. The club house Dad had built with Mark looked a little shabby. That filled her with childish pleasure. Mark said he wanted one, and their dad took off for the home improvement store for lumber and nails. Penny didn't know why it bothered her so much; it wasn't as if she had asked for a club house. Some years later Mark said that Dad told him he'd always wanted to build one with his dad, and so he was fulfilling his own dream as much as he was helping Mark. Penny reminded herself of that conversation and tried not to fertilize her patch of bitterness. Maybe it was one of his own childhood wounds; the kind that don't make much sense and that never seem to go away.

Regardless, she was glad he hadn't been able to make it home for dinner. All touchy subjects had been avoided. Well, touchy subjects involving her life anyway. Corinne had taken most of the spotlight. Along with antagonizing Archer in various ways, she tried to shock them with her new desire for a neck tattoo. Mom kept her cool though, maybe because Archer was there, an outsider.

Grandpa Cal had refused to sit at the head of the table, insisting that it was Dad's place. His face had been full of the joy of his grandchildren throughout dinner. Penny wondered what he and her mom had talked about on the porch. Neither of them would tell her when she asked, which was irritating. She had spent months being the one "in charge" of Cal, the one he confided in, the one counted on to handle the situation. As soon as a *real* adult was around, she was relegated back to her place as a child.

Penny rubbed her palms on the grainy shingles. It was definitely a relief not to be the one in charge anymore. But she was proud of the way she had handled things. She supposed she was craving some recognition from her mom.

Behind her, the window slid open fully. She knew without looking that it was Vera. They had chosen this room because of the roof access. It was like having their own private balcony. When Corinne joined them in sharing the room, the roof became a good place to escape her.

"You smell like tar and grass," Vera said, and settled down beside Penny. "Scooch over, will you?"

Penny made room for her. "Do you still come out here, now that I'm gone?"

"You're not gone, you're right here."

Penny poked her on the shoulder.

"Yeah. I come out here. It's not the same, but it's still the quietest place in the house," Vera said. "So, what's it really like?"

"What's what like?" She could have been talking about a thousand things.

"Living on your own, without the family. Being far away. Driving a car across the country. Subverting Mom and Dad. Taking care of Grandpa. Practicing life. Kissing that boy." She grinned. "Take your pick."

"Well good grief, Vera." Penny grinned back at her. "I didn't exactly subvert Mom and Dad, you know. Not on purpose."

"I understand that." She chuckled. "They've spent all summer trying to figure it out. I've heard their conversations. You were so vague, just telling them over and over that you had simply changed your mind."

Penny sighed. "When everything happened with Will, it was like a switch flipped in me. Up until that point I didn't even know anything was wrong. I was just going along, wherever people pointed me. But that night, I went somewhere I didn't want to go. I really, really did not want to go there. The fact that I did it anyway woke me up."

"I know. And I'm glad you're awake now. This way more people get to see the Penny I know. Like maybe Archer? Does he know the real you?"

Penny couldn't help but smile. "Yeah. He does."

Vera squealed. "So how did it go? Speaking your mind."

"I don't know if I really changed that much. I tried, but it was harder than I thought it would be."

"You seem different to me."

"I do? How?"

"Maybe you still aren't very comfortable voicing your opinions to everyone, but you seem more comfortable *having* opinions. You seem more comfortable in your skin."

Penny smiled. "You know what? I think that might be true. Anyway, let's talk about something else. Let's talk about you."

Vera was quiet for a moment. "Grandpa seems good," she said. "I'm nervous about seeing some of the stuff you told me about on the phone. What am I supposed to do when he doesn't recognize me?"

"Most days *are* really good, like today. He's still in the early stages. Don't be scared though. It's still just as easy to love him. Sometimes he does get grouchy. And so far, he has always remembered who I am. Sometimes he would forget that I had come to Wells Cove. I've noticed that when he's having a day like that, he doesn't usually realize or remember he's sick. We played lots of games of checkers while he thought he was healthy and just assumed I was out for a visit. I didn't have the heart to tell him, and why should I? He'd forget it later anyway. We had some good times during his lapses of memory."

Vera smiled and squeezed her hand again. Penny had forgotten she was holding it. "Wait," Penny said, "You dodged my question. I asked you to tell me what is happening in your life."

Before Vera answered, they heard the front door open and shut, and they stared at each other wide-eyed. Penny laughed nervously, and felt her heart speed up. "What am I so afraid of? It's just Dad."

"You didn't even give them a hint that you wouldn't be staying? They really think you're moving back home?"

"I think they really do. They assumed it and I didn't want to have that conversation right then. Suddenly it's now, and I have to.

"When you talk to them, just pretend you're Corinne. That girl has balls of steel," Vera said. "Anyway, what's the worst that could happen?"

"They could tell me it's a stupid mistake."

"So what?"

"Well, they might be right."

"Do you really believe that?"

"I think it's a possibility," Penny said, "in the way that anything's possible. But actually, no. I don't believe it's a mistake. I can't wait to get back there. I knew immediately that choosing not to go to MSU was the right thing, and I feel that same certainty about Wells Cove."

Vera nodded. "It's going to be fine. Besides, you already had the same conversation with them when you left the first time. This time it won't be so bad."

"I don't know. In June they thought me living in South Carolina was temporary."

Vera stood to go back inside. "Well, I'd like to take this moment to formally thank you for being born first. You have blazed a trail for us younger siblings, aside from Corinne, of course. Nothing we do will ever compare with your transgressions." She ducked through the window, laughing.

~

Penny didn't follow Vera inside the house. New thoughts and ideas were whirling around in her brain. She had a prickle of excitement in her chest, because of a new idea she'd been steeping in. She wrapped her arms around herself, and hoped maybe she'd finally found her *thing*. If it panned out, she thought her parents would be satisfied too.

Her thoughts were interrupted by a light knock on the glass behind her. She turned, and saw Archer peering at her, his hands cupped around his face so he could see out into the dark. She waved him out, and he opened the window and squeezed through.

"So there I was on the couch, cuddled up in the flowery sheets your mom laid out for me, and then do you know who walked right in?" Archer asked without preamble, and sat down in the space Vera had vacated minutes before.

Penny grimaced. "Oh no. Did he give you the third degree?"

"Nah, I have a really good fake snore."

She snickered. "You can hang out here and avoid him with me."

234

"I wasn't really avoiding him. I mean, yeah, the idea of meeting your dad scares the shit out of me and I didn't want to do it while wearing only boxer shorts. But I figured you should get the chance to talk to him first."

"Thanks. That's probably a good idea." She tried not to picture him in those boxer shorts. They fell silent. No part of his body was touching hers, but she could feel every inch of his outline. The evening was loud, and their silence made it seem louder still. Crickets chirped, bugs chattered, frogs talked. She chanced a sideways look at him, and found him looking back.

Suddenly he felt very real. Penny jerked her eyes away and scooted away from him. She coughed, feeling like she was choking. Escape. That was the only option. The feelings were too big and she didn't know if she'd ever get used to it. She pressed her palms on the rough shingles, readying herself to stand and go inside. It didn't matter if he was out on her roof, she'd just go in her bed and that would be alone enough.

Before she could lift herself, he said, "Tell me."

"Tell you what?"

"Whatever it is that is making you panic right now."

"I'm not panicking. It's just hot out here, don't you think? Maybe we should go in," she said, her words coming too fast to support her claim.

"You're different here. Back home, you were like a cannon, firing off your thoughts left and right," Archer said.

Back home. He had called South Carolina home. She settled back down against the siding. Since setting out on this return trip, her old habits *had* started to come back. That irritated her enough that she steeled herself and committed to not running away.

"You know what's weird? I felt like I was acting," she said.

"What do you mean?"

"All these months. I was saying the things I actually thought and felt. I was being myself. But it felt like an act. Maybe the real me is this one; the one who hides herself. There's nothing wrong with being a private person."

"That's true. But maybe it's just a habit that you're comfortable with."

"A bad habit?"

"If keeping your thoughts bottled up doesn't get you where you want to be, then yes."

They sat for a while, quiet again. He placed his hand on the shingles next to her hand. The air was alive between their pinky fingers.

"You don't need to work so hard to hide your feelings because you're afraid of making people upset." His voice was soft. "You're allowed to say things that might make people mad. Or me, you can make me mad if you want."

"If I make someone mad, they might not like me anymore." She looked down at her knees.

"You're afraid they might leave?"

"Yeah, I guess."

"Are you afraid I might leave if you make me mad?"

"Maybe." Her body started to shake a little bit. "It didn't matter as much when I didn't know you as much. Now it matters." She didn't want to look up at him. How could he be so calm discussing things like this? She was starting to wonder if she'd shake herself right off the roof.

"Let me tell you something about me. I grew up around people who yelled at each other and at me. I saw fights, I saw lots of shit that might scare other people. To me it was just life." He paused to smile at her. "I'm not saying that's a good thing. But arguments don't scare me. I'm not worried about people making me mad. I don't need anybody to guard my feelings. I want to hear real things come out of your mouth. I'm just going to say it. If you're regretting our kiss, or if something is bothering you about us, your only job is to tell me your feelings."

"Why on earth would you think I regret that kiss?" How could he not know the way she felt?

He shrugged. "You didn't seem to want me to tell Vera about it."

"I don't regret it, Archer. No way. I just don't know what to do now. All the things I have told you are still true. I don't know how to be in a relationship."

"I don't know how either."

"But you've had girlfriends."

"No, I haven't. I've never had anything like this. Anyway, who can ever be ready? Only people with no problems ever? Who can know what to do all the time? I don't expect either of us to be perfect."

"And that's okay with you? That I'm going to make mistakes and hurt your feelings and do dumb things?"

He smiled at her and reached out and lightly touched her bottom lip. "Everybody does those things, Pen."

"I would try really hard not to."

He laughed softly. "So you don't regret our kiss."

"I don't." She turned and sat up on her knees, facing him. She closed her eyes because she didn't want to see what he was thinking. She leaned toward him. The shingles pressed into her knees, a biting pain that she ignored. She leaned in a little more, and put her lips on his. Her hands reached up and rested behind his neck. She could feel his chest rising and falling fast beneath hers.

She pulled away and looked at him. He rubbed one of his hands on the outside of her thigh, and her belly dipped and all she wanted was to kiss him again. She sat back against the wall so that she wouldn't.

"Here it is," she said. "Imagine the moon is sitting on the ground at your feet, and you're standing in front of it, trying to look around it. I have huge feelings for you, Archer. I can't see around that moon, on either side."

"Wait, what's the moon in this scenario?" He was trying not to smile.

"Just listen. The lunar size of my feelings scares me. I have other things going on that I need to be able to see. This moon is, well, it's right up in my face and all I can focus on. That's scary." She gulped a big breath of air, and sat back down beside him.

He put his arm around her and pulled her shoulder against him. "I think I understand. But I've always imagined that one of the best parts about being with someone is that you stand beside each other while you deal with your lives. I can't save you, you can't save me. But maybe we can save ourselves, together. If I may borrow your crazy metaphor, it would be us, revolving around that moon together."

"Lunar orbiters." She swallowed. "That does sound pretty nice. I need to go slow though. Very, very slow. Slower than you're imagining."

"I've got time."

"Archer?"

"Yeah?"

"When I moved to Wells Cove I didn't plan to make any real friends. I thought I could *try* being more open, and practice on strangers."

He squeezed her to him tighter. "How'd that work?"

She laughed. "Ask my boyfriend." She looked at him with the question in her eyes. She held her breath, waiting for his response.

"He's too busy holding his girlfriend to give an answer right now."

Chapter 26

Penny woke with a visitor in her bed, snug and warm, and smelling of sweet rolls. She brushed her hand over Nedra's curls. When Neddie was born, Penny had volunteered to be the one to bathe her and rock her to sleep, even though she was a dreadful screamer of a baby.

She had loved even the times Nedra screamed, though. Her cinnamon smell combined with the solid weight of her was grounding. Plus, Penny only had to deal with her for an hour or so, nothing like the work that her parents put in.

Nedra's toddler hands opened and closed, looking for all the world the same as they had when she was a new baby. She blinked her eyes a few times, and looked up and grinned. "Hi Neddie," Penny whispered.

She reached over and pinched Penny's lips until they were fish shaped, then she kissed them. "Good mownin Penny!"

~

The kitchen was bustling with activity. Practically simultaneously, Penny's mom flipped over a fried egg, poured a bowl of cereal, and handed Blake a banana. Art's glass of orange juice toppled over, and the juice ran off the side of the table onto Vincent's pants. Vincent screeched and danced around in circles.

Penny stood in the doorway and watched as her dad shooed Vincent out the door to go change clothes, and then grabbed a dish towel to mop up the juice. He looked up, and saw Penny there. He set the towel down in the puddle of juice, and came over to give her a hug.

"Shiny Penny. It's good to have you back."

"It's nice to see you too. Can we go in the den to talk?" She knew it was abrupt, but she was ready to get it over with.

"Sure, let us get a handle on this first," he said, gesturing across the kitchen.

Just then, as though he had been waiting in the wings for that moment, Archer appeared in the doorway with Cal at his heels. "We'll take care of it." He strode into the room and peeled Blake's banana.

Grandpa slid the egg onto a plate. "Now who had the egg?"

Penny's dad didn't bat an eye, so apparently introductions had been made while she was in the shower. She felt kind of bad that Archer had met her dad without her, but by the looks of it, he had been assimilated seamlessly.

Her mom handed Archer a box of cereal, then the three of them walked down the hall to the den. She straightened her spine and closed the door behind her.

Her mom perched on the arm of the blue sofa in the den. Her dad sat in a hard-backed chair, rasping the back of his hand up and down his whiskery cheek. She used to mimic that motion when she was young. *Let me feel your bristles, Daddy.* The room smelled of books and a thick layer of dust. Morning sun made a parallelogram of light on the floor that contained the family cat, Tank.

Her mom stood up and began pacing. "Well, Papa has decided to stay. We had thought we'd put him in Art and Vince's room, but he doesn't want to displace them. We're going to clear this room out for him instead. Or rather, we'll clear a space for a bed. He says the shelves and the sofa will make him feel right at home." She looked at Penny and smiled, wringing her hands.

"It feels really good to have you home, Penny," her dad said, his voice low and raspy like his whiskers. He looked at her with warm eyes and reached out to grasp her hand. He squeezed it. "I missed you."

"I missed you, too. Both of you." She waved her mom over to sit. "Grandpa had already decided to stay, Mom. I think he just wanted you to know that it was his choice. It was what *he* wanted. He didn't come here because you thought he should."

"Penny, we owe you a huge thanks. I can't tell you how much of a help it was that you went out there and took charge of things. I know we weren't thrilled about it when you left, but you're our first baby. It was hard to let you go all by yourself."

"And I know you could have stopped me if you really wanted to. So thank you for letting me do it." She decided to get the stalling over with. She knew she was making this a bigger deal that it was. Her parents were loving, thoughtful people. "Grandpa helped me see something. I've decided I *do* want to go to college and study chemistry. I want to find a way to help people with dementia. Pharmaceutical development and research."

"That's wonderful, Pen," her mom said.

Her dad grinned, his eyes barely visible as his smile eclipsed his whole face. "I'll call the university tomorrow morning." There it was, the smugness she expected. When she didn't return his smile, he wiped his expression clean.

"I'm still not going to go to MSU."

"I don't understand," her mom said. "You're back, and you want to study chemistry. Why not MSU?"

"I'm here, but I'm not back. You assumed I was moving home and I didn't correct you. I'm sorry."

Her dad's eyes widened, and her mom pursed her lips.

Penny took a deep breath and released it slowly. "Going all the way across the country was easier than telling you

241

this." Her parents looked at her, concern now etched in every feature. "Okay here it is. I am a weak, weak person." She held her breath.

Her mom scoffed. "Penny, why would you say that? You are a very strong person."

"You only think I am. I've made a total of one strong decision in my life, which was not to go to MSU. The one decision I'm proud of is the only one you hate."

"We don't *hate* that you decided not to go to MSU. It's only that you had been so gung-ho, and then as soon as you and Will broke up, you decided not to go," her dad said. "We didn't want you to make decisions about your future because of a boy."

She took a deep breath. "If that's true, then you wouldn't want me to go to MSU either. I never wanted to go there. I only decided to because Will told me to." Her dad raised his eyebrows. "There's more. I didn't want to major in chemistry. I only planned to because you told me to."

She turned her head to her mom. "And I hated volunteering as a scout leader with you. I only did it because you told me to. I wore the clothes you picked out for me. I spent my Sundays studying because you said it was practical. I never picked the movie when I went out with friends. I got a black car because Vera thought it was the coolest color."

She flopped back in her seat. "See? I'm weak. When Will and I broke up, I began to see that I couldn't keep letting other people dictate my life. So deciding *not* to go to MSU was me reclaiming myself." She did not plan to tell them what really happened with Will. That was her personal business.

"Why didn't you tell us this, honey?" her mom said. "That's what this time in your life is for; learning how to choose your own path. We would have supported you no matter where you chose to go to school, or even if you decided not to at all. We were worried because we thought you were making a huge decision because of a break-up."

"I was ashamed."

Her dad laughed. "Frances, you need to tell her your story."

Her mom smiled. "Alright. Penny, I'm not proud of this, so I understand how you feel, I think. I never wanted to go to college at all. My parents insisted. So I chose to go to the University of Wisconsin because my friend Tina was going there. I suffered through two very long years and still they wouldn't let me quit. No matter how much I begged. So my third year, I failed on purpose."

"What?" Penny said, laughing. She could not picture mellow Grandpa Cal and sweet Grandma Ruby forcing her mom to go to college. Let alone her mother failing on purpose.

"By then I had met your father. I knew what I wanted was to marry him and start a family. So I flunked all five of my classes. I wasted a lot of tuition money that semester, but I didn't know how to get it across to my parents that I didn't want to be there. They weren't hearing my words, but they sure did listen to their dollars."

"Grandpa was holding out on me! He did not tell me any of this." She remembered back to a conversation they'd had where he told her that her mother would probably understand her situation. He was not the type to tell her what he thought she should do though. Perhaps he had learned that lesson from his daughter.

"This is partly why we tried so hard to get you to reconsider going to MSU," her dad said. "Your mom let her parents stand in the way of what she wanted. We thought you were letting Will stand in your way."

"My heart is sick because of this misunderstanding," her mom said.

"Well, it's not really your fault. I wasn't ready to share it with you until now."

"I have a question though. You really didn't like chemistry? You had me fooled," her dad said.

She shrugged. "I didn't hate it. It was easy. I've always done the easy thing. I liked how it felt when you were proud of me. That you liked that I was like you. And now I've found some meaning in chemistry, so I'm actually kind of excited to study it. So it worked out anyway."

Her dad shifted in his chair. He cleared his throat. "We're proud of you no matter what. You must know that. I did like that we shared an interest, or rather, I thought we did, but that is not the basis of my pride in you or my love for you."

Tears sprang to her eyes. "I know."

"Is there anything we can do to convince you to stick around here?" her mom said. "We miss you. We'd love to have you closer."

"When I left in June, I had to. I needed to be somewhere where I could hear and use my own voice. Around here I was so used to listening to everyone else. Not going to MSU was my first real no. I wanted to keep it. I worried that if I stuck around here, you'd convince me not to."

Her mom smiled. "You can keep it."

"I know I can. And that's what's different about this time. I'm leaving again. I'm going to Wells Cove again. But this time is different because I know the sound of my own voice. I don't have to go, I want to go."

She looked at her parents' faces. She saw something there that she craved: approval. She hoped she wouldn't always need it so desperately, but for now it filled her with relief.

Her mom arranged her face into its stern mom pose. "And now I'm going to be pushy for a moment. This boy

244

you brought. Archer. You're not basing your future plans on being near him, are you?"

"God, Mom. No. I already made that mistake. I don't know yet where I'll go to school. I'll probably take the rest of this year as a gap year. I'm going back to Wells Cove because, wonder of wonders, I have a life there. But Archer is nothing like Will. I know it's really new, but he *sees* me. And I'm different around him too. It's more than just liking him. I like how I feel about myself when I'm with him."

~

"You can have the last piece," Mark said, holding up a slice of pepperoni pizza.

Vera snatched it from his hand before Penny had a chance to speak. "When do you leave again, Penny? While you were gone, Mark put me in your place on the pedestal."

Penny stuck her tongue out at her sister. "I didn't want it anyway. The pizza or the pedestal." They fell towards each other, laughing.

"Are they always like this?" Archer asked Mark.

"No. Usually they're worse. I think they're toning it down in front of you."

The four of them were at Ramone's Pizzeria, enjoying a night away from the Beck household. "So was Dad hard on you?" Mark asked.

"He asked me a lot of questions. Wanted to know how many hours a week I work."

Vera laughed. "Seriously? What else?"

"He asked how long I was single before I met you," he said, looking at Penny.

"That is truly bizarre," Penny said. "Wait, how long was it?"

Mark and Vera laughed, which set Penny off again. Archer shook his head at their merriment. He slid his hand onto Penny's thigh, under the booth where Mark and Vera wouldn't see. "You know how long."

"Since Marissa?"

"That's what I told him. But in truth, my whole life."

Vera snorted out a loud laugh, and Mark said, "Smooth, man."

But Archer didn't laugh and neither did Penny. She knew just what he meant. She too felt a lack of aloneness so keen it was a first.

~

"Now you're both hiding," Archer said, later the next day after a chaotic lunch that included two spilled cups of juice and more questions for him from the younger kids. He pulled out a chair and joined Cal and Penny at the patio table. She had just finished giving her grandpa a hard time for not telling her about her mom's college drama. Cal maintained that it wasn't his place to tell.

"Haven't you learned yet that the only way to survive in this household is to spend plenty of time in hiding places?" Penny said to Archer. "I have several good ones I can tell you about."

"I guess I haven't been here long enough to feel the need for solitude."

"Well I've been here just as long as you have," Cal said, "and I feel the need."

"You're just preparing for what is your harsh new reality," Penny teased him.

"You're the one who talked me into coming here, my dear."

"How was your game of Candy Land?" Penny asked Archer.

"Blake won. I got the stupid gingerbread man and had to go almost back to the beginning." He looked thoughtful. "You know, I never played that game before."

Penny glanced at her grandpa, feeling guilty for not always appreciating her loud, funny, chaotic, loving family.

Cal smiled at her. He understood. "There is something I would like to discuss, now that I have the two of you alone," he said.

"Okay," Penny said. "We're all ears."

Cal looked at Archer. "Do you want my house?"

Archer furrowed his brow. "Pardon me, sir?"

"My house in Wells Cove. I'd like you to have it."

Archer looked at Penny, bewildered, then back to Cal. "I don't understand. I can't afford to buy a house right now."

Penny wasn't sure what her grandpa was up to, but she liked it.

"You wouldn't be buying it. It would be a gift. This whole trip, you've been trying to respect your elders," Cal said. "I've denied you the privilege, but now I'd like it if you did. I'm offering you a gift and it would mean a great deal to me if you accepted it."

Archer was stunned into silence. After a minute, he said, "But shouldn't you give it to Penny instead? Or sell it and do something with the money?"

"It's my house, and I can do with it what I please. I would be pleased to see you have it."

"Archer," Penny said, "It's perfect. I *want* you to have it." She pictured his disgusting apartment complex. She thought about how he wanted to stay in Wells Cove and have a hardware store. She couldn't think of a better plan, and she was overwhelmed with love for her grandpa for offering it.

Archer still looked doubtful. "I don't know. How can someone just give someone else a house? Do people even do that?"

247

"You'll have to clean all my junk out. You're welcome to what you want to keep, but there's a lot there you'll have to haul away. And it needs a new roof. That won't come cheap. The sink in the bathroom leaks. If you take it off my hands, I won't have to worry about any of that, let alone try to sell it."

Archer looked down at his lap. "It just doesn't feel right."

"It does to me," Cal said. "Archer, I'm at a stage in my life when I don't have a lot of decisions left to me. Let me make this one. Take the damn house."

Penny laughed. "Archer, you heard the man. Take the damn house."

He blew out a breath and shook his head in astonishment. "My own family kicked me out of houses, and here you are giving me one. It doesn't make any sense."

"So you'll take it?" Cal said.

"Geez, you're pushy," Archer said, and Cal chuckled.

"It's settled then. I'll get the paperwork started next week."

"Thank you, sir. That sounds so stupid to say. You just gave me a house." He still looked stunned.

"Stop right there. There will be no gushing or profuse thank you offerings. Just go back and live in it and that will be thanks enough." He shook Archer's hand, then stood up and went into the house.

"Wow," Archer said, as Cal's back disappeared through the back door. "This is insane."

"If you knew him better, you wouldn't be so surprised," Penny said, grinning at him.

"Hot damn, I have a house!" Archer's glee was palpable. They sat grinning at each other for a while.

"Do you think we could head back tonight?" he asked.

She laughed. "I know you're excited about your new house, but surely you can wait one more day."

"It's not the house. I haven't even absorbed that reality yet. I know we planned to leave tomorrow, but I'd like to add a stop to our itinerary." He suddenly sat up straight with a frantic look on his face. "Wait, are you still planning to come back?"

Penny touched his forearm tree with her index finger. "Yes, I'm coming back. Yes, we can leave tonight."

"Your parents are counting on one more day with you. Do you think they'll be upset?"

Penny figured the extra stop Archer mentioned was probably the prison, to see if he could visit his mom again. If he wanted to see her again before she died, that was more important. "We'll stay for dinner. They won't complain. And if they do, that's okay. Some arguments are worth having."

~

"Shh! If you wake up Neddie, we'll never get out of here," Penny hissed at Archer. He picked up the suitcase with two hands so it would stop bumping into the balusters.

"Sorry. Geez. It's pitch black and the middle of the night. I'm not exactly feeling coordinated," he said.

"You're the one who insisted we leave now instead of waiting until morning."

"We had to."

He was right. She'd already said her good-byes after dinner. Now her entire family was asleep, even the teenagers. It was a good time to slip out. She knew if they left in the morning, she would linger over last hugs. It felt urgent to get going. What if his mom died before they got there?

She had packed more of her things. She cleared out her part of the closet so Vera and Corinne could use it all. Vera had helped do it. Penny blinked hard, thinking of the way they had laughed and insulted each other and bumped elbows while working. She would miss her, of course, but this leaving wasn't like the last leaving. It wasn't fraught with fear and anger and uncertainty. Vera knew that too, and neither had cried.

Penny opened the screen door with a pinky finger, as her arms were laden with boxes and bags. She stepped onto the porch, the moonlight casting the yard in a silver glow. She leaned back against the door, holding it open for Archer, and about jumped out of her skin when she saw Grandpa sitting on the swing.

He smiled at her, and she regained her senses. She set down her things and sat beside him on the swing. "Out with it then," she said, and leaned against his side, expecting some sort of advice or lecture.

He patted her head with his other hand. "I forgot to give you something," he said. He reached for her hand, and opened it. He placed a chocolate in her palm, and kissed her cheek. "I love you, my dear Penny."

Chapter 27

"Look! We're in Wyoming!" Archer shouted over the rush of the wind. He had insisted that they roll all four windows down. Penny's hair was blowing like a personal hurricane about her head as they flew down the interstate at seventy-five miles per hour.

"My face is numb!" she shouted back.

He laughed. "Isn't this awesome?"

"Hair keeps getting wedged under my eyelids," she hollered, and then had to remove more hair from her mouth because she had opened it to speak.

Archer glanced over at her and pushed the button to roll up the windows. He grinned. "Well, *I* thought it was awesome."

She smiled at him, and squeezed his hand, which she was holding because he was her boyfriend, which blew her mind.

"I like your hair all crazy like that," he said.

"It's dark in here, how can you even see it?" She squinted at him, his edges lit up intermittently by passing trucks.

"I can see you, and I'm saying I like your hair. You look exceptionally appealing."

~

"We just stopped a half hour ago. Your inferior bladder strikes again," Penny said, as he veered onto an exit.

"It's getting late. Or early, actually. We should get some sleep before that extra stop I mentioned," he replied.

She looked at him, confused. Tennessee was a day away. "I thought the extra stop was visiting your mom again."

"My mom is dead." He said it with a voice devoid of emotion, a face devoid of expression.

She waited, seeing if he had anything else to say. "When did you find out?" she asked, at last.

"Yesterday morning. I got the call from the prison." He sounded like a robot.

"I'm sorry," she said, trying to hide her own shock and the cold that was spreading through her limbs. He didn't respond. "Why didn't you tell me sooner?"

"I didn't want to talk about it right then. Where we're going in the morning, that's for her. I was going to tell you then."

At the end of the exit ramp, he looked left and then right. "Which way, do you think?"

She pointed to the left, and he turned toward Comfort Suites.

~

"Would you like a room with a king sized bed, or two double beds?"

Archer looked up from his wallet, where he was wrestling a credit card free. The woman behind the counter had surprised him, no doubt. He recovered, and quickly said, "No, we'll need two rooms."

Penny placed her palm on the counter. "Actually, one room with two beds," she told the woman, who looked back and forth between them, annoyance plain on her face. It was late, she was probably tired.

Archer walked to a corner of the lobby, and paced with his hands on his hips. He motioned Penny over. "Why do you want one room, two beds?" She started to answer, but he kept going. "One room, one bed might mean one thing. Two rooms would mean something else. What does one room, two beds mean?"

It meant that his mom just died. She didn't want to leave him alone. Or did he want to be alone to cry?

"Would you prefer two rooms?"

He was quiet for a moment, then, "No. One room is good."

Archer hauled his duffel bag and Penny's suitcase up to their room. He went right to the bathroom. "I'll be back in five minutes," Penny called to him through the door.

"Wait, where are you going?"

She didn't answer. When she got back to their room, she didn't have time to get the key card in the slot before the door opened for her.

"Don't just take off alone like that, please," Archer said. "I was worried."

She rolled her eyes at him, then grinned and held up the bucket of ice. "I had to get provisions."

~

"Is it easy for you to talk to me?" Penny asked.

He looked at her nervously. "I don't really talk to anyone much. But of all the people I do talk to, it's easiest with you."

They were each in their own bed, but lying on the edges facing each other. One wall light was on, and the room glowed softly. They were tucked under blankets, and it felt impossible to sleep even though it was only a couple of hours until dawn.

"And I like arguing with you," he offered, with a smile. "Why do you wonder, anyway? From the moment we met I've been telling you things."

253

"I guess so, but in the beginning it was more like you were attacking me with your truths. Like when we played that game when we painted Irene's living room. It wasn't like you were sharing part of yourself, it was like you were trying to shock me."

"I feel sort of stupid about that now."

"Why?"

"I didn't want you to walk away just because you didn't like me, but it would have been okay if you'd run screaming." He grinned.

She smiled back at him. "A classic case of *fear of rejection*?"

"I suppose so. I never could figure out why you'd want to talk to me."

"Hey, I liked you plenty from the start. And I *also* thought about running away screaming."

He laughed.

The room fell silent but for their breathing. His eyes shined like two black marbles.

"Will it freak you out if I cry?" he whispered.

"No."

"There's something I want to tell you. I *know* it will freak you out."

"I'm used to being freaked out. It's my natural state of being. I can handle it." She tried to keep her voice steady.

He kept his watery eyes on hers. "Do you remember that day in the grocery store when you called me a dick?"

"Ugh, there's that god-awful word again. Anyway, that's not exactly how I remember it because I would not utter that word. But of course I remember the day," she said.

"I was a jerk to you another time too. Well, probably a few times. One of them was the day that Irene told you about her rapes."

Penny furrowed her brow. "I'm repeating myself, but that's not how I remember that day either. You acted upset, not mean."

"I stormed off and then ignored you."

She didn't respond, because that was true.

"Anyway, the thing is, and Irene knows this, by the way. My dad served time in prison for rape once, when I was fourteen. The woman's name was Jeanie. I'll never forget that. Her name is burned into my brain. So yeah. My dad did that. I have this crazy idea, or maybe it's not so crazy, that my dad was the one who raped Irene the second time." His voice cracked. "Logistically, it's possible. They were both in town that year. It freaks me out that it might be true."

"Well, what does Irene say?"

"She says it doesn't matter to her who did it. She has no clue who it was, no desire for revenge or even justice. She says she's at peace about it."

"Isn't that good though? It sounds like she's moved on and healed."

"I think that's bullshit. She may seem all wise and serene about the whole mess, but I know it affected her more than she lets on. How could it not? She never got married, maybe she can't trust men."

"Okay, well I think it's only fair to take Irene at her word. Everyone handles things differently. Maybe she simply doesn't want marriage and it has nothing to do with her past. And she does too trust men. She trusts you."

He blew out a breath. "It's not the same thing."

More silence.

"What does it say about me that my dad could do that?"

"It doesn't say anything about you. It says something about *him*."

He shifted onto his back. He breathed harder, sniffed. He let out a growl and hit the bed beside him with both fists.

255

Penny wanted to go to him, but she had the feeling he needed that little bit of space. After a few minutes of hard crying, he wiped his face with his palms and steadied his breathing. She waited.

"My dad is an asshole and my mom is a dead asshole."

Penny took her hand from beneath the covers and stretched it toward him. He reached out and grabbed it tightly with his own. They held hands like that for a long time, until his breathing grew quiet and she was almost asleep.

"Are you asleep?" he asked.

Instead of answering out loud, she whispered her fingertips over the back of his hand. He flipped his hand over, and they were palm to palm again. His skin felt rough and warm, and somehow he had electrified it. Sparks shot through her, and she gasped.

In an instant he launched himself across the space that separated them. She scooted over and made room for him. He crawled under the covers with her. They lay facing each other, hearts racing, breath coming fast. He reached out and brushed a finger down her nose, across her cheek. The staggering intensity of her feelings made her wonder how she managed to stay conscious.

She moved closer to him, and put her arm around him. She didn't know what to do with her other arm, there was no place for it. She tucked it awkwardly to her side and got as close to him as she could. She was wearing pajamas as always, a camisole and cotton shorts. He only had on boxer shorts. They touched along the lengths of their bodies. Even their toes touched. She did a mental scan of her body, searching for numbness. None. She was fully present, fully feeling.

He leaned his head down and brushed his lips on hers. His mouth moved slowly, and so softly. She opened her mouth. When their tongues touched, she thought she must be on fire. His hand was on her ribcage, burning a hole through her. His thumb brushed the bottom of her breast. Her senses took leave of her, and she moaned into his mouth.

He pulled his head back, and she tried to hold him to her, but he extracted himself from her grip and lay back on the other pillow. "We're going slow," he reminded her, breathing fast.

"I'm not sure what I was thinking when I said that," Penny said, her own chest heaving.

"I'm on the very edge here, Pen. If you say things like that, I might tip us both over."

She smiled at him and moved away a few inches. She let a minute go by. When she felt like she could bear it, she moved her palm across his chest and he didn't stop her. His skin was hot. After a minute, he groaned and turned back to her. He covered her mouth with his again, and pressed against her body as though trying to absorb her.

It took longer that time, but at length he managed to stop kissing her.

"I'm glad I wasn't asleep," she whispered, her lips feathering over his cheek as she spoke.

He laughed again, and rolled away. "Me too."

"You can sleep over here, if you want," she told him.

"Are you sure?"

"I want you to."

He curled on his side to face her.

"Archer?"

"Yeah?"

"You're coming to Thanksgiving dinner with me at Marissa's house."

"I am?"

"Yeah. You are."

It took him all of two minutes to fall asleep. She kept replaying everything that had happened that night, so it took her much longer. When she woke a few hours later to the sound of their early alarm, his arm was slung across her hips.

257

She didn't know how it was possible, but she had never felt more rested in her life.

Chapter 28

"You may not realize this about me, but surprises are not my favorite," Penny said.

"What are you talking about? You're incredibly spontaneous," Archer replied, confident in his assertion.

"Spontaneity and liking surprises are very different things. And actually, you're wrong about both of them. I am not spontaneous nor do I like surprises."

"Really?"

"Really. You must have made that up. I'm a planner."

He only smiled and didn't reply. She sighed and tried to enjoy the ride. The rocky Black Hills poked up all around them. They reminded her of the dribble sand castles her mom taught her to make at the lake one summer. There was a fair amount of green too. Clumps of pine and spruce trees cast a peaceful aura.

She sat up suddenly. "You're not going to make me climb one of these things are you?" She'd heard many stories through the years about excursions to the various peaks in the Black Hills.

"Penny, relax. All you'll have to do is sit back and watch something." There is nothing worse for relaxation than somebody telling you to relax, she thought.

Not long later, traffic became thick. Archer grumbled as they rolled along at 35 miles per hour. "I had no idea there would be so many people here." And a few minutes later, "It starts in 45 minutes. Why on earth is everybody going so slow?"

They inched closer, and Penny saw a sign for Custer State Park. Up the road, cars were turning into the entrance. They followed the herd into the park, past a stone wall with a metal bison on it, and wound around the park roads. That took forever too.

Finally they arrived at a big grassy field and parked the car. She got out and stretched. She looked over and found Archer watching her. He smiled and grabbed the small cooler. "Bring your quilt." She gathered her quilt and looked around. They were surrounded by cars and people, but beyond that lay what seemed like miles of gently rolling grass. A big white tent was set up, and people were sitting and standing behind a stretch of wooden fence near it.

They hiked in the opposite direction of the tent and the crowd, to a slightly less populated place at the fence. Archer took the quilt and spread it on the ground. They sat on it, looking down into a valley. Some trees across the way were turning yellow.

On the drive in she had seen signs for a Buffalo Roundup, so she had a small idea what to expect. She wanted to let Archer have the lead in explaining things though, since he had told her this event had something to do with his mom.

"Need anything to drink?" Archer asked, as he pulled out a bottle of water for himself.

"Sure." He passed her a bottle. People were filling in the empty spots around them. "When did you pack this cooler?"

"Yesterday. Actually, your dad advised me to pack these." He pulled two packages of Twizzlers out of the bag. She grinned and snatched one.

There were pickup trucks in the valley, as well as some men and women on horseback. Penny felt a rising anticipation in her chest for the bison.

Thanks to their late arrival, they didn't have long to wait. Over the crest of a hill, bison appeared. From that distance, they looked like a line of ants moving across a crack in a sidewalk. Then there were more of them. She couldn't even begin to guess how many. Riders ran at the edges of the herd.

The crowd was loud, happily cheering on the bison. Penny wished they'd be quiet. She wanted to listen to the animals. As they drew closer, she could hear the bison above the chatter of the crowd. Dust clouded the valley like a thin fog. When she felt the ground rumble beneath her, she looked at Archer with wide, enchanted eyes.

"This is amazing," she said, grinning.

"They do this every year. They'll auction off some of them, to keep the numbers manageable. The others get veterinary checkups," Archer said. He reached out and held her hand.

Warmth swirled around her fingertips, and spread like smoke up her arm.

"So are they bison or buffalo? I've seen both words used here."

"Either is fine. I think bison is correct, but a lot of people call them buffalo too."

The bison drew nearer and she felt a kernel of fear. Even from this distance she could see how large the animals were, how heavily they pounded the ground.

On the side of the hill, about twenty of the bison veered away from the herd. They rushed behind a clump of trees, as though trying to hide. The crowd laughed as the riders tried to corral them. The escapees enjoyed their romp, however, and it took a couple trucks to get them back with their brethren.

"My grandparents brought my mom here when she was eleven," Archer said, startling Penny out of her buffalo trance.

She burrowed deeper into his side.

"She had a happy childhood, you know," Archer continued shakily. "You can't blame my grandparents for her choices." He shook his head and sighed. "Anyway, one night she was drunk instead of drugged into a stupor. Maybe that sounds bad, but it was a good thing. It made her talkative instead of dazed. She acted kind of silly, even. She stumbled through the kitchen door that night. I was probably fifteen, I guess. I was sitting there eating a bowl of Cheerios. She sat down with me, and poured herself a bowl too. She teased me about my hair. She always said I needed to get it cut. Then she told me about coming here with her folks when she was a kid. How it was the best thing she ever saw. How it made her feel alive just to remember it."

Penny squeezed his arm with her free hand. His voice had gotten smaller as he talked.

"I wanted to see it too, so that when I remember it, for just a moment I will feel what she felt."

Cowboys were yelping, and the crowd was vocal as ever. Penny glanced back at the bison, then down to where Archer held her hand. He wasn't watching the bison, he was watching her.

"I wanted to see it with you," he said.

She smiled.

"The Native Americans ascribe several meanings to the buffalo. They represent abundance and strength, of course, but also emotional courage."

Emotional courage. Penny blinked.

Archer looked away for a moment, then back to her face. "So here goes a little emotional courage. Is the moon still right in front of you, blocking your view?"

"Bigger than ever," she replied. She swallowed and tried to steady her breathing. "But somehow I'm not as bothered by trying to figure everything out. It just feels like life."

Archer took a shaky breath. "I think a lot of people would say it's too soon for me to tell you this. But in my life,

262

my chances to say this have been few, and I don't have any reason to wait. Penny, I love you."

Penny looked at him with wide eyes. His eyes were warm, and nervous, and happy. She glanced at the buffalo to shore up her own emotional courage. The words tumbled out of her mouth before she had a chance to question if it was the right decision. "I love you, too." She felt the truth of the statement grounding her body to the earth.

Archer reached out and lifted her chin with his pointer finger. "Can I kiss you?"

"Yes." The rumbling in the earth intensified, and her own heart beat heavy as hooves.

In the midst of a roiling mass of bison, dust and animal scent heavy in the air and the ground shaking around them, he put his lips on hers. Her head spun. She felt his hand on her sun-warmed hair.

She wanted more, and leaned toward him. He pulled back and smiled. He gestured to two children dressed in their cowgirl best leaning on the fence a few feet to the left. When the girls saw Archer and Penny looking back at them, they giggled and turned back to the bison.

Archer pulled Penny nearer to him, and she leaned against his chest.

Soon she'd be on her way across the country for the second time that year, this time running to her life instead of away from it. She had an appointment with a palm reader. She'd let Miss Zelda tell her the future, and then she'd decide it for herself.

Acknowledgements

To my husband, Ryan, I give my warmest thanks for your support while I wrote this book. Your patience and frequent hugs during my periods of self-doubt did not go unnoticed. You are the ultimate encourager.

I wish to also thank my children, Walter and Sylvia, whose support and enthusiasm blew me away. I can't tell you the number of times I heard variations of, "You're writing a book, Mama! You get your *dream*."

Huge thanks also go to my mom, Bev, who bestowed upon me a love of reading. She listened without complaint as I chattered on about trying out this writing thing.

I had a heap of beta readers who helped me rethink and refine my story. Their feedback and encouragement was essential. Here are their names, in no particular order: Bev, Erin, Joany, Karen, Gretchen, Emmanuelle, Tiffany, Darlene, Christy, Silvia, and Amanda from Fill My Bookshelf.

Many others have helped me along the way, listening and encouraging me as I worked. In particular, thanks go to my dad, David, my mother-in-law, Rhonda, Kelly, Kim, and Emily.

About the Author

Lora lives in Indiana with her husband and two children. She spends her days homeschooling, reading, writing, and hanging out with her people. Outspoken is her first novel.

44757204R00159

Made in the USA
Middletown, DE
15 June 2017